The

Forgotten Timepiece

A historical sci-fi tale of timeless love, self-acceptance and betrayal.

JOYCE LICORISH

For information and to contact the author, please visit:
http://www.ForgottenTimepiece.com

Book Design by Licorish Enterprises, LLC

Cover Art by Olivia Pro Design, LLC

Photos of the Author by Satu V. Photography

ISBN: 978-1-387-05598-2

(Paperback ISBN)

2nd Edition: July 13, 2017

Prologue

SeRina had seen but dismissed the beatings she saw in the movies with their rehearsed agony. She almost found the scenes in the films a bit comical and felt that surely they were exaggerated. But this experience, it was nothing like she imagined it to be. Finding herself just an arm's length away from the horror, the blood splashing upon her with every lash, was a total and absolute shock to the senses. After all, hadn't they over exaggerated the struggle and what it meant to be black? She found herself face to face and now inescapably and inexplicably attached to the very label she had shrugged off and dismissed her entire life. The label of being 'black' instead of the all-American white girl she had always imagined herself to be. Being adopted by the richest Italian family in her town, it was assumed by she and everyone around her that she was like them, an Italian American, AKA 'white' by US standards girl. So as if finding out that her maternal grandmother was black wasn't shocking enough to the system, SeRina had been thwarted from her cushy life in 2009 back in time to a plantation in the antebellum South in the year 1859.

Instead of a trip to the mall with friends or hanging out poolside at her estate, where her only interaction with them was with as the help, she found herself standing there living a page from the very history book her annoying Social Studies teacher had taught her from. Standing in this new reality, SeRina had no choices, no freedoms, and no escape. So there she found herself lodged in time, hands bound and throbbing, senses ignited and forced to smell the fear and see the sweat dripping from his brow. Seeing this man she had grown to love savagely beaten until his strong rigid body grew limp from submission devastated SeRina in ways that she could not explain. The overseer joked and cackled as he twirled his whip cracking it once more across his back making a final statement as her friend had already expired from the barbarism.

At least now he was free, she thought. Every single prospect of escape dwindled away and traded itself for fear and sheer pathetic hopelessness.

She stared brutality in the face and subdued resistance just as the others had. She, the one who always said that she would never stand for such vile atrocities had not only witnessed it and done nothing, but it was all her fault. None of her knowledge of the future, and how things would someday be could save her now, she felt as if there was no escape. No one questioned the conditions or the fact that they were owned, no one stood for him or rescued him from death. The bleakness of it all was as commonplace as the tobacco and cotton in the fields to them. That is when she felt broken, that is the moment that the terror set in and the fear that she may never escape took over her very soul.

That night after his blood was washed from her face and ropes removed from her hands, she walked bemused back to the dimly lit shanty that was now her home. Her thoughts consuming her as she found herself chained to an ancestral past that she never knew. She couldn't escape, she had no idea how she had gotten to this horrible place. She was trapped in every essence of the word, and there she sat unable to sob. Her hopes of making a getaway now doomed to failure, she found herself floating adrift in a seemingly endless cycle of systematic oppression. This was her America, the one she loved and pledged her allegiance to every morning in her homeroom class. "Freedom", the once insignificant, simple, presupposed, and repetitiously uttered word now held a new value in her mind and she wondered if she would ever taste it again.

CHAPTER ONE

Give and Take

The operating room was full of light but devoid of joy despite the miraculous occurrence that had just transpired there. On this picturesque warm and breezy evening just after sunset, a beautiful baby girl was born. There were no glowing grandparents, no nervous pacing father to be, no welcoming relatives or friends awaiting this angelic child's arrival. Instead, only a mother occupied the room still trembling from the pains of childbirth.

Already, she missed her precious new baby girl who had been taken from her arms to be washed and robed just moments ago. She found it peculiar and frightening the bond that she felt with this little one after only gazing into her eyes for a few fragile moments.

She longed for her child's return, knowing their remaining moments together would be limited to just a few more hours. "They" had been called and alerted of the long awaited birth, and she knew despite the longing inside of her that she was obligated to stick to her decision. So there she lay, afraid and dreadful, her mind racing with panic, swirling with doubts. Diana knew then she need not fight herself on it, she had made up her mind and she would not falter. She was in no position to care for this child so she reassured herself that she had made the best decision.

Juanita, the nurse present during birth had ended her shift, so next, she instructed her replacement to return the now dressed baby girl to her mother's side in room 1202. Her replacement wrapped the infant in a fresh pastel blanket, scooped her up and placed her in the transparent rolling bassinet. She strolled down the hall past adoring onlookers, new dads, and grandparents to the room. When she entered the room, she took a double take at the woman resting there. She looked at the infant and back at the woman in disbelief. There was no way this fair-skinned, gray-eyed, angel with a head full of silky brunette curls could belong to this woman, this extremely BLACK woman. So the nurse apologized for the disturbance and began to turn to take the child back down the hall in time to catch the Doctor and determine her true destination. Just then, Diana turned, opened her eyes, feigned a smile and said. "Practically unbelievable isn't it? Yes, she is mine. Please, bring her to me."

The nurse paused for a second, her stare bouncing between the two for an awkward moment. This was the most uncanny thing she had ever seen. The child did not appear albino, but she was certain she was entirely too light to be born of this woman.

However, she decided it best to leave her there for a moment and go to secretly confirm with the Doctor that she had delivered the child to the appropriate locale. She did just that and he confirmed that yes, she was in the right place.

Meanwhile, in the small single patient room with pale green walls, Diana held and fed her infant. She gazed at her, taking her in, praying not to forget her features in hopes of some future reunion. They shared a moment and it seemed as if time stood still while Diana spoke these words to her child through tearful eyes and a broken heart,

"Look at you, my precious little one. Heaven knows this is the hardest thing I have ever done in my life, but it's for the greater good. I wish I could give you all the glorious things in life that you deserve, but I can't. So my gift to you, my sweet baby, is the hope for a brighter future, a beautiful future filled with all the joy and everything your little heart could ever desire. My precious baby girl, know that no matter where our paths take us, my love for you is everlasting and my heart is with you for all time."

Diana took in her child's beauty finding it hard to imagine that she played a part in creating something so magnificent. The baby who at this point, still remained unnamed, wrinkled her petite nose and cooed softly. She had the most adorable dainty features, her lashes so long that they rested on her cherubic cheeks. She yawned and strained to open her sleepy eyes.

Her mother gazed upon her noticing the resemblance to her former lover. Diana had to agree that yes, she had her father's gray eyes, his nose, and even his tiny earlobes. The mother thought to herself what a fool he was to have denied this beauty of theirs a life together as a family. It pained her to think that something as simple as the hue of their skin kept him from keeping his promise of marriage to her. She recalled the way he decided to call things off for fear of his parents cutting him off from his rightful inheritance. In this day and age, it was disheartening for her to think that some people still couldn't stomach the thought of interracial marriage and that simple fact is what had her at this crossroad.

Diana had to decide between finishing college and raising this child alone, and she had made her decision. She could barely take care of herself, as she worked at a local diner for minimum wage plus tips to support her college education. She met him her sophomore year and they had a storybook romance. She admittedly was a bit taken aback at his advances at first, as she had never given thought of dating someone outside her race, so she had turned him down several times before they had their first date.

He was handsome in a Clark Kent kind of way. Tall with dark chiseled features and gorgeous eyes. Once she gave in, it seemed they fell in love almost instantly and had been inseparable her sophomore and Junior year in college. He loved all the things she about her that she wished she could change, the gap in her teeth, her kinky natural hair, and full figure. By day they would arrange to see each other between classes, taking long walks and talking at length of their future together. Every waking moment she thought of him and he of her. Their friends jokingly told them they had reverse "Jungle Fever" and they would laugh. Others would give them dirty looks as they paraded around campus hand in hand. They had even been openly ridiculed by an older gentleman who tried to convince them that it just wasn't "natural" for them to be together. At first, she had the same doubts wondering how their children would be received in a world such as this, but with time her doubts faded and turned into more adoration for her handsome lover.

Diana had it all planned out, they would graduate together he would continue on to med school, and she would pursue her dreams as well of being a history major and political activist sharing her talents with the less fortunate and giving back to her inner-city roots. They would live happily ever after raising their children and growing old together. They had lain many nights together in the dorm room discussing it like giddy school children. Diana thought it odd that despite all of their plans for the future that she had never met his parents, nor he hers. The thoughts of their future were so vivid in her imagination that it was like she was exiled to a world of darkness when he broke things off.

Diana had only one year left of school. Just one year separated them from making their fantasy lives a reality, and he had abandoned her. She loved him with all of her heart and bared her soul to him, giving him her innocence a year after his prodding. She remembered the moment well, as it was their one-year anniversary and he made the cliché' statement that if she loved him, she would do it. So she gave in reluctantly. She had wanted to save this gift for their wedding night, but also couldn't stand the thought of disappointing him. She had never doubted that they someday would marry and have several children just as beautiful as this one. She had daydreamed a thousand times of the home that they would share and how easy life would be, given the fact that he was the son of one of the richest and most well-known families in their city.

Things happened so suddenly, she hadn't even had a chance to tell him about the baby. With the cold and unexpected way he dismissed her, he didn't deserve to know about her. In her heart, she had always wanted to save herself for marriage as her mother and grandmother had for their mates. She went into hiding because of the stigma and embarrassment of being an unwed mother. She had managed to hide her pregnancy from everyone except for her mother right up until a month prior to giving birth. Her mother had been adamant about her not giving the baby up, but she went against her wishes. She avoided her friends and didn't have much family, other than her mother. She focused diligently on her studies and made her public escapades minimal.

Diana had grown into a confident yet modest woman, with goals and ambition to spare. She was tall and beautiful, with deep cocoa skin, almond shaped ebony eyes, a full voluptuous figure and thick wavy hair that she kept natural all her life. She had a big future ahead of her, she needed to let this go and pretend that it had never happened. So a few months prior to giving birth, after praying and crying, and bottling it all up inside, she realized there was no hope for reconciliation, so she made her decision. She had already made the arrangements to release her infant to the Strahan Adoption Agency.

So, Diana dismissed the battle raging within and moved forward with her decision a mere 4 hours and 28 minutes after giving birth. She signed the last of the papers and let the emotionless representative carry away her beautiful baby girl. She had no idea what the future would hold for her. As she watched the door close, immediately her breath caught in her throat. The overwhelming ache of regret consumed her and she literally felt her heart break. She had signed away her hopes and dreams and thrown away everything she felt would tie her to her future. As the door slammed, it broke the silence. She did not know what the future would hold but just as the door had closed in the room so it had closed on that chapter of her life. In that moment, her mother's final words echoed in her mind as her tears soaked into the pillow.

"Diana, mark my words. If you do this, you will do it alone."

CHAPTER TWO

Another Saturday Morn

It was a long-standing tradition in the Salvatore household that on Saturday mornings, SeRina Salvatore would make breakfast with her adoptive father Geoffrey while his wife Darrene got her "beauty rest." This Saturday started like every other, the alarm sounded and SeRina awoke, swept her curls from her face and mindlessly shuffled from the bed to the shower and then to the kitchen to prepare some unknown culinary cuisine attitude in full effect.

Oh my God, who sets alarm clocks on Saturday?! I thought that was the whole point of it being the weekend. I am so over this ever single Saturday morning! She thought.

Disinterested, she scanned the cupboard to see what would be easy to prepare in order to make a suggestion to her dad before he could creatively concoct some sort of disdainful daybreak delight again. Just as she spotted an expired box of pancake mix, her dad popped into the kitchen wearing his favorite blue and burgundy checked bathrobe. He was much taller than SeRina, and although he hadn't shaved or combed his tousled hair yet, was still handsome with gleaming eyes. He surprised SeRina when he squeezed her from behind, kissed her on the cheek and said, "Good morning sunshine! What'll it be? Eggs Benedict? Or, I've got it, how about a delicious yogurt breakfast parfait?"

While secretly, turning up her nose and rolling her eyes she said with a half-cocked smile, "Which one is easiest?"

And he replied, "Remember this is your mother's ..."

She chimed in, and said simultaneously, "One day to rest..."

He smiled and said, "Exactly, princess, so let's do the Eggs Benedict and the Parfait... your mom has had a rough week, so she deserves them both!"

She sighed and nodded in agreement secretly not wanting to cook anything.

My mom has been on her broom lately, I can think of a few places she can shove those eggs Benedict, thought SeRina. SeRina was anything but a morning person, she had plans that did not involve slaving over a stove on a Saturday morning making hollandaise sauce. She was supposed to meet Briana and Michaela at the mall by noon for pedicures, then off to the hair salon and had planned to cap off the evening with a movie date with her best friend Alex. If she wasn't careful, her Dad would have her busy all morning and well into the afternoon overlapping with her precious "me time."

Seventeen going on twenty-seven, the adopted, spoiled, curvaceous and beautiful SeRina was lost in thought again about the coming days plans and was disinterested in her dad's mundane chitter-chatter about work, their upcoming family vacation, and whatever stupid medical fundraiser presentation dinner thing-a-majig that he the Dr. and Mrs. Salvatore would be attending that evening.

Distracted by her thoughts, she nodded and childishly giggled through the conversation, fingers intertwined in the curls that she hated. She thought she was much overdue for a date with her flat-iron and completely ignored her father's instructions to pick up her mother's evening gown from the cleaners on her way home from the mall.

Little did she know that this little oversight would cost her more than she could ever imagine and unravel a series of events that she couldn't have imagined in her wildest dreams.

CHAPTER THREE

Manicures and Mischief

"Brinky, I thought you would never get here!" said Michaela at the sight of SeRina when she arrived halfway through the mineral scrub portion of the pedicure. Michaela and Briana were SeRina's closest girlfriends, they had all given each other nicknames and had been inseparable since the 7th grade.

Briana was a stunning blonde, long legged, blue eyed and every 17-year-old boy's fantasy. Michaela, was a knockout as well, with a luscious chocolate mane of wavy hair to match her beautiful brown eyes. Michaela's nickname was "Miki" because when they were kids, she had a short haircut and always wore her hair in two curly ponytails on the sides of her head like Mickey Mouse. Briana went by "Bri" for short and somehow SeRina's ranged from "Brinky" to "Brina" depending on the tone of the conversation.

The three of them had been inseparable since elementary school. They were the 'it' girls and were hands down the three most desirable girls at Arlington Manor High.

SeRina didn't even remember how she had gotten the nicknames, but they stuck and she answered to them nonetheless.

"Yea, you don't know what you are missing," said Briana with her high pitched voice. She swished her feet around in the warm soapy water in the pedicure basin while adjusting the massage control on the chair.

"Seriously, you guys have no idea what I had to go through to get out of that house! Plus you know I had to flat iron my hair, I hate when it gets all kinky and curly after my work out!" SeRina said while rolling her eyes.

"That's OK love because you look fab-u-lous. I see you channeling your inner Kim Kardashian today," said Michaela.

"Oh my God, if one more person tells me that I look like her I'm going to lose it!" said SeRina.

"Don't be such a drama-queen, clearly if everyone tells you that, you must be gorgeous honey!" said Briana.

"Clearly," replied SeRina and all three girls cracked up laughing.

SeRina turned and said to the salon receptionist, "Hey Sharon, Is Hayden here today?"

Hayden was her absolute fave' pedicurist at Prissy's Pedicure Palace. She remembered that the other woman Phuong didn't rub her feet near as long as Hayden would. SeRina also recalled and didn't like the fact that when it came time to pay the last time she noticed she was overcharged and when she questioned Phuong, despite her previous perfect diction, all of a sudden English became the pedicurist's distant second language. She secretly vowed to boycott the salon that is until Miki and Bri convinced her to come along and give the salon another try. She really couldn't stand being around "those people." She made jokes with her friends about the fact that they had the audacity to come live amongst Americans and not bother to learn to speak proper English. She made it a point to talk louder than necessary to be understood and hated the way they would switch to their native language as they pleased. She always secretly suspected they were making jokes about her and her friends so she resented them for their imaginary insults.

"Yes, Hayden is in the back, he was expecting you," said Phuong Qui to SeRina with a Mandarin twang. "Please choose color for your nails." SeRina walked past her station remembering her as the shady pedicurist from her last visit. She laughed to herself as she noticed she was the only employee with a customer-less workstation.

As SeRina browsed the rows of polish, Miki said, "So did you ask your Dad yet about our summer trip to Miami?"

"No worries, Dad is totally wrapped!" said SeRina while wiggling her pinky. "As long as I keep my grades up, it is a guarantee! Miami here we come!" She sniffed and nervously exhaled while wrinkling her nose from the stench of the acetone, all the while selecting her favorite peachy shade of coral.

"Cool," said Bri, "Well, I guess since you have him wrapped around your little finger that you won't have to ask him if you can keep the car tonight so that we can go meet Christophe and Alex at Wes's party?"

"What party?" SeRina inquired, "Alex and I have a movie date tonight...we are going to see that new McConaughey movie. He is so hot, I can't wait... you know he is notorious for taking off his shirt in every possible scene!"

"Well, there has been a total change of plans I talked to Alex earlier, interrupted Miki, he said that this is the "party of the year" and that he doesn't plan on missing it... he told me to apologize to you for flaking and said to invite you to crash with us. I mean come on.... Wes's parents are out of town and he has the mansion all to himself... can you say pool party? Oh, and did I mention that Christophe is going to be there?"

"Yea, yea, yea, you mentioned that Christophe is going to be there," SeRina said trying to hide her grin. She had not-so-secretly had her eye on Christophe Jacobs since the first day of 7th grade and it wasn't until recently that she discovered that he too was crushing on her. "Well, my Mom and Dad do have this "thing" to go to tonight, so I'm sure they won't miss me, so why not, count me in! It's going to be a total blast!"

"Sounds like a plan," said Bri. They all laughed and made general chit chat about the hot's and the not-so-hot's at school, who was wearing Prada and who was seeing who until their toes were all dried and gleaming. Then they all got up, walked into the mall for some more chatter, stopped by their favorite boutique for an outfit, and grabbed some fro-yo from the food court before exiting Crystal Heights Mall.

CHAPTER FOUR

The Ride

"Woohoo!" Miki exclaimed as she hung out of the top of Mr. Salvatore's 2009 convertible Mercedes. Speeding down Kiley Avenue, the girls were on their way to the party of the year. SeRina didn't bother asking to borrow the car for the rest of the evening, she just turned off her cell phone "accidentally on purpose" and kept the car. She did this knowing that when she got home things would blow over in a matter of minutes with her Dad, once she fed him the story she had concocted. As storm clouds formed overhead, SeRina decided it best for them to pull over long enough to put the top up. After the short pit stop, they pulled up around 7:00 p.m. to the beautiful mansion.

"We are definitely going to be the 3 hottest girls at the party tonight," said Briana.

"I know, we look like Charlie's Angels, a blonde, a brunette and well, you know the other chick," said Michaela referring to SeRina.

"What's that supposed to mean? Asked SeRina offended at being the "other chick" who so happened to be Chinese.

"Well, nobody ever knows what you are..." said Michaela uncomfortable that what was meant for a compliment had touched a sore spot.

"I'm friggin' human! Why does that always matter?" snapped SeRina.

"And you're flawless, so forget about it!" said Briana.

After making a final lip-gloss and mascara check, SeRina, still annoyed, exited the vehicle slamming the door behind her and walking ahead of her friends.

"What's her deal?" asked Michaela.

"I know, it's not like you said she was black! Oh well, who cares...let's party!" replied Briana.

"Lets!" said Michaela and they followed her into the double doors of the mansion.

Meanwhile, at the Salvatore house, things weren't going so well. Darrene had just returned from the hairdresser to discover her daughter had not yet come home with the dry-cleaning.

"I cannot believe that SeRina hasn't come home yet with my dress!" exclaimed Darrene as she tore through the closet to find another gown for the evening's formal festivities.

"Sweetheart, I know she must have a valid reason for not being home yet, just find something else to wear. I am sure you will look lovely," he said while adjusting his bowtie in the mirror.

Mr. Salvatore was always optimistic although he quietly worried about his daughter who had recently become more detached, self-centered, and increasingly undependable. He reflected on his more conservative younger days and thought SeRina was probably just out having the fun he wished he had as a teenager. He and Darrene would just take one of the other cars from his vast collection.

His wife had a vast wardrobe and should have no trouble finding another outfit to wear for the night. She was still in the closet shuffling through her dresses becoming more and more frustrated by the minute at the thought of SeRina's blatant disobedience.

"I can't find a thing to wear that these people haven't already seen me in before!" said Mrs. Salvatore as she combed through her enormous wardrobe.

He paused momentarily, as he eyed her admiring her beauty and finding himself drawn to her even after all these years. He thought she was being a bit materialistic and ridiculous given the size of her wardrobe but loved her nonetheless. Shaking off the notion of skipping the fundraiser altogether and taking advantage of some much needed time alone, he picked up his notes and reviewed his speech for the evening pausing briefly to check his hair in the mirror.

"Darrene, we need to get going Angel, we only have an hour before my big speech." He pretended to be anxious about the fundraiser benefit he was hosting for the new children's wing at the hospital. Quietly he knew they had all the funds the board requested and that they would be breaking ground soon for the new wing, and that this was simply a formality. He walked over to the closet and picked out a little black number that he loved her in and handed it to her.

"Wear this, it is my favorite anyhow." He said eye-balling her with encouragement.

Darrene interjected, "But I wore this to the last..."

He hushed her lips with a kiss and whispered in her ear, "... and you looked lovely then too. Wear it for me, Angel."

Mrs. Salvatore smiled looking up at her husband of 20 years and said to him, "Get the car honey, I will be out shortly." She quickly dressed slipping effortlessly into the slinky black gown and fastened the string of pearls and matching bracelet he had bought her around her neck and wrist. She flipped off the light over her vanity, grabbed her purse and headed down the hall. On her way out, she peered into SeRina's room to see if she had returned, shook her head in disappointment, and headed down the semi-circular staircase toward the mahogany French doors. It looked like rain, so she grabbed her overcoat from the living room closet, and jumped into the Seven Series BMW waiting out front.

In the meantime, the girls were having the time of their lives at Wes's party. Their stylishly late arrival and Mother Nature made them miss the pool festivities. However, they made good on their promise to liven things up and had everyone on their feet dancing in every room on the first floor of the 6,000 square foot mansion.

Michaela and Briana were heading in from the patio area since the storm was about to kick up a notch. SeRina caught Christophe stealing a glance her way and nervously fidgeted as he made his way to her across the room, moving to the rhythm of Usher's smooth vocals. Without a word, he secured his lock of silky blonde hair behind his ear, took her hand, and led her to the makeshift dance floor between the sofas in the living room. She took in his scent and felt invigorated and nervous as he drew her close to him and they swayed to the music. Everyone disappeared for a moment as she lost herself in his arms and his ocean blue eyes and forgot all about her surroundings and the storm brewing right outside the window. That is until a crash of lightning snatched her back into reality when it struck a nearby tree knocking over the power lines.

Soon after, a few flickers of light put an end to the music and the electricity in the house. Christophe did not miss a beat; he pulled her even closer in the dark taking advantage of nature's abrupt interruption kissing her softly and deeply as she had long hoped for him to do. Soon after, the room erupted with giggles and wild teenagers throwing pillows, spilling drinks, and chasing one another through the darkness.

"Party's over, everybody out!" yelled Wes after a clumsy boy broke his mother's favorite vase.

"Come on, let's get out of here!" Christophe said to SeRina.

She loved the tender urgency she heard in his voice. She gave up on finding her friends in the frenzied darkness in the massive house and figured they would find a ride with someone else. They ran across the lawn, through the rain, hand in hand to her father's car, where they clumsily jumped in together to be sheltered from the pouring rain.

"Now where do we go?" asked SeRina as she secured her wet curly hair in a ponytail holder.

"I don't know. Does it matter really, as long as we're together? Come on, live a little, now move over and let me drive." retorted Christophe.

"OK?" she said and seductively climbed over him to trade places without getting out of the vehicle. She paused briefly on the way over to give him a soft peck on the lips. Next, she glanced at her cell phone and saw it was already past curfew. She ignored the blinking message light and missed call indicator. She decided to toss aside the prodding of her conscience and powered off her phone. She would come up with an excuse for her tardiness later. She knew no matter how imaginary the story, that her loving father would eat it up and that he would convince her mother that things were fine.

Much to Christophe's surprise, his heart skipped a beat as she brushed past him. She was so beautiful and he too had dreamt of this moment since the seventh grade when he saw her for the first time. He silently reminisced about her entering the classroom as a new student and remembered how he almost missed his chair when he sat down because of how taken he was by her. He remembered thinking she was the most beautiful girl he had ever seen. Not to mention she was the 'it girl' at school, always stylish, always stunning, always mysterious. After a fleeting look at the exotic beauty at his side, he drove off into the storm, no destination in mind, and felt a tingling surge of bliss at the thought that he had finally made his move on the girl of his dreams.

He ignored the crash of lightning and the wind's effects on the Mercedes and pretended to be an experienced driver. With mounting nervousness, he continued to navigate his way around the newly fallen branches through the darkness. Unable to take his eyes off of her, Christophe missed the road sign warning of a curve ahead. As the lights temporarily blinded him, SeRina shrieked in anticipation of impact ...

"Sweetheart, your speech was amazing," Mrs. Salvatore said to her husband as he returned to the reserved table at the front of the lavishly appointed ballroom.

"What can I say? You inspire me, Angel," retorted Dr. Salvatore. He stopped and swept her hair aside to place a kiss on the nape of her neck before returning to his seat.

He nodded at a few passersby, silently accepting their accolades and then stood to shake hands with Senator Oliver, one of the area's richest lawyers-turned-Senator. Scott Oliver and Geoffrey Salvatore had been friends for years. Scott's generous support of the new children's wing provided the perfect opportunity for the two to forge an even greater bond. Scott's family came from old money. They were the Jones's to keep up with in this city, second only to Geoffrey's own family.

Scott introduced his gorgeous but bimbo-ish wife who towered over him in her 6-inch stilettos. Geoffrey took a double-take at her orange tan and bulging huge fake ta-ta's and disguised his laugh with a cough. Her bleach blonde hair fell past her shoulders and rested in her cleavage. Darrene thought she looked ridiculous and trashy with all of her groceries in the window of her outlandishly low cut gown. After they exchanged hellos and fake promises to meet for dinner, as people do. They parted ways, and Darrene returned to her seat at the banquet table.

"Ah, ah, ah," said Geoffrey jokingly catching his wife just before she sat. "May I have this dance Mrs. Salvatore?" he asked, extending his hand in jest with his most impressive James Bond overtone.

She rose from the table, took his hand, and replied playing her part in the charade, "Certainly, Mr. Salvatore. Geoffrey Salvatore."

They laughed making their way to the dance floor where they whirled to the music of the orchestra until midnight. After the final song, Mrs. Salvatore mentioned again to her husband that they still hadn't heard from their daughter and although the party was still in full effect, they decided to cut the night short. The Salvatore's exchanged polite goodbyes and stopped to collect their vehicle from the valet. As they paused at the valet desk, Mrs. Salvatore said, "Are you certain she hasn't called?"

"100% sweetheart." He asserted. "But let me check my cell to see if perhaps I missed a call from her during my speech." He checked his Blackberry again and it reflected no missed calls. He again tried to call SeRina but to no avail. The phone immediately went to her voicemail and her perky voice resonated once more,

"It's me, you know what to do at the beep."

After the beep, he left a third message for her, "SeRina, its Dad. Your Mother and I are worried about you, please call and let us know what's going on. I hope you have made it home safe."

He hung up and then followed up with a call to their home.

"Still no answer?" asked Darrene.

"No answer, honey, but I'm sure she is OK, she may have left us a note at the house, or she may just be asleep or sleeping over at Michaela's or Briana's. Don't worry Angel, let's just head home and I'm sure there we will find our answer."

Geoffrey stilled Darrene from pacing and stole a kiss from her as they continued to wait on the valet to return with the BMW. They were grateful that they had opted for the valet service and watched the wind whip the nearby trees and soon the rain came pounding down upon the sidewalk. The hotel's canopy styled entrance was no match for the wind and provided little shelter as the wind ensured the rain would make its way under it.

Upon arrival, the valet driver pulled under the hotel canopy and hurriedly exited the car leaving the driver's side door open for Mr. Salvatore. Geoffrey slipped him a $20 bill at the rear of the vehicle; he then opened the passenger door, waited for her to be seated then returned to the driver's side and took his seat. Darrene thought to herself that chivalry was definitely not dead and took note of the care he took to always be a gentleman even if it meant getting drenched. She then in appreciation gently took her husband's right hand as he drove from the parking lot of the hotel. She stared at the raindrops that ricocheted down the passenger side window all the while worrying about her daughter's whereabouts.

"If she is OK, I am going to choke her!" she said sternly interrupting the silence as she glanced over at her husband.

He chuckled as he carefully made a left turn, growing increasingly worried about her as well, but not letting his wife in on that fact. He replayed the morning's conversation in his head where he reminded SeRina of the evening's events, needing the car back, and needing her to pick up the dry cleaning.

Within a few miles of reaching the Salvatore estate, Geoffrey convinced himself to relax. Surely SeRina was already home. These days, it wasn't unusual for her to disregard curfew and fail to check in. She was probably sleeping off a long night of partying and dri ... he didn't care to finish that particular thought. To distract himself, he made light conversation about the evening and complimented Darrene at how deftly she had navigated the pretentious crowd of the city's elite. He took his eyes off the road for a moment as he reached to flip the satellite radio over to her favorite jazz station.

In that instant, a brilliant bolt of lightning flashed and thunder roared just as the BMW hydroplaned and started to spin. Geoffrey fought to control the vehicle as it crossed the median, sliding passenger-side first into oncoming traffic. Beside him, Darrene gasped as the blinding lights of oncoming headlights filled the car. The Peterbilt 387 struck the passenger-side door with enough force to catapult the BMW into mid-air.

Everything came to a screeching halt, with the Salvatore's vehicle resting upside down on the embankment, wheels still spinning. Peering past the deployed airbag, Geoffrey's eyes took in the sight of his beautiful angel suspended by her seatbelt, motionless and bleeding. He reached for her, desperate to find a pulse. As his fingers touched her wrist, thoughts of how beautiful and delicate she was crossed his mind, as the world around him faded into darkness.

In what felt like a dream, an uncharacteristically giddy SeRina arrived home to the Salvatore estate. Despite the late hour, she burst into the house eager to share with her mother all of the fun she'd had at the party and the dazzling news that she had finally connected with Christophe.

"Mother! I had the greatest night!" Her voice echoed throughout the mansion.

"Mother? Father? I'm home!" Still no response.

It was so late. How could they not be home? And they haven't even called to check on! Talk about being irresponsible. They needed to take some of their own advice and... Her cell phone! That's right. She fished the phone from the bottom of her bag and pressed the button to bring it back to life. She'd shut it off so that she could enjoy a night of uninterrupted freedom with Christophe.

As she waited for the phone to power back on, SeRina flopped onto her bed and stretched out. As her thoughts began to drift, she remembered her promise to pick up Mother's dry-cleaning. Too late now. Anyway, Mother had a ton of dresses to choose from, so what was the big deal about that one dress anyway?

They must be having the time of their lives at that stupid fundraiser, thought SeRina.

The phone chimed softly, interrupting her thoughts. Three missed calls and two voicemail messages. Father didn't sound too upset, so she was fairly certain any punishment could be avoided, as long as her story was a good one. And it was a good one. Christophe, with his pale blue eyes, soft lips…their first kiss. SeRina's eyes closed and her thoughts turned to dreams as she faded into sleep.

"DING, DONG!" SeRina was startled awake by the deep chiming of the front doorbell. A quick glance at the clock told her it was 5 am. She sunk back into the warmth of her covers, hoping that Mother or Father would answer the door quickly. She wasn't ready to leave her dreamland behind just yet.

"DING, DONG!" SeRina sat up. She winced as the doorbell sounded again, this time followed by a loud, steady pounding on the heavy front door. "MOTHER! JESUS! WILL YOU ANSWER THE DOOR?" she bellowed through the darkness. Annoyed, she threw the covers aside and swung her legs over the side of the bed and realized she was still wearing her clothes from the night before. She surveyed herself in the mirror and re-secured her ponytail. Whoever was at the door would just have to deal with her rumpled look. After all, they were the ones choosing to come calling in the wee hours of the morning.

SeRina made her way to the front door, feeling caught in between a dream and reality. Groggy. Unclear. Just not quite herself. Hmmm. Probably lack of sleep. Shake it off, SeRina, she thought. She paused for a moment at the front door, steadying herself with the doorknob. The feeling of being exhausted and achy gripped her even more intensely. Why was she feeling this way? She peered through the door's side-panel to discover a police officer staring back at her, shining a flashlight on her face. Heart pounding in her chest, she swung the door open and then SeRina was given the shocking news and a ride to the ER.

CHAPTER FIVE

Unplugged and Unglued

While his decision to pull the plug on his wife of 20 years was undoubtedly the hardest decision he had ever made, Dr. Salvatore knew it was the right one. He and his wife had both expressed their desire never to be strung out on life support. Matter of fact they both had signed advanced medical directives indicating that they desired to be "let go" in a situation where only life support was sustaining them.

Although 3 months had passed, she had shown no signs of improvement and he knew the prognosis was dim and that her chances of ever waking from the coma were non-existent. He closely monitored her progress at the very hospital where he practiced, frequently consulting with doctors and trying to look for an inkling of hope. They patronized him and allowed her to stay on life support longer than the usual patient, quietly ignoring the inevitable.

Although his wife had been unconscious since the moment of the accident, the injuries he sustained in comparison were minimal. So a few short days later Geoffrey was released from the hospital with a bruised liver, fractured wrist and some minor abrasions. He wished day in and out that he had been on the passenger's side and blamed himself for everything. Thoughts of what he could have done differently plagued him constantly and although the thought entered his mind, he would not allow himself to blame SeRina for the accident. He rationalized that they would have left the party anyhow even if she were home safe and sound and that it was just a case of an unforeseen occurrence. He tried to persuade himself to believe that no matter what time they would have left that party that things would have panned out the same. He accepted the cliché notion that God must have "needed another angel." He vowed at that moment to give his all to their daughter no matter what happened to his wife.

SeRina, plagued with guilt, made her visits few to the hospital and decided instead to indulge herself in her extracurricular activities and excursions with her newfound boyfriend. She couldn't stand to look at her mother in this condition all swollen and lifeless. It was also inexcusable to her how pitiful her father had become. He spent every waking moment at the depressing hospital by her side reading, praying, talking to her, and willing her to come to. SeRina felt it was pointless him being there because Darrene would not ever even know.

SeRina continued with the cynicism from the moment she laid eyes on her laying in that hospital bed. She knew things were hopeless, and it cut her to the core, but this was an inconvenient pain that she simply could not take the time to bear. She had other things to do, other places to be, and she could not let this get her down. She had to "keep it moving" as she liked to say jokingly to her friends at school. None of her close friends wanted to shatter her reality so they allowed her to go on thinking her behavior was normal. They were somewhat used to it. This was her coping mechanism and they had seen it all too often. They all knew that she had an odd way of internalizing her fears and pains and ignoring them until they became nonexistent, and that is exactly what SeRina was doing again.

Dr. Salvatore struggled to find the words to say goodbye to his beloved wife. In her final moments, he did what he knew best. Although he was suffocating and riddled with guilt, battling a sea of uncertainty, he tried to make the best of the situation by reflecting on his most treasured memories of their lives.

SeRina had arrived the hospital but hadn't mustered up the courage to go into the room. She watched and listened quietly outside the door unbeknownst to her father.

"I remember the day we met, Darrene. I was drowning my sorrows in cheap whiskey. I had broken the heart of a woman I loved deeply and I was wallowing in guilt and self-pity. Do you remember what you said? I do. Actually, I'll never forget it. With the most matter-of-fact look on your face, you said, "Look, the only time you run out of chances, is when you stop taking them. What are you doing sitting here? Go after her, whoever she is, because she must be one hell of a woman to have someone like you acting like this." Geoffrey smiled to himself in recollection.

"And well, it was as if you were reading my mind. Somehow, you knew I was having relationship issues. I never told you who she was or why I hurt her, and after that moment, frankly, it didn't matter. Because something in me opened up after hearing you say those words to me. Somehow I knew that you were tied to my destiny.

And so the story goes... I fell for you in that moment, forgetting the past and forging you into the heart of my future. I knew after our first date that someday I would make you my wife, and God made it so. I honored every word of our wedding vows...but I've failed you, my darling..." Geoffrey took a deep breath as his head sunk. The memories were just too much for him to bear and in that moment his thoughts darkened. "I have dedicated my life to saving people, yet I can't save you! Why can't I will you through this? I want you to wake up and be angry with me for making you go to that damned conference! I was so selfish. My God, we were all so selfish. If SeRina would've just come home like she was supposed to, you wouldn't be lying here."

SeRina, overhearing her father say these words was cut to the core. She turned and without a word left the hospital not saying goodbye to the only mother she had ever known and leaving her father to do the unthinkable alone.

After a moment of quiet, Mr. Salvatore continued the conversation with his unconscious wife. "But what am I thinking? I can't blame SeRina, she made us a family." He paused for a moment smiling to himself. "That girl, what are we going to do with that girl? She changed it all, didn't she? She made it all make sense even after you put your body through hell, miscarriage after miscarriage and even after all the failed fertility treatments you never complained. I loved seeing you love her. You were the best mother she could have ever had, and the best wife a man could ever hope for. I promise to be the best father I can be to SeRina, I promise to honor your wishes and let her know about her mother when the time is right."

Geoffrey paused, shifting his thoughts and regaining his composure.

"You know, I always hear married people say they have all these regrets, or they wish they could go back in time and change this or that. Well, my Angel, I just wish I could go back in time, not to change a thing, but just to feel a few things twice. Like the way, I feel when you walk into the room, the surge of bliss that courses through me with your every kiss, the warmth of your touch ... I would give the world just to hear you laugh one more time. I would just love to relive all of the times that I fell in love with you Darrene."

He gazed upon her heavenly face and watched her chest moving mechanically up and down from the respirator that forced air in and out of her lungs. She looked so beautiful and so peaceful. He fondly reminisced about better times, all of the years they spent raising their daughter and all the laughs and love they had shared. When had it come to this? When had SeRina become so self-absorbed and cold-hearted that even a tragedy such as this could not faze her? He silently blamed himself for spoiling her through the years and giving her all the things he had and more as a child.

Never once had he called her his "adoptive daughter." From the very first moment he and Darrene brought SeRina home as a rambunctious 4-year-old, she was his baby and he loved her with all of his heart and soul. Regardless of this love, he couldn't help feeling betrayed by her at this moment. He had given her everything she had ever wanted, and SeRina chose not to be there with him when he needed her the most to ease his pain. A tear escaped his eye, he took a moment attempting to compose himself, he kissed his wife once more on the lips lingering and willing from the depths of his soul for her to awake, but to no avail.

"Goodbye Angel..." he said.

Dr. McNary entered the room and Geoffrey gave him the nod of approval.

Things happened so quickly after that. It was only moments after the machines were shut off that the whooshing sound of the respirator faded to deafening silence and the time of death was recorded.

Geoffrey stood alone in the hall hurting, lost in thought about what had just transpired. He peered in through the glass at his wife whose chest no longer mechanically moved. The attending nurse caught Geoffrey looking through the window. She then averted her eyes and reluctantly walked over and closed the shades to the room. Dr. Kwaisi, another of Geoffrey's friends/co-workers placed his hand on Geoffrey's shoulder and they exchanged glances as he entered the room with an unknown orderly.

Still frozen in the same place in the hall, Geoffrey continued to gawk hopelessly at the glass and the closed blinds. He shook his head in disbelief and finally turned his back to the window. He couldn't believe that SeRina had not shown up again, even though she knew this was the day, she knew the decision he had made.

His mind returned to the conversation from the previous evening. SeRina had just come in from school, and he had called to her as she passed his study.

"SeRina." No answer.

"SeRina, come here, sweetheart. We need to talk."
He remembered SeRina huffing into the study, yanking her earbuds

out.

"What??" she said, clearly not caring to hear the answer. She had been avoiding him like the plague lately.

"SeRina, have a seat."

"Ugh, ok..." sighed SeRina annoyed she had to stop her music.

"It's about your mother, her prognosis is dim. It's a fact we have to face."

He had studied her face for an inkling of 'give a damn', and she was fresh out.

"My heart is breaking to tell you this. Just listen to what I have to say. Tomorrow..." Geoffrey's voice trailed off as he remembered how he'd struggled to say the words that had until that point only been thoughts.

He tried again, "SeRina, I am going to give Dr. McNary permission to remove your mother from life support tomorrow. Do you know what that means?"

SeRina glared at him and screamed, "Of course I know what that means! You're going to KILL HER. 'Her prognosis is dim.' Wow, really Dad? Go on and pull the plug and treat her like another one of your stupid patients! It doesn't matter anyway. Tomorrow is Briana's party and I told her I'd help with the decorations." SeRina refused to face reality so instead diverted her thoughts to a lighter topic. Her father's face was filled with pain and she knew that her words had in part put it there. Her mission was accomplished. He had shut up for a moment.

Something broke in Geoffrey and for the first time he completely lost his temper with SeRina. "SeRina, a party? Are you serious? Are you hearing yourself? How can you be so selfish? What is the matter with you? She's your mother!

"No, she's not," said SeRina, her words cutting Geoffrey to the core and catching him completely by surprise. She had never said that before.

SeRina immediately regretted the harshness of her words, but her desire to run, to avoid this conversation and the reality of what tomorrow would bring outweighed her desire to be tactful. This time her words silenced Geoffrey completely, and with that, she jammed the earbuds back into her ears and stormed out of the study.

That dreadful morning after the argument, Geoffrey apologized for losing his temper through the closed bathroom door before SeRina left for school. She ignored him so he waited for her to come out and stopped SeRina in the hall to ask her to come with him to say goodbye. She rolled her eyes and continued to ignore him. He contemplated slapping her face moments before she rushed off to school, leaving him to do this alone.

Geoffrey found it surreal that SeRina had left him there alone to give the final nod. He had no idea that just moments ago she had watched him, longing to come to his side. He didn't know what hurt worse, the fact that he had just unplugged his wife or the fact that SeRina didn't appear to give a damn. Although he desperately needed to cry, he suppressed his tears and the rage swelling within. He shrugged away a shiver as he realized that he was all too familiar with the goings on in the sequestered room. He remained there, feet anchored to the floor staring out at the overpriced artwork that graced the wall in that hallway. He waited long enough for her death to be recorded, her face to be covered with a white sheet, and for the orderly to remove her body and cart it past him down the hall. Dr. McNary, surprised to see him still standing in the same spot as before, said, "Geoffrey, can I get you anything?"

Geoffrey shook his head "no" in reply.

"How about we go down and sit with Chaplin Mathodikus?"

Geoffrey again shook his head "no" in reply.

"Please let me know if there is anything I can do to help," said Dr. McNary placing a hand on his shoulder before walking away to complete the paperwork.

Geoffrey stood frozen and watched in complete disbelief as the orderly turned and began down another corridor with the love of his life.

It hit him at that very moment that she was gone forever.

Uncontrollable dizziness set in and he pressed his back against the window for stability. Just like that, it was over. He felt his heart shatter into a million pieces. Suddenly, there was no more pretense. He knew at that moment that the manufactured hope that she would recover had pacified him somehow. He knew that hope was no more. The chair that was just an arm's length away wasn't close enough to reach nor was it low enough for him. He needed to be on the floor, he prayed that maybe that would stop everything from spinning. He slid slowly down the wall his back feeling the coolness of the glass window, then the bump of the chair rail trim, then the smoothness of the drywall. He was grounded, but still, the hospital and the thoughts suffocated him, he couldn't scream, he needed to escape, to bolt as fast and as far away as possible, yet he had no strength to run.

The people seemed to disappear and reappear. For a moment he thought he even saw SeRina. He couldn't be sure though, he couldn't face her now, not at this moment. She should have been there! How could SeRina be so cold, how could Darrene be gone? He willed himself to pass out and become cold to the pain but still, he sat caught between consciousness and oblivion. In slow motion, he placed his head on his knees and released the deluge of tears that had been dammed and damned. The nurses rushed to him and attempted to console him there on the floor as he sat alone and sobbing outside the room where she once lay.

On the day of the funeral, the sun appeared to mock Geoffrey's sorrow, shining in all its glory and radiating in reflection on the shiny silver coffin where Darrene lay. The service was a blur. He found himself standing outside as the minister said his final words and everyone stood still in deafening silence. The wind dried the one tear SeRina felt trickling from her eye.

SeRina thought to herself that she could not cry in front of these people, these phony people. If one more of them apologized to her for her loss she would scream. How could she lose something that was never hers in the first place? How could they remotely care about her feelings and what in the hell were they sorry for?

She thought it silly the never-ending array of floral arrangements surrounding the coffin and just wished the whole thing was done and over with. To SeRina it was foolish to cut off the life of a perfectly healthy flower as a gift to someone who had no life and couldn't even enjoy it. She thought how much the flowers must have cost and what she would've done with the money instead if it were her decision to make.

She shifted her thoughts from the silly flowers and imaginary shopping spree and sternly reminded herself that Darrene Salvatore was only her "fake" mother and that her "real" mother was still alive and well and out there to be found.

She pacified herself with the thought of what new adventures she could concoct. SeRina was there in body alone, she might as well have been one of the nearby trees. She stood tall and firm and unmoving, daydreaming and playing out scenarios of how her real mother would be when she met her. She would be rich, beautiful, successful, loving, and without a doubt white. And regretful, definitely regretful. That final thought made her feel better.

So, she tucked away her pain and decided it was time to know the truth about her past. She convinced herself it was time to finally ask for some answers, but decided it best to wait a couple of weeks after the funeral to give her Father some time to just get over things. Yes, that is what she would do. She caught herself just as she was about to smile and cleared her throat in pretense. A relative standing nearby noticed SeRina's distraction and punctuated her disapproving gaze with a raised penciled on eyebrow. Despite the silent gesture of correction, there she stood, under the mocking sun oblivious to the pain of all around her. SeRina continued pondering her newest venture and tuned out the rest of the funeral service.

Things were quiet in the Salvatore mansion. Dr. Salvatore had their housekeeper move into the in-law suite to help with the daily activities. He took an extended leave from the hospital and wanted to use that time to get closer to his daughter. For a long time, he had noticed SeRina withdrawing from him and Darrene and now more than ever he wanted to rebuild the bond that they once shared.

He missed his wife more than words could express and wanted to focus his attentions elsewhere and drown away the sorrow. He needed SeRina to open up to him, he desperately needed to understand her and why she was not there for him. He had suppressed the resentment he felt toward her and dismissed it as "her way" of dealing with the pain. Nevertheless, as time progressed she did not seem to miss her mother at all. They never spoke of her, and SeRina behaved as if her mother was simply away on a vacation or business. SeRina had become increasingly difficult to find these days. She would pop in and out after school making excuses of "special projects" and group study sessions. She would gulp down her dinner and make her escape to her room where she texted and Tweeted, and Facebooked, until the wee hours of the morning ignoring him. Finally, a few months after the funeral she had taken a moment to seek him out and he was eager to hear what she had to say.

So she asked, and the room stood still, Geoffrey Salvatores' excitement for what he thought to be some quality time with his daughter was instantly turned into loathing. It was so quiet the moment after she uttered the words that you could hear the hum of the HVAC unit on the lower level.

Now? Dr. Salvatore thought. He almost uttered it aloud as he turned his back to her. *Seriously, she wants to know now, of all times?*

With a great deal of emotional angst, he remembered that not long ago he and his wife had argued whether or not to ever disclose the whereabouts of SeRina's biological mother. He recalled the passion in his wife's eyes and the finality in the resonance of her voice when she declared, "She has a right to know, and when the time is right we will tell her!"

A few years prior, his wife told him she had contacted SeRina's maternal grandmother, and that she wanted them to meet and discuss the possibility of being in SeRina's life. He dismissed the idea as a poor and unnecessary choice and remembered the disappointment on her face when Darrene realized he wouldn't budge on his decision.

Geoffrey's mind returned to the moment he and his wife had decided to adopt. They had specifically requested a Caucasian newborn baby girl but were placed on a long waiting list. When they found out that a toddler was available, they decided to move forward with the adoption. He remembered how he and his wife were amazed to see the beautiful baby girl with eyes that matched their own and how they felt she was a gift from God. Geoffrey had brilliant gray eyes, as did Darrene. Likewise, they both had beautiful olive complexions. So it was only natural for people to assume that SeRina was their biological daughter. Given the similarities. There was no need for lengthy explanations about the years of expensive infertility treatments or for all the years of trying and the heartache of two consecutive miscarriages. It all ceased to matter because they were blessed with a child who could pass for their very own.

He simply wanted to be closer to her and now she wanted to replace the only mother she had ever known with one who had abandoned her. He felt the fury raging within and could not wrap his mind around why she wanted to know this now. She had never asked before. He was afraid if he opened her eyes to this part of her life that she would slip away from him forever. He was hesitant but his wife's words resonated in his head:

"She has a right to know, and when the time is right we will tell her!"

How he wished that Darrene was here so that this moment could be a shared effort. He felt she was there with him in spirit and somehow that prodded him to divulge the truth. So Geoffrey reluctantly walked from the chaise lounge in his study over to the 10-foot mahogany bookcase and removed a dainty round hand carved wooden box. He stood for a moment unwilling to come unglued with emotion a second time. Exhaling to expel his qualms, he turned to his daughter, carved box in hand.

SeRina studied him as he moved, noticing the hesitation in his steps. She knew this was hard for him but felt it was her right to know. She was almost 18 and had wondered all her life about her "real" parents. She was tired of people she met day in and day out complimenting her beauty, but next asking her nationality, her race, her origin, her ethnicity. Honestly, this had been a looming question all her life, and she did not know the answer. It was never discussed with her adoptive parents. She had always assumed she was Italian like the Salvatores, she had always simply been SeRina Alise Salvatore.

"Look SeRina, I don't know why you are doing this. Your mother and I love you and we chose you. We have always been honest with you from the start about you being adopted, we never kept any secrets. Now look, I've never met your mother. You know the story, we adopted you when you were almost four years old. The agency told us when we adopted you that it was up to us to decide whether or not to ever disclose to you who your biological family was. And well, we put away the information and hoped that you would never ask. But since you insist, here you are dear. I hope you find whatever it is you are looking for." he said, handing her the paper he removed from the box.

This is it! SeRina thought as she held firm to the sliver of paper.

On a crisp sheet of parchment paper with an insignia that looked like an old pocket watch was a handwritten name and an address.

"Hattie? Hmm what an interesting name," thought SeRina.

It amazed her that the answers to her lifelong puzzle resided right under her nose in her father's study. She chided herself for never noticing the wooden box. It was obvious enough and did not even remotely fit in with her father's baseball collectibles and memorabilia. She wondered why after all these years he had never bothered to share the contents of the wooden box. She wondered why the paper had a clock-like insignia next to the address. She felt incensed at the thought that he had the answers all this time but had never volunteered to provide them.

She then appeased herself with the realization that she had simply never bothered to ask and without a word left the study, leaving the box behind but clutching the sliver of paper tightly in her hand.

CHAPTER SIX

A Lesson in History

Six months had flown by since the passing of Darrene Salvatore and winter staked its claim on the grounds surrounding the Salvatore estate. It was an ordinary day in February and SeRina was making her way to school. She and her classmates noisily scurried into the classroom taking their seats. For some reason on this particular day, SeRina couldn't take her mind off finally getting the courage to venture out to meet her real mom. Lost in thought, SeRina gazed out of the classroom window at the snow-draped evergreens. The sunlight gleamed off of the snow, illuminating her beautiful eyes and Christophe stole a kiss as he passed her on his way to his seat

SeRina smiled at him genuinely and returned to her thoughts. She was in such a hurry to get the information about her biological mother from her Dad but hadn't yet dared to set out to that tough part of town to find out who she was.

She missed Darrene tremendously and days like this reminded her of the only mother she ever knew. Winter was Darrene's favorite season, she loved how the snow sparkled on the trees and would take long walks trudging through the snow with SeRina when she was a kid. They would lay together in the knee deep snow making angels despite her father's warnings that she would "catch a cold." She could hear her mothers' laugh and see her smile in her minds' eye. She felt the familiar lump in her throat and dismissed the sad thought just as the bell rang.

Ms. Parker, the Social Studies teacher at Arlington Manor High wasted no time getting down to business and immediately addressed the class saying, "Good Morning class as you all know today is February 1st and this will be the beginning of our focus on Black History. I want to take a nontraditional approach to this topic this year. In doing so, I would like to challenge our countries' amnesia about a part of our history that has been swept under the rug. Unfortunately, the textbook version of the history of African Americans consists of only slavery. And although that is a large part of the history, the contributions of African Americans to society has been abridged and condensed down to a mere 28-day celebration. In order to take a deeper look at things, I have arranged for us to take a field trip to a portion of the Underground Railroad and also have arranged for a physical reenactment of the conditions under which slaves were subjected when they were transported to America. I also want to talk about the correlation between slavery and modern day African American society, and how this past has affected our present. Next, we will focus on the contributions of African Americans from the 1800's to modern day ..."

It was this pragmatic, no-nonsense way that she so matter–of-factly said everything that drove SeRina crazy. She sat staring but not listening to the teacher as she droned on and on about black history, freedom, and the past. SeRina's eyes rolled in the usual fashion, followed by her escape to her daydream. Her musings about her mother were interrupted when one of her classmates said in jest, "Why are we learning about Black History, as you can see you are the only black one in the class." It was Amy Howard, the class snob. She always had something curt to say especially to Ms. Parker, the only black 12th-grade teacher on the faculty.

The class erupted with laughter, and SeRina, although annoyed at Amy's attention-getting comment, found herself especially tickled by the outburst. It was a fact she was all too aware of. She wondered how this woman even got a job at the upscale institution and reduced her presence there to her being the token black woman on the staff as a result of Affirmative Action or something of the like. The faculty was peppered with other races. Mr. Alkandro's who was the Greek Art instructor, and Mr. Ibaraki the Japanese Chemistry teacher, but she was the only black one.

SeRina always found Ms. Parker peculiar and out of place, her diction and phrasing of words never quite sat right with her. It was as if she was too rehearsed and trying to overcompensate for herself in some way. She assumed that her teacher's politeness and special attention to her and efforts to get her to focus and "apply herself" were all a sham and really preferred to daydream her way through the history course. SeRina knew enough to get by and that's all that mattered. Her inaudible grumblings escaped her eyes and Ms. Parker used it as an opportunity to call on her or to "humiliate" her as SeRina thought. SeRina knew nothing of black history, nor did she care about it, it didn't affect her, so it was inconsequential. The point was moot!

SeRina had secretly decided years before when teased and called the "n" word by a kid because of the curls in her hair way back in 6th grade, that there was no way she could be black. Her parents never told her what her ethnicity was, it didn't matter because she could change it with the wind, and she preferred not knowing. So, when people asked, she would vary her answers from Italian to Puerto Rican, she had even been Irish once but never once had she claimed to be "BLACK."

She shrugged her shoulders in answer to the rhetorical question Ms. Parker asked, half listening, and thinking to herself, Who did she think she was anyway? She began to doodle with the mechanical pencil she had just borrowed from Michaela giving the naturally pretty full figured woman a disapproving once-over. SeRina didn't consider herself a xenophobe but just preferred to stick with people who were more like her, you know, white people. She didn't have any desire to learn about any history of any kind, especially black.

Oh and great, she came back into focus long enough to hear the teacher Ms. Parker mention an assignment that required them to trace their roots and make a family tree. This was completely ridiculous to SeRina, and she would not have any part in it, she never told anyone she was adopted not even her closest friends and she wasn't about to start now.

She figured she would let her imagination complete the assignment and dreamt of what wonderful lineage she would invent to pad her family tree.

CHAPTER SEVEN

Over the Hill and Through the Hood

SeRina had made up her mind after being given that ridiculous assignment to scratch the itch of wonder titillating her. So she removed the crumpled paper with the mystery address that her father had given her months before, from the zipper on her backpack. She had stared at this paper a hundred times, running her fingers across the name and address so much that she had smudged the ink. She affixed her eyes on the paper especially interested in the timepiece insignia as she trudged through the halls of Arlington Manor High past her giggling friends and whispering enemies. Her head had been in a fog all day imagining what she may discover if she dared to go to that address. She pulled out her phone and keyed in the address using the navigation app to plan her route. She passed on the offer to "hang out" with Miki and didn't bother to call her Dad to tell him her whereabouts. She buckled herself in, resting her phone on the dash long enough to grab her sunglasses from the visor and survey herself in the rearview mirror. This was the moment of truth, and so she started the car and began the journey to Hattie's house. She didn't know what she would find there but figured it had to be even more wonderful than she had imagined.

In a flurry of thoughts, wonder, dreams, and wishes, she made her way through traffic to the interstate and then exited the freeway. She looked around and realized this was a far cry from the dream neighborhood she had imagined that her mother lived in. She pulled over briefly to look again at the navigation and make sure she hadn't missed a turn somewhere. On the next corner was a Package Liquor store fully stocked with neighborhood drunks and homeless men, black and white, sitting on the ground and rattling their cups for change. A couple of guys pulled up next to her flexing the hydraulics on their souped-up "old school" vehicle. One flashed an 18 karat gold smile and gestured for her to roll the window down. She diverted her eyes and they sped off when the light turned green flipping her off and yelling "stuck up hoe" at her out of the window.

She was so nervous, she almost forgot why she pulled over, and just when she started to get it together she was startled when a homeless man on the passenger side of the exit approached her vehicle, tapped on the window and with a rotten toothless grin pointed to his sign that said, "Why lie, it's for Beer." SeRina dropped her phone in a hurry to pull off and almost ran the man's foot over trying to get away from him. She triple checked the door locks and sped past the Package Liquor store. "Oh my God these niggers are crazy!" she said out loud. The "n" word was one she had used before with her friends without hesitation. She loathed everything about African American culture. The music, the saggin' pants, the thug mentality, it all irked her. Who did they think they were and why did they walk around feeling entitled to the world because of something that happened eons ago. She felt that they should simply get over it and that the world owed them absolutely nothing.

She found a more secure place to pull over and double-checked the navigation directions, discovering her destination was just a few short blocks away. Then it hit her, her mother lived in this terrible neighborhood with all of these blacks. How could she surround herself with such idiots? She thought maybe her mother was like one of those white women who enjoyed dating black men but had let them live off of her and suck away all of her money. Perhaps, her mother had let herself go at the thought of having to give her up for adoption, and that in her despair she just ended up living under these horrific conditions with the blacks on the wrong side of the tracks.

SeRina recollected having a discussion with her friends and vowing together to never date black guys. She remembered one of her friends saying that black men only dated white women as status symbols and to use them, take all of their money and wreck their credit. Her friend told her that black men thought white women were easy to control and manipulate, so they reigned over them like kings over subjects. She decided then and there that they were off limits and that she would only date boys like her, white ones.

SeRina proceeded slowly down College Avenue, all the while convincing herself that although this was not the mother she had imagined, somehow her mother must need saving from these horrid conditions. So she shrugged off her disappointment with the situation and continued on to rescue her mother "Hattie" from the woes of Arsenal Avenue.

The houses were narrow one-stories painted in a series of odd color combinations. One was Pepto-Bismol pink with lime green shutters and she thought it looked like something off of a cartoon. The other one next to it was an odd shade of blue, almost periwinkle with a pink door; it reminded her of an Easter egg.

These people clearly have no class, taste nor pride in their properties, she thought as she drove by unkempt lawns sporting broken down cars, beer bottles and driveways with yellow dandelions peeping through the cracks. She accelerated past two men pushing an old car to the side of the road and slowed to watch two ladies of the night leaning into windows and holding conversations without a care that they were in the middle of the street.

Finally, she was there in front of the house. It stood out for two reasons. First, it was the only two- story on the block, and second, it was the only house that was simply black and white. She smiled for a moment thinking that at least her mother had sense enough to use a tasteful color scheme and at least she owned the nicest house on the block. That is if you could even call this nice. Unlike the other yards, there were no broken bottles, no empty bags of chips, no debris, no grass or weeds sprouting up from the sidewalk, and it was jalopy-free. The bushes sat neatly and perfectly manicured in a row framing the cozy two-story.

SeRina thought to herself how the pool house at the Salvatore estate was bigger than this house and how small the rooms must be. The sun was setting now, and she surveyed the house for parked cars in the driveway and lights in the windows. There were none.

She parked anyway and exited the car hitting the alarm button on her key fob twice to be extra cautious. The BMW chirped in response. She opened the silver chain link fence, which groaned as if it had been locked for a century. She left the gate open in case she needed to make a speedy escape and then eyeballed the mailbox to ensure the address matched the one on the faded sliver of paper.

Her eyes widened with anticipation. She cleared her throat and recited out loud her introduction and how she would ask for her mother and how she would react.

"Ahem, yes, hello, I am your daughter."

No, that sounds to direct. Ok. You've got this...

"Hi, my name is SeRina, and well, I am looking for my mother."

OK, that is a little better. Oh my God, get it together girl, you can do this!

She told herself she wouldn't be overly emotional even though the choking feeling had set into her throat. She cleared her throat in vain and nervously pulled at her blouse and skirt in preparation.

Ding. Dong. Ding. Ding. Ding. Dong. Ding. Ding.

She did it; she mustered up enough courage to ring the doorbell. She wished she hadn't, the bell was still ringing playing the longest set of chimes she had ever heard. She waited for a split second and decided it was all a bad idea. She turned to make her fast escape down the two worn chipped and cracked cement stairs, and heard a voice say "Yes, may I help you?"

She froze in place, one foot on the step below, afraid of what she would see when she turned around. She just wanted to get out of there and fast.

The sweet and subtle voice said, "Who you lookin' for?"

SeRina turned to see a very frail hunchbacked BLACK woman with brown eyes circled with gray cataracts glaring over the rim of her glasses. The woman was much too old to be her mother and much too black to be even a distant relative.

"I'm sorry; I must have the wrong address," SeRina mumbled in disappointment as she turned again to leave.

"Now how you know that when you ain't even said who you lookin' for child? I swear these children these days can't give a straight answer to save their souls," said the old lady.

"I'm looking for the lady of the house," muttered SeRina.

Just then, the old lady turned, walked away closed the door returning a split second later, she opened the door again and said, "This is she... how may I help you?" the old lady cracked herself up.

SeRina thought the old lady must have lost her mind; she thought she should just go. "Sorry, you know I knew this was a bad idea, seriously I'm looking for my mother, Hattie Rouse and you clearly are not my mother, you are too... well, you're just, you're simply NOT her."

Before SeRina could finish her sentence, the old woman had bolted through the door with suddenly mustered incredible strength and wrapped her arms around her. She was so short her head rested right on SeRina's breasts. She held her firmly although SeRina tried to step away from her.

"I always knew you would come a lookin', the old lady said smiling from ear to wrinkled ear. "Never mind me and my shenanigans, child, come on in!"

SeRina thought this must be a mistake and replayed the woman's actions the past few minutes. She seemed a bit quirky, maybe she was senile and just looking to have a visitor to break up the monotony. Maybe she was not Hattie Rouse at all or maybe she was the help? But wait, did they have "help" in these sort of neighborhoods?

"Look, lady, what is this? Do you have any idea what I went through to get here? I am here looking for Hattie Rouse and you couldn't possibly be her, so can you tell me where I can find her? I don't have time for games old lady, look I really just need to know where she is."

"Now just one cotton, pickin' minute, you come to my house unannounced, barking orders, disrespecting me, ooh child they ain't teach you no manners where you're from? You ain't even tell me your name. What's your name girl?"

"SeRina."

"SeRina, humpf, I always thought they'd name you something nice and pretty like Alice or Faith." The old lady laughed to herself much longer than she should have.

"Okay, that's it, I'm going to head out, sorry for wasting your time, I clearly am in the wrong place, because there is no way you are my mother."

"Of course not child," the old woman let out another hearty chuckle as she shuffled away. "I'm your grandmother. Your mother doesn't live here, I do. Oh, your mother, she hoped for this moment for as long as I can remember, she doesn't know I gave the agency my contact information so that iffin you ever wanted to find us you could. Trouble is, she and I had a mighty falling out when she gave you up and well, we don't talk much these days."

SeRina stood there flabbergasted; there was no way on Earth that she was a product of the womb of this senile old bag. And a black old bag at that. She stared at the frail woman looking for a hint of feature familiarity and saw nothing, nothing but black.

"Wait a minute, how are *you* my grandmother? I mean you are so…"

"Black?" the old woman said rhetorically as she laughed to herself, again. "First things first, child, run upstairs to the spare room and fetch me the hand carved wooden box on the Davenport."

"The what?"

"The box, on the Davenport, you know honey, the sofa. It's kind of like callin' a tissue a Kleenex, you know the brand name child."

"Right … OK so how will I know which is the spare room?" asked SeRina.

"Oh, trust me, you'll know in time."

"Oh, okay," said SeRina, while thinking to herself, *why can't this woman just tell me which freaking room it is, and what in the is so funny!*

Curiosity fueled SeRina's feet to move, despite her resentment. Her mind was still wrapping itself around the fact that this woman, this very black woman, claimed to be her grandmother. She hoped that this mystery box she just sent her to get would reveal the true identity of her real mother or at least help her find some peace of mind. She remembered her remarks to the black men on the street who were vying for her attention; she remembered dismissing time and time again the comments from kids growing up that suggested that she may possibly be "BLACK" or have a lil' something in her'. She was not ready to accept the possibility that she could be one of THEM.

She found herself at the top of the rickety stairs and her attention was drawn to the photos hanging on the wall in the dim hallway. She studied them for any clue of her existence and any glimmer of whiteness that would explain this anomaly. All she saw were black faces, old ones, young ones, attractive ones, not so attractive ones. She was especially curious about the black and white photograph of an old man, black as the ace of spades sitting in a rocking chair with a pipe tucked in the corner of his mouth. His skin appeared to have a glow that emanated from the frame. His overalls were tattered and only fastened on one side. He wore a checked shirt and a wide-brimmed hat. In his resting hand, he held a watch on a chain as if the photo was taken for a newspaper displaying his work.

SeRina found it odd that although the man looked refined, that he was wearing no shoes. She noticed there was a child seated next to him on the photo, her hair tied back with ragged bows with a part down the center. The child was beautiful, she was also wearing no shoes but looked content as could be in the photo. It appeared that she was playing with some sort of ragdoll. She stared, trying to figure out about how old the photo could have been when the old woman shouted up the stairs … "Did you find it, child?"

"No, not yet. I was looking at these old pictures on the wall. Who is the little girl in the photo with the old man?" SeRina asked. She was the only person from all the photos that looked remotely close to her; she was very fair skinned, round-faced, and adorable.

"Why child, that was my late Aunt Alice when she was just a girl. And the man there, that's George Abbington, my great grandfather. He lived to be 110, which was very rare in those days. Never mind all that though, I will tell you 'bout them folks, later on. Go along now and fetch me that box! " Hattie shouted up the stairs.

She sure is a bossy little thing, thought SeRina. She continued, reluctantly peering into an open room and not seeing a "Davenport" so she continued down the narrow hall. With her next step, she heard an odd twinkling, scratching, and clicking noise. Suddenly, what must have been ten dozen clocks struck simultaneously, dinging and donging and scaring the life out of SeRina.

She pushed through the door to see the tiny "Davenport" which was tattered and worn and almost too small to even be a loveseat, surrounded by what looked like 100 clocks. They covered the walls from the chair rail to the ceiling and all were screaming out that it was 7:00 p.m. That's it, this woman is LO O N Y, who the heck has this many clocks in one room? Just when she started to cover her ears, she approached the Davenport and picked up the tiny carved box. It looked exactly like the one in her father's study, the one that held the address to this insane asylum. Up until this moment, she thought she was still in the wrong place... but the boxes were identical so there must be some truth to this relationship. She was just about to open it when she heard the old lady yell "Don't open it just bring it here and make it snappy child, my TV program is about to come on. I say what I mean and I means what I say, don't open it, just fetch it and bring it here!"

SeRina took the box and made her way through the hall past the staring eyes on the countless photographs, past the happy child playing with the ragdoll and back down the creaky steps. When she reached the bottom, Hattie took the box from her hands and said, "Have a seat child, time's-a-wastin'!"

SeRina sat as she was told.

"Can I get you a drink? Some cold water, a cup of tea?" asked Hattie.

"No thanks," said SeRina, briefly remembering her manners.

"Well, where do I begin?" said Hattie rhetorically.

"How about you tell me how I can find my mother?" said SeRina.

"How about you relax and let me start where stories ought to, at the beginning." She paused a moment and looked up as if trying to remember it all in illustrious detail, and then she smiled even more as she began her story.

"You asked 'bout that chile' on the picture. Well, that there was my Aunt Alice when she was just a girl. She was born a slave. And the man sat with her, was George Abbington, my great grandfather. Grandpa George was a woodworker and a watchmaker. One of the only black watchmakers and clockmakers in his time. He made some of the finest watches this world ever seen. Some say his watches were magic. Could make time stop or rewind... never no proof, just stories, but some say that's how he lived to be so old."

SeRina thought to herself, *so that's what's up with all the clocks...*

"The best piece he created in all his days is in that there box. Folks say that watch is made of pure gold, that he took 5 years to make it just so. Folks say that watch must be worth a fortune and for me to sell it and get out this neighborhood. I say, some things ain't got no price, some things ain't meant to be touched, seen or used by people unless they special.

You special chile... I have been saving that for you all your life. I knew someday you would come to find me and your mother and that I'd have the chance to show it to you, and someday give it to you for your own children.

Now that reminds me, I baked a special batch of cookies for the children next door and there are a few left, would you like one? Oatmeal Raisin?"

"Yes, they are my favorite," said SeRina genuinely. She thought this woman was all over the place and really wanted her to focus in and just tell her about her mother.

Hattie made her way to the kitchen for the cookies.

While Hattie was away, SeRina opened the wooden carved box, it creaked and as it opened and she smelled the pungent scent of the old wood. Within it, she saw a watch, golden, beautifully ornate with an attached chain. The watch's hunter case was closed and protected its face and hands. Beside it sat a small golden key. It looked like something from a movie she had seen before. It amazed her that some uneducated black slave man had created something so beautiful.

She picked up the key and looked at it and tried to figure out how it operated the watch. Just as she was reaching in for the watch, she was interrupted as Hattie shuffled over to her and abruptly snatched the key placed it back in the box and closed it all in one smooth motion.

"Tisk, tisk, tisk, in all due time my dear; you aren't quite ready for that yet. Didn't I tell you not to open it?" she reprehended SeRina, mumbling afterward how kids this day and age don't listen.

SeRina sat there scratching her head and wondering if the old woman had lost her mind. Why would she have her to get the box if she wasn't allowed to open it or touch what's inside?

"Now your great, great Aunt Alice, she was a beauty...Grandpa George was her maternal grandfather. Through the years folks say she was the Massah's daughter, half white, so his wife sent her away so she wouldn't have to stare his sin in the face every day. Stories through the years said she had a twin, separated at birth; one sold, one kept, 'til she was sent away as a young girl. Then there's another story that once she grew up she came face to face with her long-lost twin. Ahh, yes child, there are so many stories to tell, yet there is so little time...so many people gone now but that left such life lessons for all of us. Big Sam, Grandpa George, Aunt Alice, whew, there is so much to tell you, child, where do I begin."

SeRina said, "Well, how about Grandpa George... tell me about him... how did he learn to make watches?"

"Now there's an interesting story. See folks assume Grandpa George was born a slave, but boy was they wrong. Once he opened his mouth it was so clear that he wasn't born in the South at all, no ma'am he was born in England."

"England?" asked SeRina sincerely curious.

"Yes, England. See Grandpa George was born George Robins of London, England. He was the proud and respected apprentice of a famous watchmaker. They came to the United States to do an exhibition show of fine watches and pick up connections for importing those watches and, well, Grandpa George just happened to be in the wrong place at the wrong time."

"What do you mean?" asked SeRina.

"Well, see in those days, being a free black man in the South didn't mean a thing to some folks. Folks say Grandpa George was tall, handsome, well-dressed, and had a polished and commanding demeanor that didn't sit well with white folks. He spoke to white folks like they were his equal, never lowering his eyes to male or female, never acting subservient to Massah nor trader, and the day before he was to return to his family in England, they nabbed him off the road, stole the goods from him, and took away his papers.

The slave catchers who kidnapped him, locked him away from his partner until after the ship set sail back to England. Then they took poor Grandpa George straight to the Massah who thought he struck gold and used him to make watches and fine carvings and furniture for his profit.

He lived out the rest of his years on that plantation and unfortunately, he never saw home or his family back in England again. He settled in after a time, marrying and having one child, Francis was her name and she was the mother of my Aunt Alice. He was a distinguished man, taught his trade by the best there was back in England and known and respected for his talents by folks in America. So see he wasn't uneducated at all. He just never quite figured out how to escape back to his home so far away.

Grandpa George was skilled beyond measure. He could make just about anything if given the right materials. So instead of having him do backbreaking work in the fields with the other slaves, his new master had him make furniture and fine watches and jewelry for people far and near. Folks say that in Grandpa George's spare time he carved things like that box you are holding. And he did it just to keep his peace of mind. My dear, the watch you have in that box has quite a story too, but we'll save that for another time...

Yes indeedy, it is getting late, so I won't keep you, I suppose' I will see you next time child."

"What, next time? That's it? What about my mother? You can't leave me hanging like this!" said SeRina.

"Well, sure I can!" said Hattie, "May I remind you that this here is my house, besides my stories are fixin' to start on the TV set. Go on now, see you soon, and visit anytime, anytime that is before now, 'cause that's when my stories are on child." She took SeRina by the hand and shuffled to the front door opening it and pushing her ever so gently right on out of it.

SeRina turned and said, "Don't you want my number in case you want to reach me?"

"No ma'am, you'll be back, whew; God is good, all the time!" She laughed to herself and shut the door in SeRina's face.

SeRina stood there in amazement thinking to herself boisterously.

WHAT THE HECK JUST HAPPENED?

I drove all this way and still don't know about my mother or how to find her. Oh, my God, all I did was find out about a bunch of dead slaves and people that don't matter. This woman has clearly lost her mind!

"Ms. Hattie, come on, please open up. This isn't funny!"

SeRina rang the doorbell again and banged on the door to no avail.

Hattie had gone on about her business and was watching her stories. She made it explicitly clear that she simply would not be interrupted during her stories.

You have got to be kidding!

Thought SeRina, and so she left, disappointed and furious. Dr. Salvatore had been calling SeRina repeatedly worried about her whereabouts when she finally answered on the ride home; he asked where she had been. She replied, "Nowhere," and that is exactly how she left it. She promised herself she would return, but next time she would come earlier and she definitely wouldn't leave without getting the answers she sought.

CHAPTER EIGHT

Say it!

"Brrrrrrrrrrrrriiiinnnng!!!" rang the school bell signaling the start of Ms. Parker's class. The kids were especially excited because in today's class they were to watch a video instead of listening to Ms. Parker drone on about black history. Usually, video days meant naps, love note passing, and if you were lucky making out in the back row of the classroom if the teacher wasn't paying close attention.

Ms. Parker did a brief introduction to the video they were to watch today about the Underground Railroad and SeRina and the majority of the class couldn't be less interested. Michaela passed her a note and asked to borrow her lip gloss just as the lights went down and SeRina was happy to oblige. The video started with a narrative that sounded as if an actual slave had done the voiceover, broken English and all.

The video was backed by a Negro spiritual soundtrack and a haunting voice that sang "Follow the Drinking Gourd." The dejected narrator took the students on a journey through the Underground Railroad giving them a virtual tour of Wheeling, WV beginning at 10th and Market Street at the sites of the Slave Market House and Town Hall where slaves were bought and sold clear across the Ohio River to Martins Ferry.

After the Underground Railroad tour, the video showed glimpses of plantations that still existed in modern day that had been restored to their "original splendor" big house, cook house, fields and slave quarters all still intact. SeRina thought what could be so "splendid" about a stupid plantation, and at that moment she dozed off thinking of her grandmother and picturing Grandpa George and some of the others on the plantation she had just seen on the video.

The video ended, and Ms. Anderson ended class by asking all of the students to hand in their family tree assignments. The students passed them forward to the student sitting in the front seat of each row and Ms. Anderson politely collected them all. She thanked them for their attentiveness and turning in their assignments then told the students there would be a pop quiz the next day regarding the topics covered by the video. Then the bell rang, and the students began filing out. Michaela was too caught up talking to one of the guys she was crushing on to notice that SeRina was still fast asleep sitting in her chair and that she hadn't bothered to hand in her assignment.

Ms. Parker watched as the last student filed out of the room then made her way over to the sleeping SeRina. She almost didn't want to wake her, she was sleeping so peacefully. She sensed a new bitterness in her and wondered what she could do to help.

"Ahem," Ms. Salvatore? Hello, SeRina, SeRina, time to wake up dear," said Ms. Parker tapping her gently on the shoulder.

SeRina sat up abruptly, disoriented and wiped away the drool pooling on her hand. She squinted at the brightness of the room and focused her eyes to surprisingly see Ms. Parker standing over her.

"Where is everyone?" said SeRina.

"Class let out about 5 minutes ago. Are you OK?" asked Ms. Parker.

"Yes, I'm fine!" said SeRina. She was actually not fine, she had cried herself to sleep last night after the disappointment of not meeting her mother and the realization that the only mother she had ever known was gone. She was exhausted.

"OK, well you better get going to your next period, sounds like you are going to be late," said Ms. Parker as the bell sounded.

"Great!" said SeRina sarcastically as she stood up and knocked over her purse spilling its contents on the floor including the shared lip gloss.

Ms. Parker bent to help her clean up its contents and their eyes met for an awkward moment.

"I've got it," said SeRina.

"Of course you do," said Ms. Parker as she smiled apprehensively and re-stood. She had noticed SeRina's demeanor had been especially aloof since the passing of her mother and she was genuinely concerned about her student.

SeRina rushed past Ms. Parker toward the door.

"SeRina, I will give you an extra day to turn in your family tree. Look, I know things at home have been a little difficult lately since..." she stopped herself.

"Since what? Since what? Say it!" SeRina challenged turning from the door and staring Ms. Parker down.

Ms. Parker nervously diverted her eyes and cleared her throat changing the subject. She walked over to SeRina and placed her hand gently on her shoulder.

"Look if you need someone to talk to I'm here. You don't have to go through this alone."

"Thank you, but I'm FINE!" retorted SeRina fighting back tears as she exited the classroom thinking to herself it would be a cold day in hell before she would do the stupid family tree. She didn't know her roots, and she pretended for a moment that it didn't matter.

CHAPTER NINE

The Prodigal Return

After her last class, SeRina walked through the halls of her school out to the car without uttering a word to her friends. She had been fixated on the idea of Grandpa George making watches on a plantation that looked like the one in the video and wondered what other stories Hattie had to tell. So she made her way once again over the hill and through the hood to Hattie's house. This time she remembered the route, ignored the homeless man and the cat calling men on the corner liquor store lot and pulled up in the drive of the bungalow. She opened the now familiar fence and went up the stairs, but before she could knock the door swung open and there stood Hattie. She was not quite as hunched over as before, but just as chipper and quirky and sporting her usual million-dollar ear to wrinkled ear grin.

"See, I told you you'd be back, and earlier this time... GOOD!" said Hattie laughing.

"Yes, yes ma'am," said SeRina in a feigned attempt to be respectful. She had a hidden agenda and thought that maybe this time if she played along, Hattie would finally tell her about her mother.

SeRina walked in the house, expectations high and anxiety even higher. She made her way to the same chair as before and Hattie shuffled off into the kitchen speaking over her shoulder.

"How do you like your tea?" asked Hattie.

"Well, actually, I don't..."

"Ah let me guess two sugars and a dash of cream just like me? Of course... just like your ol' Hattie," said Hattie oblivious to SeRina's declining of her hospitality.'

"So, I was hoping...well, I mean, can you tell me about ..." SeRina clumsily muttered.

"Speak up child, old Hattie's ears aren't good as they used to be!"

"I SAID I WAS HOPING YOU WOULD TELL ME ABOUT MY MOM AND HOW I CAN FIND HER!" SeRina retorted obnoxiously, severely over speaking so as to be heard.

"I said my ears aren't as good as they used to be, not that I am a deaf mute... where do these kids get their manners these days?" said Hattie.

"Well, this is my second time here, and I was just hoping we could just cut to the chase. I'm here for one reason and one reason only and that is to find out about my mother. So, are you going to help me or not?" replied SeRina.

"In time, child, in time. Now, when you left I didn't have the chance to tell you the story about your great Aunt Alice... see she was the fair skinned child you saw on the photo with Grandpa George up yonder. Your Aunt Alice, well, she lived a hard life. In those days if you looked white you could make every attempt to fool folks but if word got out that you were just passin' for white, your life would be sheer hell. She tried escaping who she was, but it just kept comin' back to bite her.

From Civil War to Civil Rights, this family has had a long line of people who suffered for nothing other than the color of their skin. When I really stop to think about it, it hit me just how ironic it is that God gave me you?"

Hattie laughed out loud cracking herself up at the irony. Just then, the clocks began to chime from upstairs with a hodge-podged melody startling SeRina.

"Oh, my God, what is with the stupid clocks?!" asked SeRina.

"You know what, I have had just about enough of your disrespect! Come on here..." said Hattie, grabbing SeRina and yanking her up the stairs. The rounded the hallway and walked into the clock just as the clanging and chiming stopped.

"These stupid clocks, these stupid clocks chime in honor of every person who has lived and died in this family. These clocks represent all the blood, sweat and tears of generation after generation, and the art of horology passed down by Grandpa George. This grandfather clock here was made by his very hands over 100 years ago, it hasn't stopped ticking for one second since he first swung that pendulum. So see, ain't nothing stupid 'bout none of these timepieces... they are one in a million. Folks come nearly every year trying to con me outta this collection. But they are priceless... just like each moment they track that ticks away. See baby girl, ain't nothing stupid about time!"

"Time is the one thing you can spend but you will never get a refund on. The older you get the more precious it becomes! When I give you my time, I can NEVER take that back. Time should be invested not spent frivolously. See you young folks are naïve they think that time and youth last forever and that they will have time to make things right with those they've wronged. But I'm here to tell you that tomorrow is not promised and life does not come with a box of second chances. So you better look long and hard at these stupid things that track and trace the thing that God gave us, seconds, minutes, hours, because baby girl at the end of the day, TIME is our most precious gift!"

Grandma Hattie's words pricked SeRina's conscious and moved her heart.

How did I never tell you how much you meant to me mom?

SeRina pictured her mother tucking her into bed. She missed the goodnight kiss that Mother always planted gently on her forehead before turning off the light. Filled with shame and regret, SeRina turned her back on Hattie to hide the tears that slid down her cheeks.

"Look here child... turn around, you had enough heart to sass me so you gonna look me straight in the eye..."

SeRina turned, locking eyes with Grandma Hattie whose eyes brimmed with tears and love. SeRina immediately regretted her disrespectful outburst. An apology was unnecessary as her eyes told the story. Hattie placed the beautiful little hand carved wooden box into SeRina's hands.

"Open it," said Grandma Hattie in a soft but urgent whisper.

SeRina obliged.

"My precious SeRina, this piece was almost forgotten when they tore down the old shanty where Grandpa George made his watches. But this one is the most precious timepiece in this room. It holds the key to unlocking your past so you can embrace your future. This watch was the last one made by Grandpa George before he died. See child, in your hands, you are holding a timeless piece of history, your history, black history."

SeRina turns away... "But I'm not..."

"What? BLACK?"

"If you have one-eighth of blackness in you, girl you are black. I told you what happens to people who deny who they are? You came here on a quest for the truth. Well, you had better be ready to embrace it. This is your truth. Your mother is black as the day is long, your father was white. He chose to live in his whitewashed society and deny your mother of the honor of marriage. So she did what she thought was best, she gave you a life. A so-called privileged life that now I wonder if it was best for you... cause girl you don't even know who you are!

SeRina was so uncomfortable with this news, that she felt her pulse quicken and immediately all of the salivae in her mouth had evaporated. She shifted her weight nervously left to right her mind racing as she tried to absorb this unsettling news.

"This watch represents a time where the color of your skin literally determined whether you lived or died! Your skin determined whether you could marry, whether you could be treated with dignity, whether you could learn to read and write, whether you could vote, whether you could sit down where you wanted to sit, swim where you wanted to swim, whether you could take a drink from a fountain, it told you who you could love, and in the days of my Grandfather, it determined whether or not you were even considered human! Most importantly, the hue of your skin it told you if you were FREE!

You have no idea the bloodshed and the sacrifices made so that you could be standing there right now holding that watch in your perfectly manicured lily white hands!"

"But I don't look black... I'm nothing like you. Black people are so..."

"So what? STRONG!? What other race has survived being chained arm to arm with one another for months in the gutter of a rotten ship, fighting disease and hunger to be brought to a place and stripped of their culture and their language? What race has seen their children ripped from their arms and sold like cattle, had their women beaten, men castrated, and hung like animals and survived?

What race was denied the God-given right to even be married and bear the name of their ancestors? You tell me child, who else has been reduced from kings and queens of civilizations to not even being recognized as HUMAN?

Black People are a resilient people who come in every shade and color from the deepest ebony to even the shade of you! So don't you ever deny who you are! You are black, you are beautiful, and you are my blood!" Grandma Hattie grabbed SeRina by the wrists looking at her hands and the box within them.

SeRina immediately broke free and said, "I, I'm sorry, I have to go... This was a mistake, this was all a mistake," said SeRina.

"Time will tell... Now go on and put that watch back in the box and put it back on the Davenport. Put it away I say!" said Hattie as she made her way back downstairs. She was still riled up and rambled to herself the whole way down about how times had changed.

SeRina, torn and riddled with curiosity, ignored the instructions and took the watch from the box, placing the key in the slot and winding it. In that moment, a tear slipped from her eye and landed on the watch. SeRina's eyes widened trying to focus as she noticed the watch began to glow. The room and the hands on every clock surrounding her began to spin uncontrollably, chimes, bells, and alarms sounding simultaneously. SeRina tried to make her way to the stairs... She could faintly hear Hattie's voice rambling on in the distance and it melded with the voice of her mother, her father, her friends. Pain and adrenaline seared through her body like lightning, her heart quickened, her breathing became erratic, her tongue frozen from speech. She tried to make her way to the stairs following Hattie, but lost her footing and fell. The light turned to darkness and all of the voices faded. The clocks chimed and morphed into to the sound of a bleak hum.

CHAPTER TEN

Lost and Found

The chirping of crickets and an unrecognizable rustling sound awakened SeRina. She was damp all over and the smell was unfamiliar. She reached down to her jean pockets to get her cell phone to illuminate her surroundings, but her phone was gone. She strained her eyes against the darkness to see where her grandmother had gone. She had simply vanished. SeRina sat up, bracing herself with her hands. The carpeting she had fallen on now felt damp and plant-like. "What? Is this grass?" she said, her voice a stark contrast to the darkened silence. The crickets answered her with the swell of their cricketing.

How in the world did I get outside? SeRina thought to herself.

She rose to her feet feeling the cool blades of grass beneath her toes, where were her shoes? What was she wearing? she thought. Her jeans and sweater had been replaced with a long tattered gown but in the darkness, she felt as if she were wearing her PJ's. "I must be losing it now," she said aloud. Just then, she heard something fast approaching and saw a dim light. She walked toward it, yelling out "who's there?" In that moment, out of the blue in the darkness, she felt the presence of someone near and before she could react or yell once more, a large and strong hand covered her mouth.

"Quiet, I say!" shushed a dark and husky voice.

SeRina's mind raced, she thought maybe when she fell she hit her head and perhaps that she then walked outside in the darkness and that someone in the hood was taking her hostage. She tried to scream to no avail. She then resorted to the self-defense maneuvers she had learned in the class her father forced her to attend. How she wished she had listened to him and just gone home after running his errands instead of venturing off to "the hood" again. She wondered what this man wanted. Was it her purse? Her cell phone? Credit card? Who knew, all she knew is she wanted to scream and run like the wind, but couldn't.

She saw the light drawing closer and heard the accompanying clattering noise grow louder by the second. It was a light moving in her direction but it wasn't anywhere near the brightness of a car headlight. She saw the light illuminate white faces, which gave her a sense of relief. She decided which maneuver to try and elbowed the man's ribs as hard as she could. He let her mouth go long enough for her to break free and turn to see he was a black man, which sent her running and screaming all the more. She bolted toward the approaching light yelling, "HELP! HELP ME PLEASE ... SOMEBODY!"

She ran as fast as she could, tripping on the hem of the unfamiliar gown she was wearing. She had forgotten for a moment that she was barefoot until her foot hit a sharp stone and she fell, writhing in pain. "Please help me!" She looked back to see if the man had followed her and saw a shadow of him approaching.

"Gal, you trying to get us killed? Get in the brush before they catch you!" The husky voice said, piercing the darkness.

"Do you think I'm crazy? You are the one trying to kill me! Get away from me!" She argued.

"Suit yourself," said the husky voice and she saw his shadow disappear into the darkness.

Still, on the ground, she looked around for a moment completely and utterly afraid and lost. Her car, the fence, and her grandmother's house were nowhere in sight. Where could she be? She reached down to rub her throbbing foot and felt the hotness of the blood run between her fingers. "HELP, please," she said. The light was almost close enough to touch. She sat and sobbed until the strange voices and clickity-clack grew closer. The closer they came the more she realized that it wasn't a car at all; it was a horse and cart carrying men who were holding lanterns. What are they doing on a horse and buggy in the middle of the ghetto? she thought to herself. Whatever the answer, they had to be able to help her get back to her car so she could go home and have her father bandage her foot. "Over here, over here!" she said motioning the men to come toward her. "Help, can you help me, please? I have cut my foot."

"Who's there?" said one of the men on the cart. The driver slowed the horses with a gentle "whoa." One of the men carrying a lantern in one hand and a rifle in the other jumped from the cart and slowly approached her. His footsteps crunched through the brush as he grew nearer to her the air's energy growing more ominous with each step, her fear intensified when the dog tied to the cart began to bark ferociously.

She thought for a moment that maybe the man in the darkness was right. Maybe she should have run and hidden with him instead of calling these men in her direction. Who walks around just carrying a rifle? SeRina said to herself.

"Ma'am, what are you doing out alone this time of night? It ain't fittin' for a lady to be traveling down these roads alone."

"Ain't fittin' for a lady?" What on God's green Earth was he talking about? He sounded like a character from "Gone with the Wind," SeRina thought.

"Well, last time I checked, it was a free country; look, I just need someone to help me find my car."

"Your what?" said the man. He rested the gun on the ground by the hilt as he spoke. His closeness to her made her nervous. She was still in darkness but felt that her clothes were different than she remembered, uncertain if he was friend or foe.

"My car. See, I parked it in front of my grandmother's house. Well, at least she was trying to convince me that she is my grandmother. Anyway, I was just bringing her the box again like last time and I fell and then... Well, I must have wandered outside and now I'm lost. I don't know...maybe I hit my head..." SeRina rambled on and on, not noticing the man looking her over with a perplexed look on his face.

"What did you say your grandmother's name was?" asked the man.

"Hattie Rouse."

"Hattie?" yelled the second man, holding a lantern on the cart. He jumped down from the cart and rushed in SeRina's direction to get a closer look.

"Yes, as I was saying, I was visiting my grandmother and ..."

"No, it can't be," interjected one of the men.
"She's 'bout white as cotton," said the second man.

"A mulatto like her will fetch a fortune," said the third man, who had joined in to see what all the fuss was about.

"A mulatto? What is this 1850?" questioned SeRina.

"No gal, it is 1859," said one of the men. His tone was more intense and intimidating than before.

"She must've hit her head!" said the man with the gun as he lowered his lantern to get a closer look.

"When did you say you saw your grandmother?"

"Just now, look, I told you I --"

"Mind your tone nigger!" warned the man holding the lantern.

"Nigger? Who do you think you are talking to?" SeRina abruptly retorted.

"Oh, she's one of those uppity niggers; I bet she got papers and everything. If you weren't so pretty I'd slap you silly. Don't you know old Mammy Rouse died last year? I thought Mr. Abbington would never stop crying over that old bag. She raised him and he was closer to her than his own mother," said one of the men. The man had gotten too close for comfort while speaking, and she certainly didn't like how he was looking at her. He reached down to touch SeRina's hair, testing the texture of it and running his soiled and smelly fingers through it. He traced the line of her jaw bone, touching her lips and making them part, revealing her pearly white teeth. "Thought you were a smart nigger, eh? Bet you were gonna try to make us think you were white so we'd let you pass, huh?" He laughed, slowly and maniacally. "I got other plans for you. Get up girl."

"But I can't," protested SeRina, her lip trembling with fear. 1859? Was he kidding? How was her grandmother dead? She had just seen her a few moments ago. What was this place? Her thoughts consumed her. She was so confused she reached up to rub her head and felt a knot forming. She wondered how it got there.

"I said get up!" the man said, grabbing her tightly by her wrists and yanking her to her feet.

"Ouch! What is wrong with you people? I demand you take me to my grandmother right now. Or better yet, just leave me alone. I will find my own way back. You just wait until I tell my father about this, you will be sorry. Do you know who I am? My father is..." The smelly hand slapped back over her mouth, cutting off any further admonishments against these strange men.

The second man with the lantern approached her with an evil grin and gave her an once-over. She still couldn't believe how the men who originally appeared helpful had now become even more dangerous than the stranger she encountered earlier in the darkness. She tried to repeat her self-defense move but this time to no avail. He was too strong and now there were two men holding her.

The tallest of the three men who originally was driving the wagon let the other two lamp holders, rest their lamps and hold her. One held her mouth and the others pinned her arms behind her back. She had all but forgotten about the cut on her foot, as the pain in her wrists and face now far surpassed that pain. The driver ripped her dress open revealing her now heaving breasts, covered in a hot pink lace bra and threw the shard of dress to the ground. She thought her heart was going to pound right out of her chest and her breathing quickened. Her mind raced thinking through all the scenarios she had seen in the movies where the helpless victim made an amazing escape. But she couldn't budge. She tried with all her strength to escape their hold but barely moved an inch.

"Well, looky here, looky here. Girl's got fancy undergarments, too," taunted the man. "Oh, yeah. I've got plans for you dear, but not before I have a little fun first," said the tall driver. He started to touch her face and her neck. A dark object hit him in the back of the head and knocked him out cold. The other two men startled, unhanded her to see where the object came from. They spotted the black man in the darkness. One ran after him while the other returned to the wagon to set loose the now yapping dog. They all took off in the darkness, forgetting momentarily about SeRina and leaving the driver where he lay.

SeRina darted toward the thick of the woods, heart racing and adrenaline pushing her legs to move faster than they ever had before. She ran wildly through the darkness and brush until she could no longer see the light of the lanterns or hear the yelping of the dog. Finally, she fell to her knees in the brush behind a tall maple tree. She felt her flesh tear again as her knees sliced against the fallen branch hidden by the darkness. Tears streamed down her face and she subdued her whimpers so she wouldn't be discovered in the darkness. Wherever this place was, it reminded her of the place in the stories her grandmother told, a place where blacks were not welcome and where "high-yellow" and "mulatto" girls were a hot commodity for whites to use as they pleased. It couldn't be...this had to be some sort of dream. She pinched herself but went nowhere.

The pain in her head began to throb in harmony with the pain in her knee and foot. She decided not to cry out again in the darkness for fear of being heard by the men again. She caught her breath and took in deep breaths to steady her mind. She had never felt this out of control. She decided to wait it out and deal with it all in the morning.

She carefully pushed aside the fallen branches and padded herself underneath with her long gown. She tore a piece of the fabric from the hem of the gown and tied it around both of her bare feet for protection. She leaned her back against the massive maple and gazed up at the twinkling stars. They were brighter and more beautiful than she ever remembered. There was no smog, tall buildings, or street lights to obscure their view.

She counted the stars, and her eyelids grew heavy. She wondered how she would ever find her way back home if she was lost in the woods...or even worse, lost in time. For just a moment, she allowed her mind to wander to Hattie's stories about Grandpa George and his watch's mysterious abilities and wondered if it had something to do with the situation she currently found herself in. SeRina had no idea what was going on.

Her head grew cloudy from the throbbing pain and soon the sound of the wind rustling the leaves and chirping crickets quieted her thoughts and lulled her to sleep.

CHAPTER ELEVEN

Rise and Shine

The sun beamed through the leaves of the ancient maple. The wind daintily carried a whirlybird seed from the tree, passed it gracefully through the boughs, and ended its journey with an abrupt thud against SeRina's forehead. She sat up, startled awake, eyes as big as saucers. She looked around verifying there was no danger. She almost smiled as she watched the countless seeds fly in helicopter fashion, carried varying distances by the wind and landing all around her. She looked down and noticed her hot pink bra exposed and smudged with dirt. Disappointed, she realized that the events of the previous evening had not been a dream.

She steadied herself against the Maple, putting her weight on her uninjured foot and stood to survey the woods. She was alarmed for a moment when she heard rustling in the nearby brush but exhaled when she saw it was just a family of raccoons foraging for food. She envied them as they nibbled on a fallen apple and limped over to join them in the feast at the twiggy apple tree. She picked an apple from the tree and polished it on her dress before taking a bite. The taste was bitter but better than nothing, and it did the trick of quieting her rumbling tummy. It was Saturday morning and she remembered the days where she dreaded making breakfast for Darrene with her father. She longed for a time machine to take her back where she could do that again, see her adoptive mother's smile, and feel her loving embrace; the one she used to shrug away. She would give up the world for a hug right now. Tears welled in her eyes at the thought of it, but she sniffed them away in the as she often did. She immediately regretted her choice of breakfast, as the apple she just devoured began to cramp her stomach.

SeRina looked down at her foot, the fabric from the dress now stained brown from her blood. She tried to remember where this dress could possibly have come from. She recalled seeing one similar to it in the trunk next to her grandmother's Davenport but didn't remember putting it on. Everything in her head felt cloudy. There were no roads, no cars, and no people in sight. Only trees, sparse plugs of grass here and there, and the occasional fallen branch. The air was crisp and warm, the wind steady and breezy. There was an unfamiliar freshness to the air and the whole moment just felt surreal. It was impossible not to take pleasure in the beauty surrounding her, but she didn't want to forget the dangers she had encountered the night before. She grabbed a handful of apples and secured them in the bodice of her dress for later.

SeRina resolved to find the road and somehow find her way back to her grandmother's house. She hobbled through the woods, balancing her weight on one foot hobbling back toward the road from the night before. She stopped a time or two to contemplate which way to go and after coming to no rational conclusion decided just to follow her instincts. She ran so wildly the night before that her only recollection was heading toward the thicker brush and woods. After mulling it over, she headed toward the more sparse area north of her. No concrete, asphalt, or streetlights were near; there was no noise of traffic from what should be the nearby interstate. There were no thumping stereos or black men with drooping pants sporting gold teeth, and no discarded 40 oz. bottles cluttering the ground. Only the ambient sounds of nature, the wind cooing softly through the trees and the birds melodically chirping broke the silence. Finally, after what felt like hours of walking, the curving dirt road was in sight as was the stump that she recalled the man resting his lantern on the night before.

Getting to the road seemed like a good idea, but that was the extent of her master plan. Now that she was there, she had no idea what to do next. Little did she know that the decision would not be hers to make. Just then, she heard the familiar clickety-clack of approaching horses and ducked into the brush. Incessant barking soon followed the clickety-clack, which drew nearer and nearer.

"There, in the brush!" yelled a man on horseback to the man on foot holding the dogs at bay. He bent down, allowing the dogs to smell the fabric torn from her dress the night before and set them after her.

SeRina overheard the conversation and took out running as fast as she could, despite her injuries.

The dogs were barking running at full pace now and were on to her scent.

It only took a moment for them to catch up to her. She tripped and fell to the ground and was staring them face to face in horror as they barked, snarled, and growled. When they were just inches from her face, the man on horseback jumped down and called them to his side just moments before they could tear into her.

"So Albert, this is the mulatto you purchased at market?" asked Massah Abbington, a tall dignified and moderately handsome man of 50 or so. He had just dismounted his horse eloquently so that he could look Albert in the eyes, as his words often had to be taken with a grain of salt.

"Yes sir, Mr. Abbington," said Albert.

"Certainly it is," co-signed Albert's sidekick Maurice.

SeRina looked at him and recognized him as the tall slender and unattractive man who had ripped her dress the night before. She wanted to slap him and spit in his face for touching her that way. Nevertheless, she sat still. This new man wasn't like the others, he didn't sound as threatening so she remained still.

"How'd you say she escaped so soon again?" inquired Massah Abbington doubting the story.

Before Albert could answer, a tall handsome man, fast approached on horseback.

"Hello son, they found her," yelled Mr. Abbington to the approaching newcomer.

As the approaching newcomer drew closer, he noticed the girl, in an unexpected way. She was very fair, with gorgeous gray eyes and full lips. Her hair was tousled and had curled near her temples from the humidity and her cheeks were rosy from the exertion. She was one of the most beautiful girls he had ever seen, not at all what he expected when they mentioned having to locate a runaway slave girl.

89

Although the man on horseback appeared at first to be a man, as he grew nearer, SeRina could see that he was just a boy probably around her age. He dismounted his horse and took another step giving her an once-over as he removed his hat. Just then, SeRina saw his face clearly and sprung to her feet.

"Christophe, oh my God I can't believe it's you!" She exclaimed crying and laughing all at the same time.

She wrapped her arms around his neck, not believing her eyes. She thought it odd that he arrived on a horse and that maybe all the other things which had occurred were just some silly game they were playing. Or some sort of role-playing, acting out various things they had learned in Social Studies class. She did not care about the explanation, it didn't matter because her hero was there to save her, so she finally let the tears flow onto his shoulder.

She was startled back to reality when he pushed her away and said, "My name is Timothy. Unhand me gal!"

Hope and courage vanished. Tears of joy turned to tears of confusion and disbelief. She felt the eyes of his father and other men around her bore through her very soul. She knew that trying to convince him was futile so she gave into blubbering uncontrollably. She stood still and welcomed the distraction as the conversation resumed about how she was lost, the events of the night before and plans for taking her back "home."

She knew that Albert, the tall man from the night before, was embellishing the story a bit. What she didn't know was that Albert Pinkard had lied to Massah Abbington telling him he purchased two Negroes at market as he had been instructed. However, he had actually gambled away the Massah's money the night before in a game of cards. Finding SeRina and the other mystery black man on the road was an all too convenient fix to his dilemma. Albert was originally supposed to bring them back the night before but claimed they had tried to make an escape together. He claimed that in the scuffle he had lost the receipts for the slave purchase and that he would retrace his steps come morning and vowed to find both the slaves and the papers. Albert and Massah Abbington's son Timothy had found the other "lost" slave moments before and had him tied in the back of the wagon. The dogs had not been as kind to him and he had multiple bite marks on his legs and thighs where they had attacked. He also had a bite mark on his hand from where SeRina had bitten him the night before.

The men continued with their conversation, debating on the fate of the captured male slave. They had earlier found the body of the slain white man from the night before and said he should hang for it. Not interested in losing his investment just yet, the Massah told Albert to keep a close eye on him and that he could take out the murder on his hide. An all too familiar task that Albert was more than happy to oblige.

CHAPTER TWELVE

The Cookhouse

"She looks hungry Dad," said Timothy, a bit concerned and still taken aback by her uninvited embrace. He was genuinely concerned. He felt remorseful about his abrupt outburst earlier which was all in pretense to impress his father and Albert the overseer. She was the whitest slave he had ever seen. Until that moment, it had not bothered him that these human beings were made to be slaves to support his family's growing cotton and tobacco business. They were some sub-human race that inhabited the land. It suddenly struck him just how wrong the entire concept of human slavery was and that these were truly people with feelings, emotions, and needs. He felt ashamed of himself for his earlier outburst.

"I'll take her to the cookhouse," he said as he rode alongside the wagon pulling down the aisle of tiny wooden shanties.

His father nodded in approval and pulled the wagon off to the side of the dirt road.

Timothy disembarked his horse and took SeRina's arm helping her to gently exit the wagon. SeRina looked at him with her steel gray eyes filled with tears and longed for something to come over him to remind him of the love they shared. It did not happen.

Timothy noticed her injured foot and was especially patient with her as she made her way gingerly down the dirt path. She wondered what he could be thinking and why his behavior had changed so suddenly. He definitely seemed more kind than before. She tripped over a small dip in the road and fell into his arms. They locked eyes and shared an awkward moment until he hastily told her "the cookhouse is this way." He wrapped his arm around her waist so she could hop on one foot up the stairs to the doorway.

He opened the door to the shanty, and as SeRina peered warily into the room, she saw a short pudgy black woman within. Her bushy hair was bound in a beige handkerchief; she wore a stained apron over a tattered frock. Her eyes were soft and inviting and her she moved and worked happily about the kitchen.

There was a chunky wooden table in the center of the room. It was surrounded by five sturdy handmade stools. SeRina sat on one of them and rested her head on her hands.

"Who this here, Massah Abbington sir?" asked the woman in the cookhouse with the warmest of broad smiles.

"This is ... um ... um ... ahem. I beg your pardon, but I failed to gather your name?" asked Timothy turning to SeRina a bit flustered by the oversight.

"SeRina, my name is SeRina." She muttered glancing up briefly.

"I will take it from here. Thank you kindly, Massah Timothy," replied the cookhouse woman.

"No, my dear, thank you," he replied and gave her a quick nod before exiting.

"SeRina. Well, chile' you look like you belongs up in the big house. I ain't never seen a field nigga light as you 'fore. Surely Massah Abbington see to it that you works in his house fair as you is..."

The woman gave SeRina an up and down assessment and asked, hands folded across her full abdomen, "Is you hungry?"

"Yes, I am," SeRina replied sheepishly.

SeRina sat quietly taking in the room, replaying the day's events and still trying to figure out how she came to be here. She gave up on trying to wipe away the tears which had now become a permanent fixture on her face. She just let them accumulate on the apples of her cheeks until they rolled down and dripped from her chin.

"Oh chile', it ain't so bad here," said the round-faced woman with a smile in her voice, "Massah Abbington mighty kind. Oh, and I can tell already that Massah Timothy, he got eyes for you, he see to it that you all right."

She walked over to the stove spooning a heap of yellow mush, gristle, and salted collards on a plate and setting it before the forlorn girl.

SeRina sat turning her head each time the woman got close enough to fully see her face. She was embarrassed and didn't like crying in front of people, especially strangers.

"My name is Tempie Mae, everybody round here calls me Aunt Tempie. Now there chile', eat up and dry your eyes, them there collards is salty enough." Tempie said laughing to herself.

SeRina missed the joke as she was lost in thought about, well, everything. Hmm, Tempie that was the name Grandma Hattie called her Aunt, but no, it couldn't be ... thought SeRina.

She walked over and touched SeRina's chin lightly and just as she went to wipe the tears from her eyes, she dropped the rag she held and stared in disbelief. Aunt Tempie remembered that cherubic face with its rosy cheeks. She had seen her as a small child and remembered her mother.

"My precious Lord, could that be you Alice Faith?" asked the stunned Aunt Tempie.

"Alice? No, my name's SeRina," she retorted, staring blankly at the slop before her.

"No child, I knows you well, your name Alice!" Then turning toward SeRina she shared her history with her as if she were reciting it from memory.

"I knowed you since the day you was born in the bitter winter of

1842. Your mother didn't know what to do with herself when her water let down. So I brought her in from the cold, lit the fire, and boiled some water on the stove. I never had to birth a baby alone 'fore.

"See your momma Francis used to birth all the babies for the Negras. But she had taken sick when it came time to birth her own. She swore she wouldn't let God call her home 'til she lay eyes on you. And she didn't. She left us when you were just four days old. Sweet Alice, it was tough on your momma birthin' a baby that was forced in her by a white man she didn't love. It near bout killed her to tell Joe that she was spectin' and it wasn't his child. Joe was heartbroken and thought you would be their first child together since they jumped the broom. He felt betrayed and secretly thought the Massah had something to do with it. He became rebellious and vengeful and tried to make a run for it time and time again. Finally, Massah Abbington got tired of having him beat constantly, so he got himself sold off.

"Poor Francis took ill during her pregnancy, heartaches what I think it was, but she got to getting around a little more and more the rounder she got. She got right excited thinkin' bout birthin' a fair-skinned baby. She loved you spite the circumstances. When you's born, black folks come by just to lay eyes on you. Said they never saw a baby as, beautiful as you were. Your eyes were always funny changing colors and such like I never seen 'fore. Your hair lay in soft curls 'round your face. You were the sweetest baby, just a laughin' and a grinnin' not a care in the world.

"We were mighty happy to have you when your momma passed on and me and your grandpa took good care of you. Things were going just fine 'til that rotten ol' Margaret Abbington lay eyes on ya. She nosing around like she does pretending to make us savages turn real Christian like. Everybody 'round here knows how the Misses feels bout mixed up young'uns. To her, it's an abomination. You were only six years old when the Massah's wife Margaret had you sold off. She thought you were the Massah's daughter since he took so kindly to your Mother and seeing as though you was so fair-skinned. It didn't set well with the Missus that Massah Abbington sold off your daddy and that you ain't look nothin' like him and to add to the doubt Massah took it the hardest when your momma passed on.

We all tried to tell the Misses you weren't Massah's. I told her myself bout your mother Francis being taken advantage of one night by some slave catcher running patrols. She was sneaking off to go see her man Joe and he caught her and pulled her into the woods. So we all know you weren't Massah's baby at all. I pleaded and begged with the Massah not to take you from us, but he grew tired of Ms. Margaret's constant-a nagging and sold you off anyways to a plantation in Carolina.

"I reckon somebody renamed you SeRina over in Carolina. But yes chile', your name Alice. Oh, I wish Francis could see you now. You was so young chile' you probably don't remember. I sent word through other slaves from the other plantation to find you but none of us saw a mulatto girl like you 'round here or there, no child, not 'til now. Your momma, she'd be so happy to know you turned out so beautiful. I guess I really is your Aunt Tempie, see chile' your momma Francis was my sister.

There was an awkward silence between them for a moment, SeRina was taking it all in and was still in a state of shock from the story she had just heard. Aunt Tempie soon broke the silence exuberantly and said, "Lord bless the day, I can't believe you sittin' here 'fore my very eyes my sweet niece, Alice Faith."

Tempie wrapped her stubby arms around SeRina and enveloped

her in the warmth of her bountiful bosom as tears of joy warmed her cheeks. SeRina wanted to push away and contest the idea that she had been in this God forsaken place since birth, but she needed this comfort right now. Especially considering all the whirlwind of emotion that she was feeling. She was so caught up in the story that she forgot momentarily that she didn't even belong in this time and place. She wondered if the grandfather who Aunt Tempie spoke of was Grandpa George and if maybe he was the answer to the mystery of how she got there.

After breakfast, which SeRina found disgusting, the cooking began again. Aunt Tempie moved about the cookhouse making this and that, cleaning up, singing and whistling as she went along, all the while telling stories of Alice's mother Francis and the times they had growing up together as young girls on the plantation. Her ramblings were soothing to SeRina and she felt at peace for the moments she sat in the shanty surrounded by the unfamiliar aromas. SeRina thought it odd for a slave to be so happy and to reminisce about the past as if it were some fairytale when she personally could find no happiness in this dreadful place.

"Now child, your foot's ailin' mighty badly, so rest yourself whilst I feeds the chirren," said Aunt Tempie. Come on out chere iffin you want. If they keeps you out here wit' ol' Aunt Tempie you g'wine need to know how to feeds the chirren."

SeRina obliged, going to sit on the front steps of the small porch as Aunt Tempie did her duty. The tree stumps outside the doorway served as the place where Tempie placed the trough-like bowls for the black children to eat their supper. They would trip over one another like little piglets, grabbing food with their hands or whatever makeshift utensils they had available to them. She fed the children like animals and it made SeRina cringe. But to them it was normal, so Tempie put out the scraps for the chirren'. As she rang the dinner bell that hung from a tall post in the center of the dirt passageway, they all scrambled to the troughs in an animalistic fashion. SeRina watched horrified as they grappled for their meals.

Although SeRina couldn't relate to these people, it distressed her to see the little ones fed like animals from a common trench. It didn't set well with her... She wished she had spoons, forks, and bowls to give them all and shoes, and clothes and combs and brushes. She felt the tears welling in her eyes as she watched them devour the mush.

The day flew by and it seemed Aunt Tempie never stopped... She cooked, she cleaned, and she sent others on errands of fetching wood and water and the like.

SeRina sat and stared the day away in a daze not being much help at all. She watched as Aunt Tempie served man and woman alike. Supplying heaps of collards and yellow slop upon their return from the fields and their inhumane day's work in the blazing sun.

Once they were all served, at the end of the day, Aunt Tempie boiled some water and soaked some strips of rags in a foul-smelling potion before cleansing and gently wrapping SeRina's foot. When she finished, a young girl followed by a massive black man entered the cabin with a sleeveless sackcloth shirt, overalls, and pants. He appeared to be wearing soles of shoes tied to his feet. His appearance alone was enough to catch SeRina totally off guard. His black flesh glistened with sweat and highlighted his bulging pectorals and biceps. SeRina had always been anxious around black men, especially large scary looking dark ones, and she found herself wishing he weren't there. He was closely followed by a young girl she would soon find out was his sister, the infamous, blabbermouth, Lillybird.

"Hey, Momma, who dis purdy lady?" dumbly uttered the mammoth male to Aunt Tempie. His voice was childlike, despite his massive stature. From the sound of his voice, SeRina instantly knew he was a couple of sandwiches short of a picnic.

"Sam, this here is your cousin, Ms. Alice, but she likes to go by SeRina."

"What she do that for momma? Alice is a fine name."

"Don't you worry Sam baby, she like SeRina better. She gwine be working in the big house. I'm gonna look after her 'til she better."

"She look white momma. She gon' cause a heap of trouble 'round here," said Lillybird, Aunt Tempie's wide-eyed blabbermouth daughter. "Annnd, she much too white to be our cousin, so how you figure dat' momma?"

"I know baby, she what they call mulatto. Her momma black, her daddy white. You remember Aunt Francis, this here her child come back from oblivion to ease our soul. Lord bless the day!"

"Bless it," said Big Sam echoing his mother's enthusiasm and clapping his hands clumsily like a 3-year-old.

"I ain't never se'ed no gray eyes on a black woman, momma," said Lillybird. She was eyeballing SeRina head to toe and SeRina was growing more and more annoyed by the second.

"I know Lillybird. Don't you worry, she black like us on the inside." That comment struck SeRina as offensive, but then she remembered the time and place she was in. As Grandma Hattie told her, if she had even an eighth of blackness in her she was black no matter how white her skin. She also remembered it from class. Hypodescent...that was the one term that stuck in her head despite the fact that she ignored most of her teacher's lesson. In her mind, she replayed her vocabulary assignment on which she penned ...

Hypodescent - *the automatic assignment of children of a mixed union or mating between members of different socioeconomic groups or ethnic groups to the group that is considered subordinate or inferior.*

I could absolutely scream, I can't believe she had the audacity to lump me in with THESE PEOPLE, thought SeRina.

They were so ignorant that it turned her stomach to sit there among them and to be considered one of them. She was so incredibly outdone that she wanted to scream!

She knew if she put her mind to it she could escape somehow and get back home, wherever that was, whatever it took, and she would get there. Her musings continued as they discussed the sleeping arrangements.

"Sam, you sleep on the floor tonight. I'm givin' SeRina yo' bed," Aunt Tempie politely ordered.

"That's alright momma. I likes the floor. It good for my aching back," answered Sam.

"SeRina, you come on child and get some rest," she said and took her to the corner of the shanty to a tiny bed covered in a dingy hand-sewn patchwork quilt.
SeRina wondered how on earth Big Sam could even fit his big body on this lumpy hay-filled mattress. However, before she could ponder it any further, she drifted off to sleep.

CHAPTER THIRTEEN

A Mother's Love

It was a new day. A Sunday. And SeRina awoke to Big Sam staring at her. She sat up abruptly.

"What are you looking at?" she pulled at her clothes, covering herself.

"You, you such a pretty lil' flower," said Sam.

"That's just weird. Go away!"

"Why you always lookin' bout so mean? Ain't nobody ever paid you no compliment?"

"It's just creepy waking up with someone staring down your throat. Haven't you heard of respecting someone's personal space?"

"No ma'am, can't say that I have," said Sam.

"Well, learn to!" SeRina said harshly.

Sam cringed slightly. "Fine iffin' you promise not to be so cross all the time." Sam stuck out his hand. SeRina got up from the bed and covered herself even more.

"Fine," said SeRina.

"You gots to shake it," Big Sam said, confused.
Everybody knowed you s'pose to shake on a promise, he thought.

"Shake what?" asked SeRina half listening while Big Sam still had his hand stuck straight out at her. She had to pee and was looking around to see find the bathroom.

"Fine!" said SeRina and she walked over and abruptly shook his hand.

"Hands sure are soft ..." said Big Sam looking at his hand as if something magical had just happened to it.

"Whatever," said SeRina "Where's the bathroom around here?"

"We ain't got a bathroom. Only a river to wash in or I can fetch you some water from the spigot for you to wash."

"No, not to wash, to pee, you know, go to the bathroom?" SeRina said wiggling.

"Oh, you don't need water, you need to go make water," said Big Sam cracking himself up.

"Yes! Where do I go?" demanded SeRina.

Big Sam got up without a word and walked out the front door of the shack.

"Sam, where are you going? Oh my God!" said SeRina as she followed him outside. "Sam!" Sam walked onto the porch and pointed to the outhouse a few cabins down. "It's 'round back of that there cabin."

"You have got to be kidding!" said SeRina, as she pee-pee danced, hopping on her good foot all the way down the dirt road over to the outhouse.

Sam thought she was the prettiest and funniest thing he had ever seen, laughing until his stomach cramped and almost until SeRina was hobbling back toward him again. After a few minutes, she came back up the step into the shack as Sam giggled holding the door wide open for her.

"Now 'dat you back it's time to get ready," said Big Sam.

"Ready for what?" said SeRina.

"Church!" said Big Sam.

"I don't do church," said SeRina.

"In dis house you do," said a gruff, grimy, husky and unfamiliar voice. Just then a tall man with the same build and stature and blackness as Big Sam entered and walked over to take a closer look at SeRina. His demeanor wasn't light and childlike like Big Sam but they looked a lot alike.

"Hey Daddy, I ain't know you were back," said Big Sam extending arms for a hug.

"Boy go on somewhere. I ain't got time to be huggin' and carrying on," said the man without taking his eyes off SeRina.

"So you's the girl everybody 'round here talkin' bout eh?" he asked rhetorically to SeRina. "Look like trouble-a-walkin' iffin you ask me!" he said as he reached over to touch and examine SeRina's hair.

"Don't touch me!" said SeRina.

"Child, me touchin' you is gone be the least of your worries 'round here pretty as you are. Better watch yo'self!" said the man without cracking a smile.

He made SeRina's skin crawl. His demeanor was so dark in contrast to Big Sam's that she wanted him to leave. Her wish was soon granted.

"See ya'll at church and don't be late. You know Missus Abbington love to oversee Pastor Edwards when he teach us savages 'bout the Lord!" said the man and then he picked up his hat and disappeared as fast as he had appeared.

SeRina's face was stoic. She didn't know whether to be afraid of the man, or to heed his warning about watching her back. Just then, Aunt Tempie re-entered the cookhouse. She was wearing her Sunday's best all spiffed up, as spiffy as a slave could be. She was followed by Lillybird who had a bushel of corn she had collected. Aunt Tempie walked in, donned an apron, and started humming and grinding the corn with a hand mill to make the morning pone. She chopped a slice of bacon from the hunk of smoked meat hanging from the rafters and threw it into the pot of boiling black eye peas. She sent Lillybird out to gather turnips and dandelion greens. She was in a pleasant mood as Sundays were her favorite.

"Hey there Sam, I see your brother Big Joe just left," said Aunt Tempie.

"Yes momma he did, he did indeed," said Sam still worried about SeRina.

"Your brother? Thought he was your father?" whispered SeRina.

"He both," said Big Sam unashamed.

SeRina's jaw dropped. She had heard stories of slave masters creating what they called big dumb slaves and she was witnessing it first-hand. Apparently in those days, it was customary for slave masters to mate mothers with sons to create sons just like them in stature, but of course, this practice created some mental deficiencies. She realized that this was the situation with Big Sam. SeRina wondered if that's where the word motherfu**er came from, and decided that now she had yet another reason to hate the people in this day and time, both white and black.

"How 'bout we skip church and you show me around?" asked SeRina in hopes that Big Sam could take her sight-seeing and give her some clue as to how to get home again.

"God don't like it when you ain't go to church, no ma'am. No momma said He don't."

"I think God will forgive you just this once," said SeRina manipulating his feelings. She reached over and squeezed his hand and his face lit up with mischief.

"Alright, but momma can't know so we go for 'lil while then we's can go look 'round!"

"Perfect!" exclaimed SeRina her face lighting up.

They washed and ate, and Big Sam helped her as she hobbled down the dirt road to the tiny makeshift church. When they arrived, the door was opened by a tall black man, handsome and mysteriously familiar.

"Hurry up and find you a seat," the familiar man he urged in a hushed voice.

SeRina looked up into his face. He flashed a flawless grin and nodded a hello.

Blushing, she nodded in return and smiled. She brushed past him and felt her pulse quicken as they touched.

Oh, my God, He's one of the most beautiful men I have ever seen, thought SeRina, surprised at her attraction to him. And those teeth, if he were in my day he could star in his own toothpaste commercial!

Pastor Edwards called the congregation to order. SeRina noticed the Master and his wife seated on the first pew, the only other whites present in the all black service. She second guessed herself when she subliminally counted herself amongst the white parishioners. Pastor Edwards urged the congregation to join in song and a wash of unexpected emotion swept over SeRina as the music reminded her of a hymn played at her adoptive mother's funeral. For a moment she was there again, this time inside the church watching the casket as it closed on her mother's face. The song ended and everyone around her took a seat. SeRina was lost in thoughts of her mother's funeral and remained standing.

"May I?" asked the familiar man, as he sat next to her and motioned for her to sit as well, snapping her back to 1859.

"Sure, sorry," replied SeRina finally sitting down, uncomfortably sandwiched between the familiar man and Big Sam. This awkward delay was exacerbated by the untimely giggles and whispers of the other slaves seated nearby, especially Lillybird.

The sermon began, presided over by the handsome, 40-something Pastor Edwards. "Brothers and Sisters, our Lord Jesus Christ sayeth to the weary 'Come unto me all that labor and are heavy laden and I will give you rest.' Our Lord says, 'Take my yoke upon you and learn of me... and ye shall find rest unto your souls for my yoke is easy and my burden is light.' Let the church say Amen."

The church said Amen and the Massah's wife gave her nod of approval to the message being delivered.

The Pastor's sermon faded in SeRina's mind after the part where he told the congregation of slaves that they are commanded by God not to steal the master's livestock and to do as the Master and Overseer tell them to do without hesitation. She knew that although Pastor Edwards meant well, the Bible said no such thing and that he was spoon fed his sermon by Mr. & Mrs. Abbington who sat nodding on the front row of the church. SeRina noticed Pastor Edwards spoke from memory and had no Bible in hand, meaning he probably was unable to read. Although she didn't care for his sermon, she had to admit the bearded, handsome man was commanding and surprisingly well-spoken. Before she knew it, Big Sam was nudging her to sneak out. Aunt Tempie caught a glimpse of the two sneaking out and got up to investigate.

Once they made it out of doors, SeRina hobbled down the steps, shooing Big Sam's extended hand for help and said, "Do you guys actually believe what he is preaching?" Then in mockery of Pastor Edwards, she continued, 'Don't steal your master's pigs, slaves be obedient to your human masters with fear and trembling as to Christ.' You have GOT to be kidding!!! I can't believe they use the bible to justify this insanity! I will never step foot back in that church again!" said SeRina with disgust.

"But Pastor Edwards, he a good man. Missus Abbington say we best listen to him or we be in big trouble," replied Big Sam hoping to sway her.

"And just where are you makin' off to?" asked Aunt Tempie stepping outside of the church with a raised brow.

Sam stopped and turned around to see Aunt Tempie. "Ms. SeRina's foot was ailing, so I's gwine take her home to rest it up a bit," he said, with a strange inflection almost as if he were trying to convince himself.

"So you says... humpf," said Aunt Tempie not believing that was the true motive. *Now I know my Sam is many things, but not a liar was he ever.* She paused introspectively and checked herself for second guessing his motives. "So go on, but you two stay out of trouble you hear? And watch out for that devil Albert!" warned

Tempie.

"Yes ma'am," said Sam as Aunt Tempie re-entered the church for the remainder of the service.

Once she was out of ear-shot, Sam said to SeRina. "Momma don't like 'dat rotten ol Albert. He does bad things to peoples. He even do bad, bad things to me even though I ain't no trouble at all." Big Sam teared up at the thought of Albert. For as long as he could remember, Albert would take advantage of him and other slaves both male and female on the plantation just to show his dominance and it made Sam feel afraid and filthy. It was a secret no one talked about, a secret Sam tucked away deep inside. He avoided Albert at all costs and hoped that the last time would be the last time that it happened to him. SeRina watched Big Sam wrestling with emotion and thought it unimaginable that little weasel Albert could have his way with this huge mountain of a man. It saddened her, for Sam was docile and childlike and had begun to make his way into her heart.

Come on, I want to show you something," blurted out Sam interrupting the now awkward silence. He took off walking with sudden urgency. SeRina tried her best to keep up with Big Sam's strides back down the dirt road, but winced from pain and slowed her pace favoring her good foot. Finally, out of consideration of her injury, Big Sam stopped and waited for her to catch up.

"Here hop on," he said hunching down so she could jump onto his back.

"Are you kidding?"

"Not at all ... your foot's ailing and it'll take us all mornin' to get there the rate you's piddling along."

"Okay. I guess," said SeRina a little uncertain as she obliged him and placed her arms around his neck.

He stood up fast and SeRina giggled. He carried her as if she was weightless, back down the dirt road and past a familiar shanty with a garden out back. He navigated the garden with SeRina in tow careful not to disturb the plants. After passing through the garden he entered the brush and headed into the forest.

"Watch your pretty lil head," he said to SeRina, ducking down to avoid oncoming branches. After a few more ducks and warnings, they arrived at their destination. He put SeRina down and she clumsily toppled over landing on the ground with a thud, which extorted a few more exuberant giggles from her.

"This here is the hush harbor, you gots to keep it down," said Big Sam.
SeRina stood up with his assistance looking all around her. She saw trees so tall she had to stretch her neck all the way back to her shoulders to see the tops. The birds and wildlife were fully awake and acknowledged their presence by scurrying away. The clearing they stood in was beautifully adorned with all of nature's best. There were a few hand-made benches about it and in the center sat a fire pit of sorts.

"Pretty, ain't it?" asked Big Sam.

"Breathtaking," said SeRina.

"I comes here to think sometimes, just to muse on all God's wonders," said Big Sam.

"I've never seen anything like this in my life," said SeRina.

"Taint seen the forest by the marsh 'fore nor the hush harbor? Then you gots to see dis," Big Sam reached for SeRina's hand, she resisted at first but then took it hesitantly. He led her to the other side of the clearing. About halfway through, he scooped her up again because she kept stumbling on her injured foot. The further they advanced, the sparser the forest became, exposing a trail leading to the beautiful and mystical Great Dismal Swamp. On the bank was a small boat nestled under a sprawling weeping willow tree. Big Sam lowered SeRina into the boat and climbed in himself as he loosened the ropes and took oars in hand.

"Let's take us a ride down the swamp. If we's lucky we may spot a gator."

"A gator? No way! Let me off this thing," said SeRina in a panic.

"No ma'am, sit tight. Big Sam won't let not a thing happen to his pretty lil flower. We is takin us a ride, you said you wants to see thangs, so thangs is what Sam's gonna show you."

"Big Sam, why are you so nice to me?"

"What reason Big Sam gots to be mean? You ain't meant me no harm."

"I know, it's just that people around here don't go out of their way to be kind to me like you have. I am so lost, I don't know which end is up and everyone just makes me feel like I'm crazy."

"You just different is all...just like Big Sam. I'm different."

"Different." laughed SeRina. "You most certainly are different." SeRina laughed again but stopped quickly when she saw Sam's face.

She had hurt his feelings. "I don't mean it in a bad way, Sam. You are just..." Her voice trailed off as she searched for words to fix her mistake. "Well, I guess what you are is ... a breath of fresh air."

"I likes dat," said Big Sam smiling.

"So, tell me. What are your dreams Big Sam?" asked SeRina as they floated past a giant tree whose stump was covered in moss and surrounded by a murky film.

"Well, I dreams, I's gwine to get me a purdy gal like you to marry, have some chirren of my own and builds me a house to live in. We be so happy helpin' round here on the plantation and raisin' up our chir'ren together."

It saddened her to hear how simple his desires and dreams were. She wondered how an enslaved wife and children born into slavery could be anybody's dream. *That would be no life at all.*

Big Sam and SeRina floated lazily downstream, surrounded by the peaceful sights and sounds of the swamp. She was surprised at how close she felt to him and how much he genuinely cared for her.

"Tells me about where you from," Sam requested, wide-eyed with anticipation.

"You won't believe me," said SeRina. She sighed and thought,
It would be amazing to share the bizarre events of the last few days with someone. But no, he definitely won't believe me and even if he did, who would ever believe him?

"Course I will," Big Sam assured her. "Pastor Edwards say, 'With God, all things is possible.' "

The look on Big Sam's face was so genuine and caring, that SeRina opened up and shared with him all of the emotions she'd carried inside for so long. She told him of her Mother and Father, her Grandma Hattie, and all of her friends back home, ever mindful to avoid any specific references to the fact that all of that existed in the year 2009. She was encouraged by how intently he was listening and so she continued, laughing and crying her way through the journey that had brought her to this God forsaken time and place where she had become the very thing she never claimed or desired to be... BLACK.

CHAPTER FOURTEEN

A Tromp Through the Garden

Several days had passed and they all seemed a blur, each one much like the next.

SeRina had found little joy in the passing days other than her occasional interchanges with Sam after a long day's work in the cookhouse with Aunt Tempie. He would always find something silly to do or say to get her giggling. Once she had gotten past his menacing outer appearance, she found that underneath all the muscle, lay a man who was childlike and full of joy and laughter. SeRina felt a connection with Sam. Although she felt sorry for him, he made her laugh. She thought she'd never smile again in this horrible place but he somehow made things more tolerable. She couldn't dare let him know that she liked his company, so pushed him away every given chance. Although she was distant and intentionally cold toward him, she secretly looked forward to him coming home from the fields in the evenings and having dinner with them in the cookhouse. Quietly, she felt safe in his presence, she knew he would do anything to protect her.

On this particular morning, SeRina awoke at the crack of dawn to the sound of clattering pots. Tempie was at it again. She had enlisted the help of her daughter Lillybird. SeRina needed to use the bathroom and dreaded the long trip past the three cabins out back to the foul outhouse. She bid everyone she passed good morning on her way and held her breath when she arrived, just as she had the days before. Crying wouldn't get her home, she needed to focus and think of a plan. That in mind, she made a quick exit and found a quiet spot near the cookhouse where she sat on the ground to clear her mind and give herself a pep talk.

SeRina, stop the pity-party! If you are stuck here, then you are stuck here. Deal with it, focus on what you CAN do, and keep it moving quitting is NOT an option!

She surmised from the conversations that she must be somewhere in the cotton belt. She remembered her teacher telling the class that the belt stretched from North Carolina down to northern Florida and West to California. SeRina hadn't seen any palm trees so she knew that Florida and California were out of the question. She thought maybe she was in the Carolinas. She then was confused because she cheated her way through that history test. Was Florida even a state yet, or was it still a part of Spain? She thought of the swamp and Big Sam's tale of 'gators possibly lurking in the swamp and thought she must be pretty far south. She decided to worry about that at another time. Where didn't matter nearly as much as how and when, so her thoughts shifted to the moment at hand.

She looked down at the lacy frock that Aunt Tempie had given her to wear and felt vaguely ashamed of thinking so negatively of her the previous night. She was simply a product of her environment, a slave woman whose only function in life was to feed the field "niggas" when they come in from a hard day of planting or harvesting and slop the chillun' like pigs. It was not her fault.

If she can find happiness, so can I, thought SeRina.

She returned to her musings about her whereabouts and plans to escape when Big Sam came barreling out the back door.

"Sam?"

"Yes, pretty lady."

"Where are we?"

"You know where we is, we's on the Abbington Plantation."

"No, Sam. I mean where are we, as in, what city and what state, for Christ's sake?"

"Oh pretty Ms. Alice, you shouldn't call on the Lord in vain."

"For the last time, my name is not ALICE! Can you just tell me when and where the heck we are?" SeRina shouted at Big Sam.

"Momma said if you can't be nice to folks when you talk, that you shouldn't say nothin', so I'm gonna talk to you when you not feeling so spiteful Ms. Alice, I mean pretty Ms. SeRina. Good day ma'am."

He shuffled away toward the fields with the other men and women leaving her to bask in her own negativity.

"Whatever, just forget it!" SeRina yelled after him. She couldn't believe God was cruel enough to put that small of a brain in that big of a body.

"What an idiot!" she said under her breath forgetting their connection and returning to her self-centeredness.

"What's that child?" Aunt Tempie asked from the doorway with a sweet voice. "Did you call?"

"Nothing," said SeRina. Unless your name is 'idiot', she thought.

"You ain't ate your breakfast," said Aunt Tempie.

"I don't want it!" replied SeRina. She hated the taste of the bland boiled, coarse cornmeal mush that was served day after day. She hated the carved out wooden tray it was served on and the makeshift fork she had to eat it with. She felt like an animal eating such slop and was appalled at the way the children lined up in the morning to eat from a trough out in the center of the shanties. It was so dehumanizing. She was flabbergasted to see one of the young boys push a dog away from the food so he could dive back in with his grubby little fingers. Biscuits, cornbread, mush, pot liquor from collards... that was food for animals as far as she could see it. And she was no animal.

"Well, tonight we havin' bean soup. I's soaking the beans right now and Massah Abbington done gave us some ham hocks to put in them. Them niggers and pickaninnies gonna eat mighty fine this evenin'."

SeRina couldn't believe her ears. This woman sounded so proud to serve them slop, beans, and ham hocks. She had to be clueless referring to her own people as niggers and pickaninnies with endearment. It blew her mind. SeRina always hated how blacks referred to themselves with the "n" word in jest, making it the hook of a song like it was something to be proud of. She thought it was especially degrading and showed their ignorance. It was yet another reason why she hated them and wanted no part of this day or time nor any part of their world when she returned to her own time. It was another reason why she simply was NOT black.

"Your foot ought to be healed enough now chile. Enough of that sittin' round. Go out to the garden and fetch me an onion and some taters," said Aunt Tempie from the doorway, as she handed SeRina a makeshift short-handled tool to dig them up with, and a basket to tote them in.

Lillybird giggled in the corner at SeRina.

"Okay," muttered SeRina as she turned to walk away, rolling her eyes at Lillybird who stuck her tongue out when Aunt Tempie wasn't looking in response to SeRina's eye rolling.

"What's that? Speak up now!" said Aunt Tempie.

"I'm going!" said SeRina staunchly.

"Oh chile' we got to get to work on your manners. It's a shame for such a pretty gal to have such a foul disposition. You ought to be grateful somebody took you in, fed ya, and gave you a dress to wear... And you got to eat meat two days running. Some chirren I tell you don't 'preciate nothin', humpf." Aunt Tempie slammed the door and returned to her bean-soaking.

SeRina rolled her eyes and ventured off to find the garden.

She asked a few slave men passing by her on the way to the fields if they had seen the garden. One of them wouldn't make eye contact with her and the other couldn't take his eyes off of her, neither of them uttered a word in reply.

Just then a little girl chocolate as a Hershey's kiss with hair twisted in rags came up to SeRina. SeRina stared at the girl for a moment and then said, "Hello."

"Hello, is you lost?" asked the chocolate girl.

"No, I'm not lost. Just trying to find the garden," said SeRina, almost smiling at the irresistible tyke.

"Why you talks like white folks? If you's white, what you doin' out here wit' us?"

SeRina rolled her eyes in reply and kept walking.

"I know where da garden is. C'mon I takes ya!" said the little girl, quickening her pace to catch up with SeRina.

She grabbed SeRina's un-extended hand and took out, skipping through the shanties across the dirt road that separated them and down four more shanties. She stopped and pointed to the rear of the wooden cabin and said, "It's in old man George's backyard; he takes care of the garden in 'tween fiddling' with watches for Massah's friends and makin' things outta wood, like furniture and such."

SeRina stood still, staring at the porch attached to the shack in disbelief. It looked exactly like the one in the photo at her grandmother's house. It had the same chair and the same cane leaning against the house. All that was missing was the old man and the doll-faced little girl. SeRina never made the connection before when she went through the garden to the clearing with Big Sam. It was like she was sucked into the picture on the wall at her grandmother's house.

Just then, SeRina heard Aunt Tempie's voice in the distance calling the children to eat and as quick as she appeared, the little chocolate girl disappeared. SeRina made her way to the back of the house just as the child advised and there she saw a small garden. There were a few rows of corn, some carrots, and what she supposed were onions and potatoes. She had no clue what they looked like on the upside of the ground because she had never picked a vegetable in her life. So there she stood in the middle of the garden looking plant to plant, not knowing where to begin. A familiar dark voice startled her.

"You are a mighty fine wench indeed. Best thing I've ever found in them there woods."

A chill went down her spine as she turned to face Albert Pinkard. Her wrists were still bruised from the night he had found her and held her so tightly. Her mind raced, not knowing whether to stand still or to turn and run.

"Stay put girl. If you run I'll make you regret it!" he said reading her mind. He slowly approached her and she backed away from him, tripping over a vine in the garden. She turned and ran but didn't make it far before he caught her by the back of her hair. A dog like yelp escaped her throat as the searing pain in her scalp met the chill in her spine.

"I said stay put!" The stench from his breath made its way around to her face from behind and burned her nostrils. He ran his hands through her hair and down her back to her waist and pulled her close to him, holding her by her hips. She felt him firmly pressed against her pelvis and it disgusted her to know he was aroused.

"Don't you touch me!" SeRina yelled, trying to pull away from him so that she could run again. She remembered the tool she had stuffed into her apron pocket. She took it out and spun around, raising it to strike him.

Albert saw it coming and grabbed her wrist, slapping her to the ground with his free hand.

"Now, girl, I asked you nicely to stay put. I could've had you whipped for what you said to me out in the woods the other day, but I didn't. I could have you killed for raising your hand to me, but I've got another way to teach you a lesson. You had better learn your place and learn it fast nigger. I could take you right now, right here in this garden if I wanted to and your place is to lay there and take it. I will have you one way or another. I was going to ease into it kindly like, but you've got it coming now girl! Hold still and shut your mouth!"

He forced himself on top of her, and she scratched and pushed him with all of her strength, screaming as loudly as she could. Just then an old man came out of the back door of the cabin and yelled with a distinct accent, "What's all that ruckus?"

"Mind your business, George."

"George? Grandpa George?" thought SeRina out loud. "Help, help me!"

"Shut your mouth girl!" said Albert.

"Unhand the girl. There are plenty of women here you have had your way with, why do you need another?" asked Grandpa George as he stood tall and refined.

"George, mind your business nigger and go on back in that house if you know what's good for you!"

Grandpa George went back inside.

Albert got up and grabbed SeRina by the arm, dragging her off as she yelled for help again to no avail. He covered her mouth, pulled her through the garden, and remounted the now squirming SeRina. He was attempting to take down his trousers and hold her down at the same time. Grandpa George reappeared at the cabin door with a large shovel in hand, the business end resting on his shoulder, and began heading toward Albert when Massah Abbington approached on horseback.

"Albert, what are you doing with that negra?"

"He was attempting to have his way with the girl," replied Grandpa George.

"George, go on back inside. I can handle this," said Massah Abbington.

"Yes sir," said Grandpa George." And then he did just that.

"Well, sir. She sassed me, sir. I'm gonna beat her," Albert muttered in disappointment as he removed his hand from her mouth.

"Please, sir, he's trying to rape me! Help me please!" SeRina pleaded. The moment he took his hand from her mouth, she tried to break free from his grip.

"Let me be clear with you Albert. Your place is to oversee the niggers in the fields and that is all. If you have vile intentions to defile this gal, I won't stand for it. If you don't understand my meaning, test me and you will learn just as the slaves by the end of a whip that I mean what I say! You stay clear of her until I say otherwise!"

"Yes sir," said Albert, defeated. He let go of SeRina and headed toward the fields to do as he was told. He gave SeRina a freezing glance that said he was not done with her yet. He had long had his way with any slave woman he pleased and she would be next. He craved her, for she was smart and sassy, quite unlike the others. She was a challenge for him; he longed for her scent and loved the curve of her hips and full supple breasts. He smiled to himself as he turned to walk away, accepting this temporary setback.

"Now girl, you are a peculiar one. You don't talk like the other niggas. You have an air about you," said Mr. Abbington, speaking down to her from his horse.

SeRina, still shaken from the encounter, exploded with emotion and said with earnestness, "I am not a slave! I do not belong here! I'm from West Virginia and the year was 2009 when I left there. I don't know how I got here. Please just let me free so I can go home to my father. I'm not black, look at me! I'm almost as white as you are. How could you do this to me? Please just let me go!"

"Now mind your tone girl, you are mine. I bought and paid for you fair and square. Albert gave me the receipts for you and the other nigger. I already lost one a few weeks ago runnin' away, so ain't no way I'm gonna set you free and lose another investment. So you can get that out of your pretty little head. Now you stay clear of Albert. If he touches you, you let me know. I won't stand for the raping of my property. I don't want you bearing any children just yet. I want

to get some work out of you first."
SeRina's resolve melted into defeat, his words stung and revealed the cruel reality that reduced her from human to mere property.

"My daughter's birthday is fast approaching and you'd make a mighty fine gift for her as a personal slave girl. In your spare time, you could help out in the kitchen. But now girl I need you to keep your head about you. Stop with this foolishness. You are in the year 1859. If that bump on your head tells you otherwise, you remember what I tell you. That's enough with the fancy theories. Mind me well and get back to the cookhouse with Tempie!"

SeRina nodded in agreement and watched Mr. Abbington ride off. Her heart still racing in her chest from the insanity that just transpired and still aching with disappointment. She couldn't believe she had actually laid eyes on Grandpa George from her grandmother's photos and that he was willing to try and save her. She almost wished he had a few more moments to go upside Albert's head with that shovel before Massah Abbington rode up.

She returned to the garden and pulled up a handful of vegetables from each row, not knowing what was what until it was on the other side of the ground. She picked up the basket she had long dropped and put the vegetables within it holding them close to her for comfort. The reality of everything that just occurred weighed on her heavily. She turned to look at the house hoping Grandpa George would make another appearance. He was nowhere to be found. She wanted to knock but instead, did as she was told and returned to the cookhouse and the temporary comforts of Aunt Tempie and Big Sam. In an instant, she made up her mind despite the consequences that she would run at the first given chance. She had to flee for her life before Albert Pinkard took it.

CHAPTER FIFTEEN

Rude Awakening

Back in the cookhouse, SeRina slept restlessly that night and awoke time and time again. She dreamt off and on about her friend Michaela's nerdy little brother Isaiah being fascinated with time-travel stories and rambling on about quantum physics and the space time continuum. She wished for the life of her she could remember the formulas and theories of Einstein, Copenhagen, and Paul Dirac the British physicist that he used to quote. However, between noddings, she could remember nothing more than a few scenes from "Back to the Future" which did her absolutely no good seeing as though there were no DeLoreans invented in 1859. "Ugh, what was that he said about subatomic phenomena?" She put her makeshift pillow over her head out of frustration. She was trapped inside of Pandora's Box and there was no refuge.

Morning came seemingly earlier than ever and it was day sixteen in 1859. SeRina longed for the basic necessities of a teenage girl's life. She had bathed the night before in the nearby stream with Aunt Tempie and some of the children. She wished she had a toothbrush, toothpaste, some deodorant, and lotion. And what she wouldn't do for a tampon! Aunt Tempie had given her some lard to rub on her skin and sooth her chapped lips, and sunburnt skin, but she had refused thinking it gross to rub pig fat on her body. There she lay lost in her recurring daydream and not wanting to budge from her makeshift bed.

"Child, you sleep longer than any chile' I ever seen in my life! Rise and shine and give God your glory! The day is slippin' away," said Aunt Tempie.

"Sorry, I didn't sleep so well last night," replied SeRina.

"What's the matter, bad dreams?" asked Tempie genuinely concerned. She sat on the end of the makeshift bed and moved the curls from SeRina's face. SeRina immediately started sobbing uncontrollably and between sobs replayed the story about Albert in the garden the day before.

"Ooh chile, that rotten Albert is known far and wide for breaking in the slaves 'round here. He is as vile a character as the Lucifer himself! You sit right 'chere, and stay clear of that devil and I will fetch the water from the cistern dis mornin'." Tempie headed out mumbling to herself about the rotten scoundrel. She soon returned to the cookhouse with the water ready to prepare the day's vittles and was shocked to see the 'Devil' himself fast approaching.

"Good morning, let me get that door for you Ms. Tempie," said

Albert with a faux chivalric tone.

"No sir, I's capable sir, I get it myself," retorted Aunt Tempie, trying to keep him as far away from SeRina as possible.

"Oh, it will be no trouble at all. Why I insist," said Albert.

"No sir..." but before Aunt Tempie could finish he had swung the door open and there stood SeRina chopping carrots.

"Morning there, you ready?" asked Albert.

"Ready for what? I'm not going anywhere with you!" said SeRina with feigned confidence. Inside she was shivering with fear of the thought of him finishing what he had started the day before. She held tightly to the knife in case she needed to use it for something other than the carrots,

"There you go sassin' again. Ain't you learned your lesson gal? Keep your mouth shut!" said Albert.

SeRina didn't utter a word but held on firmly to the knife staring Albert dead in the eye for what seemed like an eternity.

"You best be puttin' that knife down if you know what's best for you."

"SeRina, put down the knife baby," admonished Aunt Tempie.

After an intense moment, SeRina complied but placed it within reach in case she needed to take hold of it again.

"Mr. Pinkard sir, she fine here with ol' Aunt Tempie, she helpin' fix the vittles. She ain't no trouble, no trouble at all. She ain't mean that sassin' boss!" said Aunt Tempie.

"Oh you right mammy, she won't be any trouble at all," said Albert to Aunt Tempie.

"It's high time you put those pretty little hands to some real work! Tempie, fetch this girl some working clothes. We can't have her dirtying up her pretty little dress now can we?" Albert enjoyed the fear he saw in SeRina's eyes.

"Oh no, sir. Please, sir. Won't you please, let her help old Aunt Tempie? I's feeling poorly, she's gon' cook today sir. Just let her stay here, please sir." Aunt Tempie knew the tender young SeRina would not last through the backbreaking work in the fields. She knew Albert would try to make an example out of her for spite since he hadn't been able to have his way with her. She knew SeRina was no match because it took her a day or two just to learn to chop the carrots and peel the potatoes as she wanted. Her hands were that of a white woman's. They were smooth, dainty, and callous-free. Aunt Tempie knew wherever she came from that she had done little to no work, so was afraid for her to be put out in the smoldering sun to harvest with the other slaves.

Aunt Tempie pleaded to no avail. Albert stood and watched as SeRina undressed, standing just inches from her. She tried to change discreetly without showing him what he so desperately wanted to see. She felt Aunt Tempie's presence was the only thing preventing him from ripping the work dress clean off her before she could even get it all the way on. His eyes never left her as she slipped cautiously into the rags fit for the field. Once she was dressed Albert escorted her to his horse.

He mounted and pulled her up in front of him, holding her tight against him as he made his way to the field. She could feel his breath on the back of her neck and it made her hair stand on end. She inched away as far as humanly possible while on horseback and he abruptly pulled her back into him. SeRina swallowed her pride and figured she would not resist further. She would give it her all in the fields and thought that was better than what he could have done with her. She would run before he had the chance.

CHAPTER SIXTEEN

Hot White Gold

The sun had barely risen in the sky, but the humid summer's heat was already taking its toll on the field workers. It was late August in this time, although SeRina remembered it being chilly the weeks before when she was at her grandmother's house in 2009. The slaves stopped for a moment to stare at her when she arrived on horseback, personally escorted to the field by Albert the overseer. They were all startled that he had let her ride his horse instead of dragging her behind like he always did the others.

"What are you gaping at? Get back to work niggers! It's too early for me to have to crack the whip 'cross you!" he yelled.

They all quickly dropped their glances and resumed the work. SeRina was surprised, as the crop was a leafy green one instead of white. The farm also had what they referred to as "white gold" by way of acres and acres of cotton fields with newly planted Egyptian seed. However, this was tobacco harvesting season, so instead of picking cotton as she anticipated, she was to prune tobacco. Albert had taken her to the center of the gorgeous acres and acres of land that made up the Abbington tobacco crop.

Albert dismounted the horse, his freshly oiled whip tucked neatly in the back of his pants. He extended his hand to SeRina. She refused and clumsily dismounted the horse without assistance, falling with a thud to the ground face-first.

"Suit yourself, nigger!" Albert laughed at SeRina and extended his hand again to help her up. When she refused, he kicked a clump of dirt into her face. She coughed from the dry dust and wiped her face, her sweat blending with the dirt leaving a brown smudge on her face.

"Now you look more like a nigger should!" Albert said to her, laughing once more. She stood up to see the slaves staring again, just as Albert caught one of the slaves across the back of his neck with his whip.

"I said back to work nigger 'taint nothing to see here!" ordered Albert.

The fallen slave answered, "Yes sir, Massah boss!" After returning to his feet, he wiped his hand across his bloody neck. He swiped his now crimson palm across his trouser leg and bent to resume priming the withered yellowed lower leaves of the tobacco plant.

"Rose, come here. Show her the way to prime that tobacco. Just so, ya hear?!" Albert motioned the nearby slave woman to come closer. She looked to be about 45 or so. She had broad shoulders and a wrinkled forehead with wide-set eyes. The woman's biceps looked like they belonged on the cover of a fitness magazine. SeRina thought she looked like she belonged here; she surely couldn't imagine a woman like this living in the year 2009. She looked like some sort of savage beast. The only thing missing were fangs and claws. SeRina thought the woman's mother must have been delirious after childbirth to name her "Rose" because she was a far cry from any flower, in fact to SeRina she looked more like a thorn. SeRina almost laughed to herself momentarily, forgetting the gravity of her situation. Her desire to giggle quickly subsided after the glances of the other slaves working nearby and fear set in. SeRina thought there was no way that she would ever be able to keep up with this woman who was built like a power-lifting man. She hoped Albert would leave so she could work at her own pace, but she wouldn't be so lucky.

SeRina surveyed the slaves and their technique. Rose explained to her that today they were priming the plants and pulling off the lower leaves of the plant that had yellowed. SeRina thought it would be easy work until the sun came out in full force and change her mind. Albert watched her closely waiting for her to make a mistake, he hovered over all of them, whipping anyone who complained of thirst or who moved "a might too slow to his liking."

SeRina shrieked when she pulled a leaf and a huge worm just as green as the leaf crawled onto her hand. It was the strangest thing she had ever seen bright in color with a red horn-like protrusion on its nose and eye-like markings on its back.

"Oh chile', that's just a tobacco worm 'taint gone do you no harm. They send the turkeys through here to pluck them off the leaves but now and again they miss one or ten," Rose explained laughing at SeRina's squeamish behavior. SeRina didn't like the idea that there could be more of them lurking about. Furthermore, she resented the fact that this beastly looking woman had the nerve to be clever.

Around mid-morning, the heat had already become unbearable. SeRina felt her skin began to tighten under the August sun. She needed sunscreen to protect her fair skin, a luxury not afforded to her in 1859. She regretted refusing the lard. Her lips cracked from thirst and her stomach rumbled with hunger. She had foolishly refused the meals offered to her by Aunt Tempie and now realized that she had only spited herself. She bent to pluck a leaf from the bottom of a plant just as she had been trained, but instead of putting it in the trash bushel she stood and began to fan herself with it. She had never worked so hard in all her life and it was still morning. Since she saw the worm, she had been working at a much slower pace in hopes to avoid another encounter. But even at this pace, the sun had drained her energy, she was hot, tired and thirsty and felt she could not go on. She needed food and water and she longed for air conditioning. She stood fanning herself and staring off into the fields daydreaming in hopes of catching a glance of her vehicle in the distance.

She thought, *these people are insane, there is no way I am doing this all day. I mean they are such idiots there are easily 40 slaves to one scrawny overseer out here, so why don't they just band together and ...*

WHOOSH! CRACK!

The daydream was interrupted abruptly SeRina's eyes involuntarily shut tight, the shock of the blow from the overseer's whip surged through her body like electricity. She had never felt such pain.

The lash landed rigidly across her back, ripping the rags she wore and the flesh beneath it, and snatching her clean back into reality. Her back was ablaze, pain searing up her spine and again she was knocked to her knees. She hoped that if there were another blow that it would kill her to keep her from feeling this pain again.

"Get up, girl! Get up and get to pluckin' 'fore he lash you again!" urged Rose never breaking her plucking and pruning stride. SeRina could faintly hear the words and willed her legs to move but was frozen from pain and fear.

WHOOSH! CRACK!

"You heard her, get to pluckin'!" yelled Albert.

Another blow struck her this time lower on her back and she went from her knees to lying face first in the dirt...again.

"Massa Albert, go easy on her. She green, she ain't know no better," said Rose.

"Shut up gal and mind your manners or you'll catch one too! Get up I say!"

WHOOSH! CRACK!
WHOOSH! CRACK!

SeRina nearly fainted from the pain of the second lash. The throbbing was so intense now that she couldn't move from the spot she lay. By the time the third and fourth lash hit her, she was out cold lying in a pool of her own blood. Albert lost interest in torturing her when a nearby slave complained of thirst as a distraction.

"Massah Albert, I's powerful thirsty, can I fetch some water? It's past time now for the water to come." Although he was right and Lillybird, who usually came out to water the slaves had not shown up for some reason, a blow from Albert's almighty whip soon silenced his request.

One of the fit and brawny male slaves began a song with a heavy and low baritone voice and the others chimed in willing themselves to keep working and not retaliate to the brutality.

Soon after, Lillybird came to call the field hands in for water and the midday meal and it was then that Big Sam saw his pretty little flower sprawled out laying in a pool of red. The other slaves had been warned by Albert to "LEAVE HER BE, OR GET THE SAME!" so they let her lay there unattended and roasting in the burning sun as they moved on in song not looking back to another part of the field.

Sam rushed to SeRina's side and gently cradled her limp body in his arms, careful not to touch her open wounds. Despite the anger growing within, he made his way back to the cookhouse. Tears stained his face, paying tribute to this mountainous man's emotions about what had just transpired. Someone will pay for this, he thought. But he knew wrath was God's and God's alone, so instead, he said a silent prayer, steadying his mind, subduing the rage, and focusing on the most important thing in that moment...his precious SeRina. Lillybird followed him fearful and quiet back to the cookhouse.

"Mama, Mama, come quick!" Big Sam called as he approached the cookhouse holding SeRina as if she were weightless. Aunt Tempie came barreling out of the front door answering his call. Aunt Tempie gasped when she saw him carrying SeRina's lifeless body. Sam ran up the stairs into the cookhouse and lay SeRina face down on his bed. Sam's father Big Joe was seated at the table when Big

Sam entered the cookhouse. He walked over to where SeRina lay and said to them all, "See, I told you 'dat girl gon' be trouble." He put on his hat, shook his head and left the cookhouse.

CHAPTER SEVENTEEN

Healing

"Oh momma, that old dirty rotten Albert done beat her good! I didn't knowed it til' waterin' time. I happened across her in the field laying there still as a rock momma. Is she dead?" Big Sam asked desperately searching his mother's eyes for the answer.

"No chile, she ain't dead. She just ailing badly. I knowed it gon' be trouble when that ol' devil come for her this mornin'. Poor chile she ain't never worked the fields a day in her life. She so burnin' hot, she probably had heat stroke. Lillybird, bring me some fresh cold water for her to drink. Sam, put some water on to boil and fetch me some tobacco leaves to make the salve quick-like ya' hear!"

Big Sam did as his mother asked fetching some water from the spigot; some to drink, some to boil and the leaves she requested. He carefully made the ointment by boiling the tobacco leaves in lard and water. When he finished, he soaked strips of rags in the salve just as he had countless times before to sooth the oozing wounds of other whipped slaves.

Aunt Tempie choked back her tears as she cleansed SeRina's cuts. SeRina lay motionless taking short shallow breaths, she had long since come to but was willing herself to pass out again. She recalled briefly her desire to escape and a tear slipped from her eye as she realized there was no way for her to leave in this condition. She was so lost in hopeless thought that she barely winced as her wounds were cleaned and dressed with the salve-soaked rags.

Aunt Tempie prayed over her as she covered her dressed wounds with the patchwork quilt.

"Father God, please if you will reach yo mighty and powerful hand down and touch 'dis here chile. Heal her heart, heal her spirit, and mend her body. Protect her Jehovah from the wicked hand of that rotten Albert. Forgive her father for her wayward ways and sins against you, she young father and she know not that she is a child of your'n and owe all thanks and praise to you. Help dis chile finds her place in dis cruel world father. Don't let the world just suck her in and spit her out like her poor mother. Help dis chile finds her way and herself. Put her mind at ease and grant her comfort and healing. I comes to you father a simple ol cookin' woman, but a woman of a mighty faith and I leaves dis chile in your worthy hands. Thank you, Father, in advance for your grace and mercy in the name of your precious son Jesus... Amen."

She ended her prayer, wiped the tears from hers and swept the curls from SeRina's angelic face with her rough hand. She sat by her side into the night neglecting her duties in the kitchen for the first time. Slaves came by complaining of the lack of supper and wondering why this woman had received special attention. Beatings were the norm and it was her own fault in their eyes since she didn't work as hard as she was told. Sam handed out vegetables, corn meal and scraps of meat as the slaves stopped by and instructed them to cook for themselves as they did on occasion in their individual cabins.

Big Sam watched from the stubby stool as his mother prayed and rocked, she hummed softly as she stroked SeRina's face. He couldn't stand to see his mother so distraught over SeRina's condition. In his mother's mind, SeRina was her long-lost niece, and she wanted to cherish that connection to her and her deceased sister. Aunt Tempie had failed to protect SeRina so blamed herself for the incident. Sam's simple mind was more active than ever before. Although he was full of fury and hatred toward Albert and had thought long and hard about ways to get even, his bible trained conscience wouldn't let him.

It was one thing for Albert to do the rotten things he had done to Sam but SeRina was off-limits. Sam felt Albert had crumpled his flower. Sam secretly loved SeRina, he hadn't minded giving up his bed for her. He loved her smile and her curiosity. He saw through the rough and tumble facade' she put on to her broken heart within. They had shared a couple of precious moments where she really opened up to him, talking about the home she was from and all of its beauty and things that he could never imagine. It seemed like a distant dream to him, like something that was out of a storybook in the big house, a book that he could not and would not ever read.

He hung on her every word in those moments, trying to imagine this amazing place she described. He wondered if she was a bit "touched" as he was and if she had imagined it all. She had opened his mind up to things beyond his wildest dreams and he couldn't imagine his world without her. If she did choose to go, he secretly longed to escape with her to the "home" that she spoke of so vividly.

It had now been just a few weeks since she arrived but he had fallen madly in love with her. She hadn't bothered to notice. She was so tied up in her thoughts of escape, she ignored his compliments and insisted on rambling on about her world and the life she left behind.

He knew that given the things that had just transpired, he needed to look out for SeRina and protect her more than ever. He secretly hoped she would someday see his love for her and be the wife he had dreamt her to be.

Although Albert had managed to get Sam alone a few times in his life and had his way with him to supposedly teach him to be 'submissive,' many years had passed since the whip had touched Sam's flesh. He was loyal and true and never created trouble. He was also one of the biggest, strongest, and fastest workers and had earned the respect of his Massah Abbington. He wasn't the smartest of the slaves, but made up for his lack of brains with brawn.

Days had passed and SeRina hadn't made any improvement. In fact, she had taken a turn for the worse. Infection set into her open wounds and she was feverish and delirious. She faded in and out and had haunting dreams of home, her parents, her friends, and everyone from 2009 morphing into the people in this place. Flashes of light and voices from home swirled in her head and for a moment she almost thought she was there. In a feverish stupor, she called out in vain for her father and for her precious Christophe. She dreamt of their kiss, the night of the storm. She remembered riding in the car and then the light came again and the pain and the agony clouded her thoughts. She dreamt that she was at her adoptive mother's funeral, only this time she cried uncontrollably. This time she apologized for not picking up the dry-cleaning and she was so remorseful for not going home on time. It was all her fault, the accident, and her father's pain. She had left her father when he needed her the most. She called out to him again and this time almost felt the touch of his hand against her forehead.

SeRina awoke to the sound of a knock at the door. It was Christophe. She saw his face. Yes, it was Christophe or was it Timothy? She hoped it wasn't Timothy, the one who had pushed her away and treated her like a nigger. To her, they were one and the same; the past and the present combined in her clouded mind. The difference was that Timothy had no idea who Christophe was and had no memory of the year 2009 or of her. His image faded and then she heard Aunt Tempie's voice.

"Rest easy chile, don't you fret' Aunt Tempie here now..."

Why was she here? Wasn't she home? She fought against the cloud coming over her, pulling her back into the darkness long enough to realize that Christophe wasn't there at all, it was Timothy. She was not home, she was still lodged in 1859.

"Tempie, Father has sent me to get the mulatto. She is to serve in the house for my sister who is returning soon from visiting our cousin. Can you get her ready for me?" asked Timothy.

"Sir, she's not so well, you see she..." Tempie's voice trailed off as she turned toward the girl choking back her tears.

"Massah Timothy, 'dat ol' dirty Albert near bout beat her to death her first day in the field," Interrupted Big Sam stammering over his words as he did when he was upset.

"What?" asked Timothy, surprised. He knew Albert could be a beast, but thought his father had set him straight when he heard about the incident near the barn a few days prior. Timothy rushed to SeRina's side, reaching his hand out to touch her forehead. Sweat beaded on her brow as she was burning with fever from infection. Her hair tangled in soft curls around her forehead framing her angelic face. His heart nearly melted at the sight of her. He had tried to shake off the effect she had on him but had lingering thoughts about her for days after they first met. His conscience bothered him from pushing her away before. Even in this condition, she was the most beautiful woman he had ever laid eyes on.

Anger swelled within him. He couldn't imagine raising his hand to such a gorgeous woman. He took her in head to toe and despite her newly tanned skin tone was still amazed that she was a mulatto. Her face, neck, and arms were bronze with a tinge of red from sunburn. He admired the curve of her breast and the dainty tapering of her waist. He saw her hand and caught himself before he reached out to hold it. Timothy longed to pick her up from the bed and the squalor of the shanty and take her to his room in the big house. He wanted to take care of her and shelter her from any further harm. He wanted to find Albert and string him up and beat him with his very own whip.

For that moment she wasn't a nigger or a darkee, she was a beautiful woman who had been shamefully abused at the hands of his father's hired overseer. He would see to it that Albert pay for hurting her like this. He tore his eyes from her long enough to state the obvious. "She is riddled with fever, she needs a Doctor."

"Massah Abbington lets me doctor the slaves. He never sent for a real doctor to help none of us. But maybe you can fetch me some whiskey to help with the pain?" answered Aunt Tempie.

"She needs more than whiskey. I'm going to fetch the Doctor. My father will just have to understand. Have her moved to the big house, I will be back shortly," ordered Timothy without hesitation. "Have Millie see to it she is put in Eliza's room until I return."

"Yes sir, yes sir," answered Big Sam and Aunt Tempie, echoing one another both shocked that SeRina would not only get a real doctor to tend to her but that she would get to lay in Eliza's room the daughter of the Massah.

Sam's sadness was a bit released at the thought that Timothy was looking out for his precious flower and would see to it that she made it to the big house.

Timothy lingered and gazed at her once again before leaving her side. He found himself caught off guard when she opened her eyes and reached for him. He sprung to his feet and turned to walk away. SeRina inaudibly mumbled, "Christophe, I love you." her thoughts then spun out of control into light and then back into darkness. He turned, vaguely making out the words she uttered and wondered why she kept mistaking him for this "Christophe."

Without hesitation, Timothy ran out of the door, mounted his horse, and rode into town to get the Doctor.

Aunt Tempie wrapped a blanket around SeRina's shoulders, doubling it to cushion her back for the trip ahead. SeRina opened her eyes briefly and nodded off again, still feverish and weak. Big Sam effortlessly carried SeRina to the big house as instructed. He was greeted by Millie the main house maid who showed him to a room near the back of the house on the 2nd floor. He lay his precious flower across the bed and left her with a kiss to the forehead. Sam knew SeRina was in good hands, so he left her there resting peacefully closing the door behind him.

CHAPTER EIGHTEEN

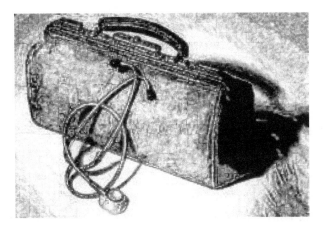

The Doctor and Timothy arrived in record speed to the Abbington estate. He rushed past Millie the housekeeper and up the staircase to the room where SeRina lay. She had faded in and out of consciousness multiple times since Big Sam laid her in the bed. She lay fretful, writhing in pain, disoriented and burning with fever.

The Doctor turned her onto her stomach despite her thrashing and cleansed her wounds using water to loosen the rags now adhered to her back by dried blood. Timothy held her arms against her will holding her still while the Doctor worked. When her cuts were clean, the Doc wrapped them in a gauze-like cloth. He then prescribed his usual dose of an opium-based concoction also known as laudanum, which he made into a tea for SeRina to drink.

Timothy gently rolled her onto her side and propped her up on pillows. He held her head as the doctor administered the concoction. SeRina, half-awake, grimaced at the bitter taste of the tea and opened her eyes fully to Timothy's surprise. Despite the taste, she was too weak to resist, so she swallowed, closing her eyes once more.

She re-opened her eyes briefly and felt at ease at the sight of Timothy. She could see the shielded worry in his eyes. She mouthed the words "Thank you Christophe," mistaking him again for her lost love.

The doctor assured Timothy that the medicine would ease her pain and break the fever. He left enough on the nightstand for a few more doses and a bottle of castor oil for the impending constipation it would cause. The Doctor excused himself and left Timothy alone with SeRina who was now fast asleep from the medication.

Timothy looked at her in the semi-darkness longing for her to open her eyes again. He walked over to the dressing table and lit the lantern sitting there.

He returned to the chair at her bedside and sat relieved that the doctor had come so quickly. He leaned forward in the chair rubbing his temples to relieve the tension. He was still surprised at his own emotion and newfound hatred for the cruel overseer that put SeRina here.

SeRina was calm now and in a deep sleep but was still sweating and burning with fever. Timothy dipped the end of a cloth into the basin of water the Dr. left on the nightstand and dabbed SeRina's forehead hoping to cool her. He couldn't take his eyes off of her as she lay there battered, helpless and breathtakingly beautiful.

How could someone hurt something so beautiful? Timothy thought as he gazed upon her stroking her hair.

Just seeing her lay there made him question his way of life. Timothy always felt his father was a fair Christian man. His father studied the Bible regularly and often quoted its contents to justify the institution of slavery. It never bothered Timothy until this very moment that his Father had built his fortune on the backs of these helpless people.

He knew his Father wouldn't approve of SeRina being up in his sister's room but he didn't care. She needed a clean, safe place to rest, a place where he could keep an eye on her, a place where Albert wasn't welcome.

In spite of all he had believed and was taught through the years, he saw SeRina, this mulatto woman as just that, simply a woman, simply a human and the equal of his mother or sister. He realized she was the equal of his future wife. It was the sobering fact that her skin was just a shade off from his own, and nearly the same as his mother's and his sisters that made him feel this way. If she were cleaned up and dressed differently, she could pass for a white woman on any given day without a second glance. However, the circumstances in which she arrived, although questionable had branded her as BLACK.

He pondered the thought for a moment and played back the many times he had stood by and watched the cruelty. He questioned his integrity. He questioned why slavery and all that accompanied it seemed to bother him now after so many years.

It occurred to him that it wasn't right to chain and treat these people like chattel working them day in and out under the unforgiving sun for nothing more than scraps of food and squalid living quarters.

Slavery to him had been a life-long reality, a natural sort of reality that now seemed malicious and appalling. A tear escaped his eye, slithered down his cheek and landed on his shirt.

Time escaped him as he sat and pondered his existence and his role in the lives of the slaves around him. He reached into his pocket and removed his watch leaning toward the lantern to decipher the time. He placed the watch on the nightstand near the medication and water basin, then stood to stretch his legs. He bent slightly and carefully pulled up the quilt over SeRina's shoulder, gently kissing her on her forehead. Stealing a final glance at her, he blew out the lantern and tiptoed from the room carefully closing the door behind him.

CHAPTER NINETEEN

The Box

Four grueling days passed before SeRina's fever broke. Timothy personally tended to her night and day, administering the laudanum, followed by castor oil, and dabbing her forehead and neck with cool water. He kept her from lying on her back as much as possible turning her toward him so he could keep an eye on her as she slept. When she awoke in a fit, he calmed her humming lullabies to her and soothing her to sleep again. He read her poetry as she slept imagining her as his muse.

During SeRina's few waking moments, she felt safe with him, even though the opium concoction had her especially disoriented. She did not know the year the day or the time, all she knew is that she was with her love and he was taking care of her. It soothed her and the medicine was her lullaby when he wasn't. Timothy fed her, read to her, prayed for her, and longed for her to fully awake. He wanted to know her story.

Timothy sent for Millie on the fourth day to fetch a fresh gown for SeRina. When Millie returned, he left the room long enough for her to bathe SeRina, change her dressings and dress her.

"Humpf, Massah Timothy done clean lost his mind havin' you up here in Eliza's room. I bet you think you high and mighty up here resting and such while we hustle and bustle around waitin' on you hand and foot. Now, you listen and you listen well..."

Millie lowered her tone and looks SeRina square in the eye as she heard Timothy approaching.

"You best enjoy this while you can, little missy, because you gone do your share of the hustlin' and bustlin' when the Massah and the misses get back here."

On the evening of the fourth day he came to her as usual, prepared to read aloud as he had the nights before but was surprised to see her awake and staring at his watch.

"This is the same as my grandmother's," said SeRina softly as she continued to stare at it.

"What is the same?" asked Timothy, not understanding. He was surprised and glad to see her looking well and fully awake.

"The watch, maybe that is how I got here," said SeRina blankly. She contemplated winding the watch with its key, wondering if that would send her back home again. The watch in the wooden box was the last thing she remembered from her time. Touching the watch was the last thing she fully remembered doing before she ended up here. She was afraid to wind it in case it sent her to a place even more horrid than this one. She wondered what would happen if she did wind it. Would it send her back to medieval times or even worse, the dinosaur age?

"What do you mean?" asked Timothy, "I don't understand."

"Christophe, don't you remember anything? Now that we are alone, please be honest. Do you remember me?" *Please remember me*, she thought.

"I'm sorry dear, I cannot say that I do, and Christophe, why do you keep calling me Christophe?" asked Timothy truly bewildered. He sat on the chair next to the bed and turned to face her. He wanted so desperately to understand her, where she was from, who she really was, why she felt she knew him as someone else, and why she spoke so differently than the other slaves? Could it be that she truly was a free woman, taken into captivity against her will as she had tried to explain to his father?

"Well, I guess it doesn't matter since you don't remember," SeRina said a tear gliding down her cheek as she continued to stare at the watch. She wanted to be home now more than ever. She missed her friends, her father, and even her wacky grandmother Hattie. This place made no sense to her. The one person she was so happy to see had no idea who she even was, so there was no way that he could possibly love her. She was in love with a boy from a different time, a boy who just so happened to be the spitting image of this one from 1859.

"SeRina, please tell me what's the matter?" Timothy asked softly.

"It's all so pointless, you would never believe me." SeRina turned to him searching his eyes for a glimmer of recollection but finding nothing there but tenderness.

"Try me, I am all ears," Timothy said smiling supportively.

"Christophe...I mean Timothy..." SeRina paused to wipe away the annoying tear. "I'm going to tell you everything, even though I know you will never believe me. Please just hear me out and don't judge me until you have heard the entire story."

She paused for a moment, closing her palms together securing the watch and key within.

"Surely darling, I promise you that I will hear every word before I pass judgment." She intrigued him and he needed to hear this story no matter how farfetched. There was something truly unique about her, a special something that made him feel connected to her and that made him yearn to be closer to her despite the consequences. He adjusted the chair so he could face her fully and gave her his undivided attention.

"I promise..." he repeated.

SeRina had to tear her eyes from his. She was so drawn to him it was difficult to hold it together while staring into his eyes. She reminded herself that this was NOT Christophe'. It was some stranger in his body in another world, another time. She thought to herself that if she had to be stuck here, it wouldn't be so bad if she could somehow convince him that she was not a slave. If she could be with him and he could find a way to love her despite their contrived differences, it could possibly be worth it.

And so, she told him. She told him everything about 2009. She told him all about Christophe', how they met, and about the night of the storm and the party. She told him how he made her feel things she had never felt before and that although it may seem silly, she felt she loved him after just one night. She told him about her parents and her search for her real mother. She went further to tell him how she had found her grandmother and discovered she was black, and shared stories her grandma Hattie had told her and how they had now become her reality.

She tried to tell him of the future, about cars, the Internet, cellular phones, and all the things that made 2009 so different from 1859. Initially SeRina was successful with pulling him into her world but then she noticed it all became too much for him to grasp so she went back to the basics.

She also shared how peculiar it was to her that Aunt Tempie had mistaken her for Alice. She told him about her being thrown from her time into this one out of the blue and how she ended up in the woods. She revealed how Albert had found her that night and lied about buying her at market. She told him that unlike the other slaves she could read and write and could fully understand the politics and goings on in this day and age. She even ventured to tell him she felt as if God had somehow decided to punish blacks with the curse of slavery and that although she never claimed to be religious she remembered discussing this at school when other students were sharing their thoughts on the bible verses that condoned and even predicted slavery.

She told him that slavery didn't exist any longer in her time and that men and women were free and for the most part treated equally. She told him her adoptive parents were Italian or by 1859 standards "white" and that she had always thought of herself as white until she met her grandmother. She ended by telling him about the wooden box with the watch in it at her grandmother's house and that she took the watch from the box and that was the last thing she remembered. She went on to surmise that she must have fallen or that the watch took her back when she wound it with the key, and that she believed that to be the way she ended up here in 1859.

When SeRina finished, she looked at him to get an idea of how he felt about her deliberation. She could not read him, and assumed he needed a moment to take it all in. The room grew quiet for a while.

Timothy was in shock. He thought at first it was the laudanum talking and that she had lost her mind. However, she told her story with such heartfelt conviction that it was impossible to toss it all aside. She was fully awake and aware of all that she shared with him. It almost sounded like some sort of fictional novel about the future. He took it all to heart and wondered how it could possibly be true. None of it sounded sensible, not a word of it plausible, but her eyes exuded nothing but passion and truth.

"Thank you for your candor. I honestly found it difficult to believe at first, after all, I've never heard such a tale. But I believe every word. I've never seen anyone speak with such sincerity. I see now why you've been so upset with me for not answering to Christophe'."

Timothy stopped to smile, his eyes following suit washing an unexpected an unexpected tidal wave of warmth and relief all over SeRina.

"Although Christophe' is a fine name, I have no recollection of meeting you in another time and place. I believe I would recall falling in love as I don't believe I have had the pleasure of falling in love at all and especially not with a beauty such as yourself."

SeRina was surprised; she didn't expect him to believe her. In addition, in 1859 she honestly didn't expect him to find her "beautiful." After all, she was just a nigger here like the others... a forbidden entity... an article of possession whose sole existence in this time was to pluck, cook, wash, and serve and eventually bear more children who would do the same.

Now that she had bared her soul, there was an awkward moment between them. She felt he was coming on to her a bit with the "beautiful" comment but didn't dare to assume they were on the same level. She also was fighting an internal battle trying to convince herself further that he was NOT Christophe and that she would be starting from scratch if she wanted to pursue a relationship with *this* man. She wondered how he would feel about her and if he could ever love her despite her "nigger" status.

Timothy on the other hand thought it odd that technically he was over 100 years her senior and that she appeared to be more educated than he. She could even read. She picked up a book of poetry he left lying on the night table and rambled off the title effortlessly. She couldn't be from this time or she would have never revealed the fact that she could read. It was forbidden for slaves to learn to read and write. He found her existence a contradiction as she described being black as a bad thing but was admittedly black by heritage. Quietly he understood why she loathed that part of herself because it is what landed her here in this bed, bandaged and bruised. Even though the attraction was evident and he had stood and watched her his every waking moment the days before even feeling a flutter every time she looked at him; he wondered if he could ever love a girl who obviously did not fully love herself.

"Where did you get this?" SeRina asked, breaking the awkward silence and reopening her clasped hands to look at the watch.

"Oh, the watch. It was made by Old George as a special gift from my father for my seventeenth birthday."

"George, as in Grandpa George?" asked SeRina.

"The one and only remarkable Grandpa George?" replied Timothy curious where this line of questioning was going.

"Did it come in a box?" asked SeRina.

"Yes, as a matter of fact, it did," answered Timothy.

"Interesting, my grandmother kept hers in a box, too. And strangely enough my father had a matching box on the bookcase where he kept her contact information. Is it a wooden box?"

"Why, yes," said Timothy, intrigued. He knew she wouldn't have a clue about that since she hadn't left the bed since Big Sam carried her there four days prior, and since she had never stepped foot into his parent's bedroom.

"I bet I can describe it to you. Then you will have to believe me," said SeRina.

"I already believe you," he replied with a steady gaze that said he was sincere.

"So you say, but this will prove my story even more. There is no way for me to know about the box. Is it a small wooden box, hand-carved with a star-like flower etched in the top of it?" asked SeRina.

"Just a moment," said Timothy. He was really floored now. How could she possibly know that? He stood, leaving the room for a brief moment to retrieve the box she had described.

"That's it, that's the box!" said SeRina when he returned to the room. She was so excited that she sat up too suddenly, stretching her healing wounds. Shooting pains went straight through her, sharpening the moment she sat up. "Owwwww."

"Darling, do be careful. You haven't healed yet," warned Timothy as he adjusted a pillow behind her to make her more comfortable.

"May I see it please?" she asked as she straightened her back against the readjusted pillow.

Timothy handed her the box. It looked the same as the box her grandmother had kept the watch in; and very similar to the one her father had. The wood was lighter and not as aged. It was smoother and smelled fresh. She removed the lid and examined the inside. It was empty but had the same markings as the one her grandmother had. How could this be? The same watch...the same box...what could it mean? Was this her ticket home? Her thoughts were interrupted by the return of searing pains in her back. Her face reflected her discomfort.

"It's time for your medicine dear," said Timothy. He called for Millie to boil some water so that he could prepare the tea for her laudanum dose. She returned a few minutes later and prepared her medicine pouring it into a teacup. Millie gave SeRina the oddest of looks, obviously annoyed that she had to tend to her and equally annoyed that Timothy was by her side seeing to her every need. Despite Millie's freezing glance, SeRina hurried to grab the teacup and swallowed down the concoction with haste to alleviate her pain.

"I'll let you rest now," Timothy said as he took the teacup from her hands and pulled the blanket over her once more. He took the watch from her hands and placed it on the bedside table and stepped out of the room. SeRina lay still on her side looking at the watch and wishing her pain would subside. She was in tremendous pain but also felt a sudden surge of excitement at the thought of a moment alone with the watch. She tempered her curiosity waiting just long enough for the door to close behind him and for his footsteps to be heard going away from the room, then she reached for the watch. She had it, in her hands, all to herself. This was the moment she had been waiting for. She shut her eyes tight and wished for home winding it twice.

An ethereal light flooded the room. SeRina heard voices all around. First her father's voice, and then others... Strange, hurried voices. Who were these people? *What's happening? Father?*

"Father, is that you?" she cried out. SeRina reached toward the sound of her father's voice, fingers grasping nothing but air. As her pain grew to an intolerable crescendo, the voices and sounds around her faded. Bright, piercing light flooded her face and sucked her into a bright white void. *Father? Am I finally going home?*

CHAPTER TWENTY

THUD!

SeRina hit the floor hard. The sun peered through the window and she sat up squinting from the buttery light. She had fallen out of bed. Her back ached from the fall although she could tell it had healed a bit more than the days before. There was no doubt; she was still there, in Timothy's house, in his sister's room. She was still stuck in 1859. What happened the night before? She felt she was traveling back to her time. She remembered hearing her father's voice and then being sucked into what felt like a vacuum of light. The memory was so vivid to her, it had to be real!

She was so confused. The watch was on the floor next to her, the sun's light reflecting from the golden cap that covered its hands. She picked it up, wanting to throw it across the room. She stood up stretching her legs and her back. It had been nearly a week since the beating and that long since she stood on her own two feet. She didn't realize how weak she had become from the fever. Millie had tended to changing the linens and keeping her clean and dry when she was too weak to make it out to the outhouse. She had heard that house-slaves used the outhouse, and weren't afforded the luxury of a chamber pot like the whites. SeRina grabbed the watch, climbed back into bed and covered up rolling over to catch a few more winks, just then, Millie walked in.

"Chile is you alright?" asked Millie.

"Yes, I'm fine." SeRina replied.

"What was that loud thumpin'?" asked Millie, irritated.

"I fell out of bed," retorted SeRina, laughing at herself despite the pain.

"Well, it's high time you got out of the bed anyhow. Massa Timothy said your fever broke, so I reckon' it's time you get back to work. He say you are to work in the big house now. Although I welcome the help, I'm not one for making merry all day long. So enough of the foolishness, rise and shine!" she said, and in a swift motion snatched all the covers off of SeRina. SeRina wanted to slap her silly, but instead she sat up and rubbed her eyes forgetting the watch on the bed.

"What have we here, a thief huh? Massa Abbington would have a fit if he knew you had this watch. I can see now you gon' be trouble.

"Yea, I keep hearing that," said SeRina sarcastically. This woman was really getting under her skin.

Millie found zero humor in SeRina's sarcasm, so bluntly replied, "Hear me and hear me well girl, on my watch, there will be no thievery, there will be no foolery, there will only be respect, and dedication to duty!"

Before SeRina could say a word in response, Millie had snatched the watch up and walked out of the room. SeRina sat there for a moment still a bit dazed from the laudanum the night before, so still never stood from the bed. Just then, in popped Millie back into the room with a clean dress and apron for SeRina to wear. "Get cleaned up and come on down you hear?"

"Yea, I hear..." replied SeRina.

OMG, who, couldn't hear, she was loud enough to wake the dead! SeRina thought.

Millie was pretty enough. She was tall and had a caramel complexion, unlike the other slaves who were much darker. Her hair was meticulously styled and matched her neat appearance. It was a silky and wavy texture. She wore it braided in one long braid that she wrapped and pinned up into a bun. She was long and lean and could've easily have graced the cover of Vogue magazine. But despite her appearance, SeRina had made her mind up not to like her. She hated the staccato way she ordered her around.

"How dare she just assume I'm ready to *get to work*!" mocked SeRina out loud.

"What's that now?" said Millie, her head peeking around the door she peered in one eyebrow raised.

"Oh nothing," said SeRina, startled.

"What do they call you girl?"

"Since I've been here I have been called everything but a child of God. But my name is SeRina."

"So Ms. *SeRina*, get to gettin'!" ordered Millie, slamming the door behind her. She had surely had her fill of SeRina's remarks and preferential treatment.

"This is going to be a long day." Muttered SeRina as she washed from the basin of water on the night table and dressed. She took a moment to clean her teeth with the end of the rag she was given to wash with. Although it seemed trivial given everything else she had been through she still longed for deodorant and toothpaste and a HOT shower. She used some of Timothy's sister's scented talc powder under her breasts and armpits in place of deodorant and left taking the stairs slowly down to the kitchen.

Millie was a multi-tasker, a workaholic of sorts, and sometimes she tended to start too many projects at once. This would be one of those days. She was overly ambitious to say the least, often seeking to go above and beyond to the praise of Massa Abbington and the Misses.

Millie prided herself on keeping the other slaves in line and was a no-nonsense kind of woman. Although she was in her early thirties, she carried herself as a woman twice her age. Well respected and sought after by many of the fine tall and strong field hands, she turned down many proposals. Millie opted instead to keep to herself, her household duties, and her God. In her mind, she was married to the Lord.

SeRina had never seen her before she came to the big house so she
wondered if Millie and Aunt Tempie ever crossed paths. It was
strange to her how different their worlds were. The house worker
was just as her teacher had taught, lighter, better spoken and better
treated than the field hand or the "Mammy." It was so unbelievably
cliché. Millie even carried herself as if she were of a higher class than
her darker/harder working counterparts. To SeRina, she talked,
dressed and behaved as if she were 'almost' white.

SeRina worked diligently as she was told helping Millie clean. She
was dusting the banister when she saw Aunt Tempie outside the
window. SeRina surprised herself with how excited she was to see
her. Aunt Tempie was one of the only people who made her feel at
home. Tempie was busy as usual, this time carrying a bushel of
potatoes to the cookhouse. SeRina flung open the front door and
trotted down the stairs to greet her.

Aunt Tempie looked up and smiled at SeRina. She waved and a few
potatoes rolled off of the top of the heap onto the ground. SeRina
bent to help her pick them up and placed them on the top of the
mound.

"Thank you kindly, oh chile, you looking well." Tempie smiled
sincerely.

"So glad to see you feeling better. The Lord always has the final say."
Aunt Tempie oozed of sugary sweetness. SeRina almost wanted to
hug her.

"Yes, Timothy took good care of me," said SeRina nearly boasting.

"Well, you watch yourself. Keep yourself clear of those white men, they'll use a pretty thing like you clean up."

Aunt Tempie paused a moment giving SeRina a forced stern look. It was hard for her not to smile and wrap her arms around her. Tempie had seen slaves die from infections, and was worried sick about SeRina. Although their time together was limited, she really missed her company out in the cookhouse.

"So, Aunt Tempie, do you know Millie?"

"Of course I know that saditty ol' heifer. She can hardly get her work done for lookin' down her nose at the rest of us! She's another one to look out for. All she cares about is savin' her own hide!"

"SeRina, SeRina!" called Timothy from the side of the house.

SeRina turned to him her eyes lighting up. And just like that, she tossed aside Aunt Tempie's advice.

"Mind what I told you chile," said Aunt Tempie with a motherly gaze as she continued with her bushel back to the cookhouse.

"Oh Aunt Tempie, he's not like the others," said SeRina ignoring her advice. Her voice trailed off into a smile. She was so happy to see Timothy that she almost felt back to her old self. Seeing him made her feel warm and tingly all over. He was the only thing that kept her sane. She wanted to run into his arms but decided to play it cool so walked instead.

"I was just going to check on you, and here you are," said Timothy with smiling eyes.

"Here I am." Echoed SeRina, flirting.

"Hmm, looks like Millie got you all prettied up!"

"Pretty as can be expected in these old clothes," said SeRina, wishing she was wearing jeans and a tank top. She missed her jeans almost as much as her cell phone, iPod and her Dad.

"Are you hungry?" asked Timothy.

"I could eat," replied SeRina playfully.

"Well, meet me by the big oak tree by Old George's cabin in say 20 minutes?"

"I don't know the time," replied SeRina.

"Ah, but you do ..." said Timothy stepping closer to her and placing the watch in her hand. He closed her hands around it and stared into her eyes. He felt as if he could lose himself in them sometimes.

SeRina couldn't believe it. She thought surely Timothy would think she had lost her mind when she told him about her past. She wondered why the watch seemed to be a recurring theme. There it was again in her hands. She remembered what happened the last time she wound it so decided to tuck it away instead. She would hold onto it until she needed to escape and then she would give it a whirl again.

She counted the minutes, returning to the house through the back door and avoiding Millie. She ran upstairs for a moment to check herself out in the cheval mirror in his sister's room. She loosened the tie around her hair letting her curls cascade around her shoulders. She wished for makeup, hairspray something but decided natural would have to do. She glanced at the watch and only 7 minutes had passed. She freshened up with more scented talc and tiptoed down the stairs in hopes of avoiding Millie. She knew if Millie caught sight of her, she'd be trying to put her to work again.

"That child is good for nothing! Nowhere to be found, just when I need her. You just wait 'til I get my hands on her!" Millie was having a conversation with herself in the kitchen when SeRina tipped by and out the front door. "Oh and that Lillybird, she sure is a good for nothing gal' probably running hither and thither telling grown folk's business. The two of 'em together might be worth a penny!"

SeRina took the back road between the shanties to the garden she recalled so well. It was the garden where Albert had found her and almost had his way with her. The big oak tree was just a few feet away from there. She wondered why he chose to meet her there of all places. She refocused herself being careful as ever, looking over her shoulder every few steps and not making eye contact with any of the whistling male slaves she passed on the way. The last thing she needed was another confrontation with Albert, she wasn't fully healed from their last encounter.

When she arrived at the garden, she was surprised to see Timothy taking a bushel of chopped wood to Grandpa George's back door. She stood far enough away not to be noticed. Timothy knocked twice on the back door and was greeted by a smiling Grandpa George. He took the wood inside the cabin and exited soon after. They exchanged goodbyes, and Tim walked over to the oak tree to wait on SeRina. Although she found his nervous pacing and continuous adjustment of his neckerchief adorable, she didn't want to keep him waiting, so made her way over to him with suppressed eagerness walking delicately around the garden's perimeter. They locked eyes from across the garden and he smiled coyly, relieved to see her there. She made him uneasy in a good way, a nervous kind of way.

"Hello there," said SeRina.

"Hello dear, shall we?" he asked.

SeRina answered silently by locking arms with him and walking off with him into the familiar brush. They made small talk as they navigated the dirt path weaving childishly around the trees. It felt amazing to escape the prying eyes of the other slaves into the solace of the woods. The sun peeked through the leaves and cast a golden glow on the ground between them. Their shadows danced as they galloped through the trees laughing out loud at nothing and everything. They felt alive and free and finally at ease with each other. He playfully lifted her by her waist up onto a fallen tree and held her hand as she teetered and balanced down the bough one foot in front of the other making the tree her tightrope. She tripped and fell into his arms and time stood still for a moment. He slowly placed her feet on the ground but she barely noticed for she was on a cloud. She cleared her throat and readjusted her dress and they continued on a few feet ahead to the beautiful clearing in the woods. She could hear the ducks on the water nearby splashing about and pollen from the endless blooms tickled her nostrils.

SeRina was shocked at what she saw there in the clearing. A lovely pastel patchwork quilt laid out on the ground with a beautiful basket sitting on top. Next to it sat two glasses and a bottle of wine. She was blown away by his thoughtfulness. He had created a picnic for them in this special place.

Her mood darkened despite his gentlemanly notion... she reflected back on a lesson from her teacher about the urban legend that the word picnic was derived from parties whites had back in slavery times where they "picked a nigger" to hang or torture while eating with the family. Although her teacher dispelled that myth, it was still ironic that here she was having a 'picnic' with the son of her

'Massah'.

Timothy, immediately picked up on the mood shift and said, "I'm sorry darling, have I upset you?"

"No, of course not, why would I be upset?" replied SeRina as she snapped back into the present. She smiled genuinely, deciding to just relish in the moment, after all, the *picnic*, was beautiful. They stood there together for a moment taking in the beauty. He stood close to her his breath sending a tingle down her spine as it touched the nape of her neck.

The clearing was almost a perfect circle. The jade green grass sprinkled with colorful wildflowers. The bees made their way flower to flower followed by a hummingbird whose wings fluttered invisibly, just as the breeze combined with a squirrel foraging for his lunch sent a few leaves scurrying down. The air had a floral fresh scent and the weather was absolutely perfect.

As they stepped from the wooded brush into the clearing, the sun warmed SeRina's cheeks and illuminated Timothy's brilliant blue eyes. They were holding hands and neither of them could remember when they had begun. The giggling ceased and they locked eyes for a moment as their souls spoke one to another in a language devoid of color. The breeze blew her curls into her face and she swept them aside. He placed a kiss on her forehead tenderly and then led her to the blanket for their afternoon picnic.

She couldn't believe this was happening to her. It was all so odd, so surreal. She was swept away to this place in time, confronted with her biggest fears, but rescued from bleak oppression by the man of her dreams.

He waited for her to sit first, as gentlemen do and then he helped her straighten her skirt to keep her legs covered as ladies do. He sat, leaned against the tree and opened the basket to reveal a mixture of bread, cheeses, homemade marmalade and two jars of milk. It was some of the best food she had tasted since she arrived. He found it endearing to watch her as she devoured the spread before her.

She caught him watching her and flushed a bit, embarrassed at her ravenous appetite so quickly diverted.

"Beautiful isn't it?"

"Breathtaking," he replied obviously talking about her.

"Why were you taking wood to Grandpa George's house?" said SeRina, diverting again.

"He is getting old, I like to help him out every now and then," said Timothy.

"Aren't their slaves to do that?" said SeRina.

"Well, yes, but Old George is special to me. He looked after me a lot when I was a boy. I guess you could say he's like a father to me," said Timothy.

"Or like a grandfather?" said SeRina

"Yes, of course, more like a grandfather," said Timothy. "He makes things with the wood to stay busy since he usually doesn't get his hands on material to make his watches anymore. He is pretty handy, he makes most of the furniture the slaves use in their homes. The tables, the chairs and if they are lucky, the beds," replied Timothy.

"Did he make the box?"

"What box?"

"The wooden box that the watch was in."

"Well, yes, yes I believe he did."

"Interesting..."

"Why is that?"

"Well, the box, the one you had on the dresser is just like the one my grandmother had in my time, and really similar to the one my father had. It's just all too coincidental."

"I'd say."

"I would like to meet Grandpa George."

"You haven't met?"

"Not really? We've seen each other but we haven't talked."

"Well, I'll be certain to make the introduction," smiled Timothy. He had the most amazing smile. His dimple dancing as he spoke under the setting sun's light. "It's getting late, we better get back. I'm sure Millie is wondering where you've run off to."

"Yes, I'm sure she is," said SeRina

"Oh, and the watch, do u still have it?" requested Timothy.

"Sure, here you go." SeRina reluctantly reached into the pocket of her apron to get the watch...

"Good, I trust that it is in safe hands, keep it for when we meet again."

The sun was low in the sky and he wanted to get home, he knew his parents would be arriving soon and didn't want them to see him coming back from the woods with a slave girl. He wanted to be with her, but he knew they would never understand. He remembered what his mother had done when she suspected his father of having relations with one of the slave women, and he didn't want anything bad to happen to SeRina.

SeRina was disappointed, the time had slipped away so fast that she could hardly believe it. The sun hung even lower now and was nearly out of sight. The colors cascaded through the clouds in shades of pink, orange, and lavender. It was breathtaking. Finally, the time had come, they needed to head back to beat the darkness. Timothy helped her to her feet then neatly folded the blanket placing it inside the empty picnic basket. They went back the way they came only with regret this time, they walked slowly and frolic free. His hand never left hers. SeRina felt safe and at home with him even in the woods, he was such a gentleman. He wrapped his arms around her shoulders and she in turn, wrapped her arm around his waist and they navigated side by side through the trees.

The clearing would be their special place, the place where their hearts, minds, and souls could dance free without judgment.

SeRina walked around back of the big house trying to sneak in the back door as she had before. She hoped to avoid Millie at all costs.

"Where have you been?" asked Millie, her voice coming out of nowhere.

"Well, hello to you too Millie," responded SeRina sarcastically.

"Who you think you are chile, runnin' round like you's free. There's work to do, washin', cookin' and cleanin'."

Big Sam's wide-eyed little sister Lillybird was peering around the doorway watching the exchange while pretending to tidy up. She was the plantation gossip and always seemed to pop up during juicy moments such as this.

"You best be glad that Massah Abbington and the Misses sent word that they were off to a wedding up North and that they wouldn't be back for a few more days. You can't just run off when you get good n ready. You'll learn your lesson one way or another. Tonight you can forget about having any supper!"

SeRina didn't care. She wasn't hungry, she was fuller than she could ever remember being. She was on a cloud, and so she floated on up to Eliza's room.

"Not so fast missy, you ain't ailing anymore," said Millie following close behind her. "You can sleep in the attic with the rest of the house hands. Ms. Eliza would be a might upset to come home and find a negra lying in her bed. And the misses certainly wouldn't have it!"

What a killjoy, thought SeRina. She had just come off cloud 9 and landed abruptly back into this ridiculous reality.

"Go on in and gather your things and I will gladly show you *your* room." Millie said. SeRina would learn her place one way or another and she would see to that.

SeRina wanted to plant one right across Millie's face. Instead, she followed obediently getting her things and heading up the set of rickety stairs to the attic she never knew existed.

It was damp and musty in the attic and much warmer than the rest of the house. In the winter that would be a good thing, but in the humid summer, not so much.

SeRina made a pallet on the floor with her things, balling up an extra gown she saw nearby to serve as a makeshift pillow. She lay there on her side staring at the candles dancing flame and reflected on the beautiful day she had. Even though her back was still sore, she didn't even mind the hard floor, her thoughts had her in another place, so there she slept and dreamt of her precious Timothy.

"Why are you sleeping on the floor in this ratty old attic?" asked Timothy startling her awake. He had looked all over for her and one of the other house slaves told him she was there.

"Well, Millie said I had to..."

"Forget that old, battle-ax," he interrupted. "She is always trying to impose the rules. You can stay there in Eliza's room until she returns. And I will ask Grandpa George to make you a bed. You are far too beautiful to rest on the floor. And your back isn't fully healed. You need to rest on a nice soft bed. Come, now my darling," he said softly, taking her hand and helping her to her feet. When she stood, he caressed her face for a moment and gently kissed her upon her forehead. A few of the slaves nearby watched with strained eyes in the darkness shocked at the openness of his affection.

He escorted her with the same things she just took up a few hours before back down to Eliza's room. SeRina thought it odd that she never even knew his sister's name yet she had slept in her bed, worn her perfume, looked in her mirror and used her powder. She laughed to herself since she had even drooled on her pillow, the one with "Eliza" hand embroidered on it she had hardly noticed it before. She wished Eliza would stay away so she could enjoy her bed a bit more. The floor where she briefly slept had run its toll on her back and the soreness had returned. She almost longed for the laudanum again but remembered the seemingly endless sleep it brought and the unpredictable side-effects so opted to endure the discomfort in hopes for more time with Timothy. She smiled to herself when she realized it had to be nearly 2 a.m. and he had looked for her..."how sweet" she thought.

"Timothy..."

"Call me Tim, all my friends do." He said.

She thought it odd, 'friends' she considered herself more than a friend, but she would take whatever she could get from him...so friends it was. "Friend" beat nigger any day.

"Tim, why are you so sweet to me?" she said sincerely, her eyes searching his for an answer.

He hesitated, he didn't have an answer for her. Before slaves were slaves, whites were whites. Before he wouldn't have given her or her injuries the time of day. He couldn't answer. So instead he smiled, his pearly whites gleaming and distracting her from the question.

"Here you are dear, goodnight," he said in an undertone as he handed her the oil lamp to light her room.

"Goodnight." She closed the door behind him perplexed. She wondered why he obviously avoided the question. She undressed removing the watch from her tied handkerchief and placing it again on the night table. She walked over and extinguished the lamp. She put the watch on her pillow so that she could have a part of him near to her and the ticking lulled her back to sleep.

CHAPTER TWENTY-ONE

For a Moment

This day started like any other, the sun rose and beamed through Eliza's window past the pale blue curtains and radiated in reflection from the shellacked pine floors. SeRina awoke to the sun on her face with a daisy on her pillow and a note from her precious Timothy.

Even before reading a word, she felt her heart nearly burst with excitement. His thoughtfulness was something she could definitely get used to.

The note read,

My Dearest SeRina,

I hope the morning greets you with the same beauty you bring to the world. Please join me in the kitchen my dear.

Yours, Timothy

SeRina was nearly healed from the beating in the field but her back ached slightly when she sprung from the bed to wash up and dress for the occasion. She was genuinely surprised to see a 2nd note laying on top of a gorgeous green frock that said,

A Little Surprise,

You are far too beautiful for the rags Millie gave you to wear. They will all be green with envy when they see you wearing this. A special gift for a special someone. Wear this for me darling.

Yours, Timothy

Green was Timothy's favorite color and he had picked up the dress for her when he was in town days before wanting to replace the bloodied rags she had come to the big house wearing. He imagined her in it all the days he sat by her side in Eliza's room.

The frock was just the right size and fit her amazingly showing off her full breasts and thin waist. She dressed, and put on the new slippers and undergarments that he gave her. It took her longer than usual to dress, as she was not accustomed to all the layers of petticoats, corsets and under stockings. She was tempted to call for Millie's help but knew that would ruin their moment together. She wondered why Millie hadn't come already barking orders. After all, Millie wouldn't be content that SeRina was happy; she would try to ruin it with talk of the Massa's returning and what the Misses would think of her gifts.

SeRina decided to go at it alone and struggled to get all the garments on right side up and in the right order. She wondered why women wore so many layers in this day and age, but once she had it all on, the dress looked amazing on her. Although it was so tight she thought if she sat down she would either sever herself in two or not be able to breathe. She giggled and admired herself in the mirror jokingly speaking to her reflection using her best Scarlette O'Hara accent.

"Why dahling, you look simply mahhhvelous."

Meanwhile, there was quite a hubbub at the cookhouse. LillyBird had spent the night in the attic at the big house and had some juicy news but no way was Big Sam open to hearing it. He had big plans of his own, and well, they didn't go over so well with the family.

"I's gwine' to tell her and dat's dat," said Big Sam to his dad, and his little sister. Aunt Tempie was busying herself cooking as usual and tried to tune out the conversation which at this time had become quite heated.

"Boy, I's telling you that gal ain't but a barrel of trouble fixin' to run you clean over! You will do no such thing. You think she wants a man big and dumb like you? She runnin' round with Massah Timothy like she's one of dem white folks, that gal ain't thinkin' bout you boy. You needs to focus your mind on them fields and maybe you find you a fine gal out there. A fine gal like dat Rose, now she been needin' a man for some time now she be happy to have you," said Big Joe in his gruff and usual manner.

"No sir, Rose twice my age daddy, she can't bare me no chillun' plus she not so pretty like my SeRina, folks say she even look like a man," said Big Sam.

"Daddy right, I se'ed her rompin' round with Massah Timothy out in the hush harbor like they is courtin', then I saw Massah Timothy lay one right on her in the attic' reported Lillybird.

"What you doing rompin' round in the hush harbor, gal, I told you 'bout dem gators down yonder!" said their father.

"She ain't did no such thing. She knowed she gwine' be my girl, Lillybird. Now look here, I ain't gwine' sass you daddy, I never have and I never will, but I got's my mind made up and dat's dat!" said Big Sam making his way toward the door.

"You mark my words, you old ugly fool, she ain't want you, you ain't fit to be her man, she gwine' find her a quadroon like she is or better a white man! So, go on and make a fool of yourself if you want, I ain't gwine beg you not to! She don't want no big stupid nigga like you!"

Big Sam for the first time in life, stood up to his dad and walked right on out the cookhouse door ignoring the echoing insults. He had a fire in his soul that could only be quenched by his SeRina.

Meanwhile, what SeRina didn't know was that Timothy's parents were away on a trip up to New York to attend a wedding, and for the first time they had the entire house to themselves. Timothy arose early that morning dismissing all the house slaves from their daily work. They all murmured amongst themselves speculating on the motivation for his generous offer. A few of them peeked in the windows periodically to see if they could spot the two of them "at it." Millie was absolutely beside herself and tried her hand at ordering the other slaves around outside the big house to no avail.

Up in Eliza's room, SeRina perked up her breasts in the corset so that they looked like two perfectly round peas in a pod. She then looked on the chair next to the dressing table and saw a 3rd note that read,

Rose scented perfume for the most beautiful flower in the garden of my life.
Yours, Timothy

She smiled and sprayed two sprays lightly on her wrists and rubbed it from her wrists to her neck just as her mother used to do. She decided not to go for the "natural" look this time, so snuck into the master suite long enough to put on a little of his mother's rouge and lipstick and to pin up her hair. She then slowly descended the stairs and made her way to the kitchen to meet him.

On the way down, she smelled bacon burning, and she wondered if Millie had gotten distracted trying to boss someone else around and had burned the breakfast. She peered in the kitchen expecting Millie's abrasive reaction to her new dress but instead saw Timothy. He was trying to cook eggs, bacon, and biscuits and had miraculously managed to burn all three and totally wreck the kitchen in the process.

"You need some help with that?" SeRina asked, surprising him.

"No, I have this absolutely under control. You gave me such a fright." Timothy said turning slightly to look over his shoulder.

"A fright?" said SeRina giggling, she still had to get used to Christophe, or rather Timothy talking like this.

"Yes dear, a fright, you startled me. I thought you were still asleep. I wanted to surprise you."

He turned completely around this time putting down the wooden spoon and stepped toward SeRina. He absolutely took her breath away, he was so incredibly handsome. His hair had fallen just over his eye from the kitchen's heat, and he was also covered in flour. She loved how his smile just seemed to light up the entire room and make this place and time feel like home again. He stood 6 foot 4 with broad shoulders that tapered into a 32-inch waist. SeRina caught a glimpse of his forearms and knew that they led to toned rigid biceps. These were the arms that kept her safe and rocked her to sleep through the nights she was ill. She remembered that his hands were strong yet gentle when they needed to be. Those were the hands that cooled her fever and nursed her back to health. She grew more and more nervous with every step he took nearer to her.

He gauged her reaction from the quickening of her breathing as he drew closer. He couldn't find the words to tell her how beautiful she looked at that very moment wearing the gift he had bought her. He wanted her kiss now more than ever but didn't want to rush into things. He knew there was major chemistry between the two of them and longed for her more than any other woman he had ever known, yet he was still torn about how he would handle telling his parents or if he would tell them at all when they returned. These feelings would simply not be tolerated, his family would feel betrayed and he wasn't certain if these forbidden desires would outlast the consequences of giving in.

He knew that a war would begin the moment his parents stepped foot in the house and found her there sleeping in his sister's room. He knew that he would have to put up the façade of hating her or at minimum just viewing her like the other slaves, or risk losing his family, especially his mother. All this battle surged within him as he drew nearer to her but it was all surpassed by the desire to kiss her tempting lips.

Would he dare? wondered SeRina as he drew closer, he was just steps away from her and hadn't said a word. Their eyes had locked in the most awkward of silences and their souls spoke to one another. She was drawn to him like a tiger to prey and she wondered if her hopes for a future with him would vanish the moment his parent's returned. They shared the same unvoiced fears. In 2009 their relationship would be virtually inconsequential but now it was purely forbidden.

Just inches from her lips, his kiss was interrupted by a knock on the door. It was Big Sam. He had chopped some wood for the stove's fire and was dropping it off. *Could his timing be any worse?* SeRina thought. On the other hand, Timothy felt momentarily relieved, thinking that maybe Big Sam was saving him from himself. Timothy stepped away to answer the door.

Big Sam was peering through the window envious of Tim and how close he and SeRina had apparently become. Although he was warned by his mouthy little sister, he still wasn't prepared to behold his flower being remotely intimate with anyone else. He sheepishly entered; nodding toward SeRina and after three trips had delivered enough wood for the stove to last a week. Sam paused for a moment tipping his ragged hat once more at SeRina.

"You lookin' mighty fine Miss SeRina," said Sam, wondering what he had just interrupted.

"Thank you Sam" said SeRina obviously annoyed at the interruption. She smiled mouth closed, and waved impatiently; hoping Sam wouldn't stick around and continue to spoil the mood. Sam stood there shifting his weight from left to right and smiling sheepishly. She shot him a buck-eyed glance that screamed "GET LOST," and he did just that. Just before Timothy could notice, her glance softened and she recomposed herself as she waited for Timothy to plate the burned breakfast and then push up her chair. She went to the table to be seated and served.

That moment made her remember the times she would dread making Saturday morning breakfast for her mother with her father. She stared at the plate, a tear dropping from her eye into her rubbery eggs. She missed home. She missed her parents. With each passing day, she wondered if she would ever see home again. She was ashamed of herself and how selfishly she had behaved.

"SeRina are you alright dear?" Timothy asked, concerned. He had been so busy cooking and trying to get everything on the table just right that he hadn't noticed her crying.

"Oh I'm fine..." she said, her voice trailing off as she choked back the tears and wiped her eyes. She felt silly sitting there in her Scarlet O'Hara dress and her rouge and lipstick. She had given herself permission to be numb since she arrived at this place. She tried to toss aside all the emotions welling within her. As she looked around at the silver platters, the woodwork, the tapestries, and the finest things that money could buy, it made her realize just how much she missed home.

"What is it dear?" asked Timothy lifting her chin to face him.

"It's my mother. I miss her so much. I pushed her away and when she died, I turned my back on my father. Now I am stuck here, and I will probably never even see him again to tell him I'm sorry." She bawled right in the middle of her plate.

"Oh please don't cry, I'm certain your father knows you love him. Go easy on yourself. All things heal with time. It will all work out."

She looked up at him her eyes welling with tears. She wondered if he really understood or if he had some sort of hidden agenda. What could he possibly want from her, the *"nigger?"* What did she possibly have to offer him? Why did his words remind her of her grandma Hattie?

She stood to dismiss herself from breakfast, but he wouldn't let her off quite that easily.

"Just live here, in this time, in this place, allow yourself to be here and only here and pretend all is well with the world if only for a moment."

He lowered his face to hers first kissing the tears away from both eyes, then kissing both cheeks, then their lips met. His kiss was velvety smooth, his lips soft and inviting. He caressed her face, and she his, running her fingers through his hair. A wave of passion swept over them both and for a moment they were far away from master and slave. He grabbed her by the waist and pulled her nearer deepening his kiss and stroking her back. SeRina winced and cried out in agony from the pain her wounds still not fully healed.

"I am so incredibly sorry darling." He apologized and held her in his arms, gently this time, kissing the residual tears away. She lay her head on his shoulder and he kissed her ever so gently on her brow. He was falling madly in love with her and had a million doubts bombarding his conscience. SeRina had opened his eyes. With the brief moments that they shared, he saw something in her that awoke him, something he didn't understand. She wasn't like the other slaves, she was more than beautiful, SeRina was bright, intriguing and fearless. She didn't' seem to fit in with the others and he knew quietly she didn't belong in his world.

Big Sam intentionally returned to the big house *again*, this time with a surprise for SeRina. Trouble was he was the one who was surprised as he observed the kiss from outside the back door. He didn't want to believe his eyes. SeRina was *his* little flower, and now she belonged to the white man. Didn't they have enough? He dropped everything right there on the stairway stood in total and utter disbelief. It was such a disappointment to him. He had big plans. He had stopped on the way and picked some wild flowers and had them waiting on the side of the house. He wanted to surprise her with them. He had made up his mind to finally tell her how he felt about her, but now he realized that they would never be.

He walked back to the side of the house leaning against it. His knees gave way as he felt the weight of the world on his shoulder at the mere thought of that kiss. She couldn't possibly know what she had just done to him, his spirit was crushed beyond measure. He picked up the surprise flowers, smelling them and replacing the scent of them in his mind with the scent of her and memories of their ride down the swamp.

His arms dropped to his sides and he released the wildflowers on the lawn and the wind took them away and dried the tears on his cheeks. Slowly he turned and walked defeated and as blue as the sky above him back to the cookhouse.

CHAPTER TWENTY-TWO

Timothy and SeRina's escapade lasted six days until the Abbington's returned to the plantation a few days after schedule. They had taken walks, had picnics, gone horseback riding, lay and stare at the night sky and had almost forgotten the slave/master relationship entirely. They had fallen completely in love with one another. SeRina flaunted her relationship in front of the slaves to the point that when she saw Aunt Tempie, she chose to ignore her and not acknowledge her disapproval or even her presence.

The day the Abbington's arrived, things were busy as ever. Slaves were off to harvest another crop, Millie was polishing the silver, Aunt Tempie was cooking up a storm in the cookhouse and Grandpa George was busy building a bed for SeRina per Timothy's request.

SeRina pretended to be busy in the kitchen with Millie when the Abbingtons arrived giving her forbidden lover a peck in the hallway before he ran outdoors to greet them.

Millie had been abnormally somber with little to say the past few days, and SeRina took it as her being jealous and a bit perturbed at being ousted from the big house during their exploits. SeRina had no idea what was wrong with Millie and wouldn't for quite some time.

Curiosity got the best of SeRina, and she wanted to see Timothy's sister, Eliza. She wondered if she were as attractive as her brother. She wondered if they would be "friends" or if she would be a snobby racist. Just then, Massah Abbington stuck his head in the kitchen looking more cheerful than usual.

"Hello there Millie, fetch us some vittles, it's been a mighty long journey. The Misses and I want to have a bite then get a little rest before our guests arrive."

Millie did not appear to hear him, so SeRina called her name.

"Millie, Millie, did you hear Mr. Abbington? Millie still didn't respond, SeRina tapped her on the shoulder.

"Whew!" Exclaimed Millie, frightened by SeRina's touch. "What is it, girl?"

"Did you hear Mr. Abbington?" asked SeRina.

"No, huh, oh no sir, I'm so sorry Massah Abbington can I help you, sir?"

Massah Abbington repeated his lunch order this time annoyed. It was funny to SeRina how fast his expression changed. It wasn't like Millie to not to be on top of things in the kitchen, It was in disarray and had a lingering burnt smell. She seemed aloof, and careless which was also not like her. Millie was definitely off of her game. Massah Abbington gave her a look that said *"Get it together!"* as he went to catch up with his son. He found him staring out of the window in the study. Timothy had a blank look on his face and seemed lost in thought. The Master smiled at the sight of his son, so tall, handsome and studious. He felt a sense of pride knowing he had left things in his capable hands and wanted to see how all had fared the first time in his care. The house was disheveled, and he hoped that the fields fared better in his absence. He knew overseeing Albert alone was a full-time job. He could have a heavy hand when it came to discipline with the slaves.

"Son, how is that new negra working out in the kitchen?"

"Negra?" said Timothy, offended at the reference.

"Yes son, the mulatto, how is she in the kitchen? Can she cook?"

"She is fine I suppose." He replied suppressing his annoyance.

"Suppose? That doesn't sound too encouraging. Did anything interesting happen while we were away?"

"Nothing at all Father."

"Is Millie alright? She seemed distracted and out of sorts. I was thinking of giving her some time to rest up for our guests. There will be more washing, cooking and cleaning to do the next few days than usual," he paused, carefully considering his next words, "yes, I think I shall give Millie a rest and allow the mulatto to prepare supper this evening." He said answering his own question. He crossed the room and seated himself at his hand carved desk opening the drawer.

"Millie's fine," mumbled Timothy still staring out of the window. Massah Abbington was on to the next topic, so didn't notice his response.

"How are the field hands?" asked Massah Abbington as he seated himself and prepared the tobacco for his pipe.

"Fine sir, I suppose," muttered Timothy. His mind was racing with all the thoughts and new emotions he was feeling about slavery and the morality of it all.

"You suppose? You know son, you seem different too. What's going on around here? The house smells of burnt food and the kitchen is an absolute atrocity. And son, it seems you may have a bit on your mind, do you wish to speak on it? What's troubling you?"

"Nothing at all Father, I'm fine, just a little tired is all. So, do tell me, who are these guests you spoke of?" said Timothy trying to divert his father's attention to another topic.

"Your cousin Morris from Maryland and his new bride," said Massah Abbington between puffs with a raised eyebrow still sensing something was off with the son he knew so well.

"Son, I know things have probably been a bit difficult for you managing the plantation and making sure the house is kept as well but remember you have Albert's help with the field hands."

"Yes Father, heaven forbid I forget the loyal assistance of the king of the whip! Erupted Timothy, surprising his father enough for him to put down his smoke. "That son of a..."

"Timothy James Abbington! Don't you use that tone with your Father, now get over here and kiss your dear Mother!" interjected Mrs. Abbington half serious and half joking as she entered the room right before he blurted out the expletive. She grabbed her son by the elbow, swinging him around and wrapping her arms around him. His scowl soon turned into a closed mouth smile. His mother had a way about her of demanding everyone around her to be in better spirits.

Timothy definitely had her eyes. She was heavyset, honey blonde and outspoken with a broad toothy smile. She had been listening from the corridor in between instructing Henry. Henry was one of the older house servants who wasn't good for much these days. He was the step and fetch it type that despite his ailments would jump and ask twice how high when it came to the Abbingtons. He was born and raised on the plantation and knew nothing outside the walls and fields nearby. Despite his arthritis, Henry was busy unloading the carriage and slowly, but surely carrying the things up to the bedrooms.

Following the Misses was Eliza. "Hello brother, how are you?" she said dry and disinterested. She turned quickly to run up to her room without awaiting his response. Luckily, SeRina had made a special point to tidy up and put things back just as she had left them in her room, or she would have definitely noticed. SeRina heard her voice vaguely from the kitchen and was slightly disappointed that she wasn't able to catch a glimpse of her yet.

Timothy excused himself after pretending to listen to his mother babble about their trip. He responded "wonderful mother, so happy you are home safe," before giving his mother a quick kiss on the cheek and exiting mid-sentence. She stood there shocked and looked at her husband who shrugged and continued to puff on his pipe.

Timothy was really in no mood for his mother's ramblings. Just the mention of Albert had sent his blood boiling! He hadn't seen him one on one since SeRina's beating but when he did he knew it would not be a cordial interchange.

Meanwhile, back in the kitchen, SeRina began to worry more and more about Millie. SeRina was trying to make the best of the situation, so tried to strike up a conversation with her but to no avail. Millie was working at half her usual pace and had said little to nothing all day. No orders, no demands, no sly comments. SeRina almost missed her smart remarks, she longed for anything to kill this silence.

The quiet gave SeRina too much time to reflect on her mysterious arrival and inability to escape. The silence made her long for home. She wondered how her Father was if he missed her as much as she missed him. She wished there was a way for her to send a message to him to let him know she was all right. She missed her friends Briana and Michaela. She wondered how they had spent their weekend if they had looked for her, and if time had somehow stood still when she left or if instead, she had actually been missing for as many days in 2009 as she had been trapped here in 1859.

She wondered about Christophe'. She felt like she was somehow trapped in a parallel universe. Christophe' wasn't Timothy, she knew that. Sure, they looked the same but their personalities were totally different. She wondered if maybe they were somehow distant relatives. She was in love with them both but felt even more drawn to Timothy. She wondered how she would explain all of this when she got home again, or if anyone would even believe her. She swept the kitchen floor, concentrating on the same spot longer than necessary as she daydreamed.

"Hey, girl, Ms. Eliza needs some tendin' to!" Henry said for the 3rd time, clearly irritated. *Great, another person to order me around*, thought SeRina. "I'll be right there." SeRina ran up the stairs to Eliza's room. Eliza was seated at the dressing table her back to the doorway. She removed her earbobs, and bonnet, and let her hair down. She was wearing a beautiful blue and cream colored dress. SeRina held her breath in anticipation of seeing her face. There was a familiarity in the air, she hoped desperately for a connection.

"Girl, in the bag there you will find some soiled items that need tending to," said Eliza as she critiqued herself in the looking glass.

Eliza turned her head to reach for her hairbrush and SeRina caught a glimpse of her profile. She could NOT believe her eyes. Eliza was the spitting image of SeRina's best friend Briana from 2009. She was just as beautiful, with chiseled features, blue eyes, honey blonde hair and the exact same figure. It couldn't be.

SeRina knew better than to run and squeeze her like she longed to, she had learned her lesson that although the people here may appear the same, they absolutely were not. So, she waited for a moment asking, "This bag?" knowing full well what bag it was, after all, it was the only one in sight. She just wanted Eliza to look up in hopes that she would recognize her. Eliza put down the brush and walked over to her with a sneering head to toe assessment.

"Yes stupid, that bag! How typical, my Father has bought me a dumb mulatto. If you are going to be my servant girl you need to know a few things. First, do not ask me to repeat myself and second, do as you are told when you are told. Am I clear nigger?"

"Absolutely," said SeRina. She felt something inside her break and struggled to hold back the floodgate of tears dammed inside. She picked up the bag and took the contents outside to be washed as she was told. She hadn't ever hand washed clothes before, so had no idea how to do it, but by the time she got to the washboard and tub she could have filled it with her own tears instead of the water from the spigot.

She sat on a log near the wash basin and looked out into the middle distance of the tobacco fields. She had been taken down so low by that one sentence. Reality stung as the tears slid down her cheeks the heat of the sun drying them before they could hit the dusty ground. She wanted her Timothy to hold her right now to take it all away, she wondered where he could be and how he would be now that the Abbington's were home. Would she be his love or just another nigger?

CHAPTER TWENTY-THREE

The Reflection

Cousin Morris and his new bride arrived in style in a double horse drawn carriage. Henry took the horse and carriage to the stable to water and care for them after their long journey. Mrs. Abbington embraced Morris, her first cousin and welcomed him and his new wife to her home. SeRina was almost done preparing dinner. She had a little help from Millie before she went to lay down, but was left alone when it was time to serve the family. She hadn't seen or heard from Timothy since his parents had arrived earlier and wondered if he would be joining them for dinner.

SeRina had dug deep to recall some of the recipes her mother used to prepare. She made roasted chicken, carrots, and mashed potatoes. Millie helped prepare cabbage and cornbread. She felt disgusted as she had to hand pluck the feathers one by one from the scalded bird.

Ugh, where is a good old fashioned grocery store when you need it? SeRina thought. Plucking the bird made her even consider becoming vegan as the fad was in 2009 but she knew she would never survive in these times without meat.

Big Sam had made a brief appearance bringing even more unnecessary firewood and fresh milk from the stable. Dinner was ready and smelled amazing. SeRina had earlier mechanically set the table with the best china and silver and rounded up another servant girl named Mary to help serve. Mary poured the wine and took out the roasted chicken. The Abbington's and their guests ooh'd and ahh'd over the scents wafting from the kitchen. SeRina followed Mary out as she carried the carrots and potatoes with the cornbread and cabbage. She sat the cabbage on the table and stepped in between the guests to place the cornbread on the table in the only remaining empty space. She paused for a moment as she was greeted unexpectedly by one of the guests.

"Hello, and thank you kindly," said cousin' Morris' bride while glancing up at SeRina.

When their eyes met, they both were in absolute shock. SeRina dropped the silver tray that held the cornbread and the pieces crumbled all over the floor.

Morris's bride jumped up from the table and joined SeRina as she gathered the crumbled pieces from the floor. Between the crumbles, their reflections were mirrored one upside down the other right side up on the silver platter.

SeRina was so shocked she couldn't even apologize for the mess she had made. His bride looked identical to her. She and SeRina could be twins. Time stood still as they saw one another for the first time. Why no one else had noticed the striking resemblance, bewildered SeRina.

The only differences in their appearance were that his bride's eyes were a stunning jade green and SeRina's were gray and the fact that she was dressed as the ladies of that time dressed whereas SeRina was dressed as a slave, her hair pinned neatly beneath a white headscarf. That and her skin tone was a shade lighter than SeRina's sun-kissed tone.

"Dear, let her get that," said Morris in staccato fashion, through clenched teeth, embarrassed that his bride was helping this clumsy slave girl. He grabbed her arm tightly and gave her a look that brought her quickly back to her seat. He faked a smile to everyone else at the table. He didn't bother looking at SeRina so hadn't noticed the resemblance. It was as if everyone in the room was blindfolded for that moment. But she noticed. Morris' bride was utterly shocked to see someone identical to herself serving her dinner as a slave. She returned to her seat and rubbed her arm where Morris had grabbed her. She knew there would be trouble later that night. His bride hoped no one else noticed the resemblance and avoided eye contact with SeRina when she returned moments later with a replacement batch of cornbread.

"Father, where on God's green Earth did you find that incompetent slave girl?" asked Eliza.

"Now, now dear, it's her first time preparing dinner, everything looks so delicious that I think I shall forgive her for dropping the cornbread, plus there's plenty more to go around," asserted Massah

Abbington. He had the tendency to be naturally understanding and empathetic, in most cases. Not to mention, SeRina had already replaced the cornbread she dropped so he felt there was truly no harm done. He preferred to avoid drama and confrontational situations at all costs so quickly put the conversation on track shifting the nervous energy in the room.

"Dear, where is Timothy?" asked Mrs. Abbington with a feigned smile. She was all about keeping up appearances and thought it rude of him not to join them for dinner their first night back, especially since guests were involved. Since their return, he hadn't been himself. He had avoided the family all day and when their paths did cross he was distracted and disinterested in their conversations.

"I'm certain something important must be keeping him," said Massah Abbington. He gave SeRina an uncomfortable once-over and waved his hand dismissing her back to the kitchen. Mrs. Abbington noticed how her husband watched SeRina and made a mental note to deal with the situation soon after. She kept quiet to save face during dinner. It was obvious that he found her attractive and Mrs. Abbington would most definitely have to put a stop to that.

The family sat for what felt like hours, the women making idle conversation about Morris' wedding and how they originally met their husbands, and the men about the expectations of the crop in the upcoming harvest. Mary stood by, refilled the wine and removed the used utensils and plates as the guests and the Abbingtons finished their meals. Timothy came in during dessert spoke to everyone briefly, then apologized for his absence and retired to his room without eating and without a word to SeRina. She wondered where he had been and what was going on.

Everyone demolished his or her dessert, and when the meaningless drivel finally dwindled down, the guests retired for the evening. Massah Abbington made his way back to the kitchen to pay SeRina a visit. Mary had returned to her cabin, so SeRina was alone cleaning the mess from dinner.

"Absolutely delicious," said Massah Abbington, unannounced. He had a glass of brandy in one hand and his pipe in the other. He looked SeRina up and down his eyes stopping when they reached hers insinuating that it was she who was 'delicious'.

He had long noticed her beauty and had secret yearnings for her. He didn't want Albert spoiling the goods, so would keep a close eye on her and quietly hoped to keep her in the house, if only to admire her beauty from afar. The fact that she was a good cook should make it an easy sell for his wife. She was an excellent complement to Millie, younger, prettier, and perhaps an even better cook.

SeRina nodded in response to his compliment feeling uneasy as he undressed her with his eyes. He was the last person she had worried about making advances at her, especially since he dealt with Albert so harshly for doing the same.

A loud noise by the front door took the unwanted attention off SeRina momentarily.

"Who goes theeeere?" slurred Massah Abbington, obviously tipsy from the brandy and wine at dinner.

"Father, it's me," said Timothy.

He and Henry were carrying in the wooden bed Grandpa George had made for SeRina. They had apparently bumped into the wall on the way up the stairway.

"What's all the gosh-darn racket?" inquired Massah Abbington.

"No worries Father, it is just a bed me and Old George made for SeRina," Timothy said.

SeRina overheard the ruckus and smiled in relieve to know that her Timothy was away creating something for her which explained his disappearance.

Timothy and Henry disappeared up the stairs and then Henry followed with a mattress filled with hay. By the time SeRina finished her work in the kitchen her back was especially grateful for the bed and for her precious Timothy. He kept his word; she had a bed and didn't have to sleep on the floor although several of the other slaves in the attic lay there every night. She felt remotely guilty in her bed as they lay on the floor with their makeshift pillows. Soon, guilt faded into dreams and she wondered how her next meeting with Morris' bride would go.

CHAPTER TWENTY-FOUR

The Prodigal Return

SeRina arrived unannounced to the guest quarters with a basin of warm water and fresh washcloths for Morris and his bride. No one told her to go, she simply went out of curiosity but needed to legitimize her nosiness by pretending to be of service. She rested the basin on her hip and knocked lightly on the door.

"Come in ..." said a soft sweet voice.

SeRina entered with the basin of water and towels. Morris was nowhere to be found.

"May I get you anything else?" asked SeRina, hoping to make eye contact with the nameless bride of Morris once more. She hoped that she was just being delusional and that really in the light of day they weren't as identical as she remembered.

"No, thank you, dear," sniffed the bride almost inaudibly.

"Are you alright?" asked SeRina. The woman was obviously crying.

"I'm fine, thank you," the woman weakly replied.

"Are you always so polite?" asked SeRina.

This time the woman she didn't answer. She turned her face to SeRina and stared. SeRina nearly dropped the basin of water, startled this time to see her spitting image with a bruised cheek and blackened eye. There were also bruises on her neck as if she had been choked.

"Oh my God, what happened!" said SeRina not believing her eyes for more reasons than one.

It was as if SeRina herself sat there bruised and battered it unnerved her to see her like this. Immediately the bride began to cry, uncontrollably. SeRina rested the water basin on the table and put her arm around her to comfort her. She sat on the upholstered vanity bench next to her and waited a moment before asking any other questions. SeRina knew in her heart of hearts exactly what had happened. Morris! He had given her the "*look*" the night before, speaking to her in an undertone that said 'GET UP OR ELSE!' when she came to SeRina's rescue with the dropped tray. However, SeRina could not believe he had it in him to be this vicious. It angered her even though she did not even know the girls name; no woman should have to endure such pain at the hands of the one that they love.

"I'm here if you want to talk about it," said SeRina. "Did your husband do this to you?"

"Yes."

"Why?"

"Because he doesn't want anyone to know," she replied.

"Know what?"

"I don't even know you, why do you care so much about my well-being?"

"Because I don't want to see anyone hurt. Especially since you were so kind to me. Most whites won't go out of their way to help someone like me... you know a *"mulatto"* ... said SeRina sarcastically. But you are right. You don't know me. I don't even know your name. My name is SeRina," SeRina took her arm from around the mystery bride's shoulders and extended her hand in a gesture of friendship appealing to her polite and sensible side.

"How rude of me. How do you do Ms. SeRina? My name is Alice, Alice Faith." The mystery bride said finally raising her eyes to meet SeRina's and accepting the handshake as she sniffed back her tears.

SeRina couldn't believe her ears. This was *the* Alice Faith, the one everyone had mistaken her for. She couldn't wait to tell Aunt Tempie. She almost wanted to hug her. Somehow finding out that this Alice existed reconfirmed the fact that she didn't belong here and that this was all some huge mistake. Not that it would get her home, but it was a bit of relief. She was NOT Alice. SeRina was so lost in thought she didn't utter a single word in reply nor did she withdraw her hand from the handshake. It was even remarkable how their hands fit together perfectly as if they were extending from a single pair of arms. A tingle made its way from Alice's hand to SeRina's and they locked eyes, gray with green. The resemblance was so striking that it sentenced them both to a moment of silence. Alice waited for words from SeRina but they never came.

SeRina could find no words to say, she didn't want to scare away this new friend by saying too much too soon, so without a word, she turned and left Alice Faith right where she sat and wandered back purposelessly to the kitchen.

CHAPTER TWENTY-FIVE

Unlikely Ally

SeRina awoke in her bed face toward the ceiling for the first time in weeks; her back was finally healed enough for her to lie on it without excruciating pain. She had seen Timothy sparingly since the Abington's return as he had to 'keep up appearances' but occasionally he would steal a kiss or give her a flower. She was still holding on to the thought that someday they would be together and that hope is what got her through her days and nights.

The visitors were still there and she had become so intrigued with Alice Faith that her plight of being stuck in a distant past and the not so certain future with Timothy didn't seem so bad. Luckily, Alice had managed to stay clear of her new husband's fist for the last two weeks so was in the best of spirits this sunny day. On SeRina's daily trip to the guest quarters with fresh towels and warm water, she was invited to steal away to town accompanied by Alice for some shopping.

The sun this particular day had risen in exquisite fashion painting the sky an array of sherbet-like colors. Despite the scorching heat on this sweltering morning, SeRina had dressed in the green gown Timothy had given her with all the layers she hated so much. She had to "fit in" with Alice Faith and to her surprise when she arrived at her door, Alice emerged also wearing a green gown. The resemblance was so eerie it was like looking in a mirror. SeRina just a shade darker with hair just a tad curlier than Alice smiled as their eyes met. Both ladies subdued the eerie feeling they felt from the uncanny resemblance and covered the uncomfortable moment by babbling on about the weather until the driver pulled up with the wagon.

"Morning ladies, ready to head into town?" a husky low and masculine voice inquired.

SeRina immediately recognized his voice as the man from the woods when she first arrived. She often wondered what had become of him after that night. This was her first time laying eyes on him in the light of day, and she had to admit for the first time she found this man, this very black man extremely attractive. He was tall around 6'2 with broad muscular shoulders and a smooth-shaven face. His eyes were bright and inviting, his teeth pearly white and straight. He had a strong chiseled jawline and a Denzel-like swagger she had only seen in the movies. She thought to herself he looked like a tall glass of chocolate milk and she felt her cheeks warm at the idea of him possibly reading her mind. She blushed and looked away as she noticed him, noticing her, noticing him.

He was gentle as he helped both ladies Alice then SeRina mount the carriage and then climbed aboard with a "Yah" to urge the horse to lunge forward. SeRina was now staring at the back of his head and had noticed his firm buttocks as he mounted the carriage. Alice giggled at her and said "handsome isn't he?" which jolted her back from her daydream.

"Yes, well, I suppose for a negro," said SeRina.

"For a Negro? How about for a Man?" said Alice.

They both giggled and nodded answering the question unanimously and without words. At that moment they felt like sisters. He let out another masculine "Yah" as he slightly grinned and pretended not to hear the interchange. He felt flattered that these two beauties found him attractive but wouldn't let on that he had overheard. He smiled a pearly white and impeccable grin flashing a set of deep dimples.

They made their way down the winding dirt road, past the big tree where the whirlybirds had first introduced themselves to SeRina. SeRina was distracted daydreaming about this fine black man and how if she knew he was so kind and handsome she would have gladly let him lead the way in the dark that night she arrived at the plantation instead of screaming for help like an idiot and being captured. She wondered if instead of being captured, they would have run away together and fallen in love and made a life together... then she thought of Timothy and how she'd much rather live life as his wife the wife of a black man especially if she was stuck in this day and age. She then snapped out of her daydream and tuned back in to Alice's ramblings.

"I heard there is a marvelous hat and dress emporium in town. I want to go there and buy the most amazing gown. A gown so fine that Morris will never want to take his eyes off of me!"

"I'd be more concerned about him keeping his *hands* off of me," said SeRina without thinking. She caught herself and immediately apologized when she noticed the impact her statement had on her friend.

"I'm sorry, I shouldn't have said that," said SeRina.

Alice averted her eyes, which were now tearing up and said convincingly, "It's all right dear. He only wants what's best for me. He thinks I am much too empathetic to Negroes, and well, there is much more to the story. We have much to talk about," said Alice.

SeRina wondered what she meant and would soon find out. Because at that moment they had arrived at *Stanley's Emporium*, supposedly the finest source for modern adornments for the modern woman, or at least that's what the sign said. SeRina thought it silly that they considered anything in this little shotgun town in the middle of the antebellum South "modern."

As the handsome driver assisted the ladies down from the carriage, he made eye contact again with SeRina and this time nodded as he tipped his hat. She had a strange feeling that he had overheard their comments because his eyes now had a sly little smile in them that wasn't there before. SeRina again blushed and averted her eyes and resumed conversation with Alice. It was definitely not her style to feel so out of control of her emotions and he had a mysterious edge to him that made her brain and body involuntarily respond in ways that made her extremely uncomfortable.

"Do you enjoy sweets my dear?" asked Alice.

SeRina thought some chocolate would be nice but wasn't at all thinking about the candy.

"Yes, yes I do," responded SeRina clearing her throat.

"Come, let's walk down the way to the sweet shop first," replied Alice this time not detecting SeRina's musings.

They walked down the sidewalk sharing Alice's parasol and gentlemen, white ones, one by one stopped and tipped their hats at them and wished the ladies "Good Day." SeRina had hardly noticed they treated her the very same as Alice until one particular gentleman struck up a conversation.

"Well, I'll be, you two ladies have got to be the most beautiful set of twins I have ever laid eyes on. A most fabulous day to you two fabulous ladies," said the gentleman. He tipped his hat as did all the others and continued down the sidewalk after turning completely around and looking over the top of his spectacles to observe the ladies pass him by.

"Have you noticed that no one treats you differently when they don't know?" asked Alice.

"Don't know what?" asked SeRina, knowing full well what Alice meant. She just wanted *her* to say it.

"When they don't know *we* are Negroes," whispered Alice.

"We?" retorted SeRina, quietly remembering the sold away little girl Aunt Tempie told her of named Alice. She was surprised that Alice was revealing what she thought to be her darkest secret to her outdoors in the light of day. SeRina looked around to see if anyone had heard.

"No one knows, and no one heard," said Alice. "You can stop pretending now. When we first arrived, I went to visit my Aunt Tempie in secret at the cookhouse and she told me everything about how she had mistaken you for me. I figured maybe would we just resemble a little and that her memories may have faded since so many years have passed. But when I saw you at dinner I was as shocked as you were to see that not only do we slightly resemble, but we are nearly identical. Aunt Tempie is the only relative I know of, so imagine my surprise when my husband Morris told me the Abbington's were his relatives and that we were to visit them on their plantation for our honeymoon when we were married."

"Wow," said SeRina, genuinely surprised at her revelation.

"Now, Morris and I met under a pretense. When I was sold away as a young girl, I ended up at a plantation in North Carolina. My missus had just buried their 7-year-old daughter who passed away from yellow fever. So when her husband brought me home with the other slaves, she saw me there frightened and sobbing and pulled me from the bunch and raised me as her own. She felt I was a gift from God and a replacement for her lost daughter. She wouldn't allow anyone to call me black or Negro, and she never allowed me to slave in the big house.

After years passed, my true identity became only a distant rumor. She made the slaves swear to never tell it and her husband, my father obliged her since it seemed to ease her grief. They raised me as their own, like a proper white lady and I was courted by Morris as such. It wasn't until after he married me that I revealed the truth to him in confidence, and the man that I loved so much who I thought would always protect me and never hurt me turned into the violent creature you see today. He felt I betrayed him and now am beneath him. But I know in my heart that deep down he loves me still, he just is so afraid that this secret will be revealed. I told this to him in confidence, thinking he would not care because of his love for me, but I have learned that love is not enough to conquer some evils. He had long noticed that I always treated slaves as my equals, but he never knew it was because they are just as I am, Negro. He has warned me he will divorce me if anyone finds out, and he has decided never to return to my hometown for fear that the truth will get out into our small community."

At that moment, Alice paused and sniffed away the tears welling in her eyes. Her eyes met SeRina's for a moment before she continued.

"So my dear, I find myself here with you, on the very plantation where I was born a slave, seeing you treated as property and it sickens me. I want to help you. If you'll let me," asked Alice.

"Help me get back to 2009?" SeRina asked.

"No I'm no magician, Aunt Tempie told me of that dilemma and I thought she was making merry and did not take her seriously. So although I cannot do that. However, I can do a bit of magic and help you break free from the bonds of slavery and live as I live, as a free *white* woman. But only if that is what you wish."

The unspoken truth was that Alice loathed having to pretend to be something she wasn't. She hated that the blackness inside of her was despised by the very man she loved. She had a fear of whites knowing that if they knew her secret that she would be doomed. She desperately needed to escape the stigma of blackness so she could have their approval. So since she was light enough to pass, she did just that. In the race-based society in which she lived, she chose a carefree life over accepting herself for who she truly was.

SeRina wanted so badly to confide in Alice her secret romance with Timothy, but couldn't find the words. So instead, she listened intently hanging on Alice's every word, searching for an inkling of hope and means to escape to a better life.

The two beauties entered *Stanley's Emporium* and walked past a counter covered with glass canisters of assorted treats to the rear of the store where the "modern" clothing was. Alice saw a beautiful calico print blue dress which she fell in love with and touched and admired the fabric.

"So what do you think?"

"It's pretty I guess," said SeRina.

"Perfect, I'm glad you approve. It's yours… now something for me…"

She walked a few steps where she lay eyes on a yellow and white dress that suited her, the bodice had an eyelet lace overlay and cinched waist she thought would catch Morris' eye. She took both of the selections to the candy covered counter and handed them to the storekeeper. Alice then grabbed a small ladies satchel and placed it on the counter to purchase as well. She turned to SeRina and said, "This is also for you."

"Ah, I almost forgot the sweets…how for heaven's sake could I make such a mistake?" Alice giggled to herself. She selected a striped candy stick that matched the frock she was buying and SeRina picked the most expensive chocolate bar in the store. Alice paid for the items and the storekeeper nodded and wished them a good day.

Just then an older black woman stepped up, placing her goods on the counter to be rung up and bagged.

"Beautiful day isn't it sir?"

"Yes, ma'am it is, prettiest I've seen in a mighty long while."

"Indeed," replied the woman.

Overhearing the conversation, SeRina turned around shocked to see her Grandma Hattie standing before her very eyes at the shop counter.

"Grandmother? Grandma Hattie?" she said overwhelmed with emotion, surely she would remember her.

The storekeeper looked at the two women in utter shock as he had assumed that SeRINA was white. His pipe nearly fell from his lips.

"I'm sorry dear? Do I know you?"

"Grandma, it's me, SeRina!"

"Well, last time I checked, I didn't have any grandchildren...perhaps you will find your grandmother in time, but as you can see, there is no way you could be related to well someone like me." she paused to look SeRina. "No, you wouldn't be kin to me, no, not at all. Good Day Ma'am."

SeRina's only other connection to 2009 hadn't recognized her and had disavowed their relationship. SeRina froze in place tears welling in her eyes as she watched the woman walk out of the store front. And just like that, she was gone. Alice grabbed her by the arm and pulled her down the aisle of the store out of earshot of the storekeeper.

"What are you thinking?" said Alice sternly to SeRina but low enough that the nosey shopkeeper couldn't hear. "I am teaching you a very important lesson today in passing. If folks think you are white, you never let on that you are not, no matter what!"

"You don't understand, I thought..."

"You mustn't think or feel, you must only do, and act as if you are white your very future depends upon it, now do you want your freedom or don't you?"

"I do," muttered SeRina, still shaken by Grandma Hattie's appearance. She wiped her eyes and squared her shoulders confident in her decision.

"Fine then," said Alice, guiding SeRina back to the counter with a feigned smile.

"Sir, do you have a tonic for headache? My sister is clearly delusional with pain and needs something immediately to bring her back to her senses..."

On cue, SeRina started to rub her head and smile and nod in agreement with her 'sister'.

"But of course ma'am," said the storekeeper grabbing a bottle from the shelf behind the counter.

Alice paid, and they bid their goodbyes to the storekeeper. As they exited the store, they encountered more hat-tipping gentlemen and proper ladies who acknowledged them and wished them good day. This was the best treatment SeRina had received since she arrived in this day and time and she thought to herself she could definitely get used to it.

The handsome driver was there waiting to lean against the wall of the next store front. The horses were roped and tied to the post next to him. He had his hat off and was holding it against his thigh. He was there conversing with another driver. His profile was so regal, his eyes caramel brown and his hair wavy and jet black. The sun kissed his skin and it seemed as if he moved in slow motion as SeRina approached. She couldn't take her eyes off of him, she watched him talk, nod and smile. He turned and saw the ladies coming toward him and locked eyes with SeRina for a moment. She quickly turned away and struck up a more idle conversation with Alice. The driver then walked over to greet them and take the packages from Alice to load on the carriage.

On the carriage ride back to the plantation, Alice didn't speak a word about "passing" but instead rattled on and on about her husband. As she spoke she slipped a note and some money into the satchel she had purchased in *Stanley's Emporium* and handed it to SeRina.

"Now my dear, this is a gift, a gift with one stipulation. It cannot be opened until you are in private." She quietly placed it in SeRina's hands and continued with chatting until they arrived at the front steps of the plantation.

The handsome driver helped both ladies down from the carriage. He grabbed both packages to take into the big house and Alice stopped him. "This one is for her." He then handed the package to SeRina.

"Excuse my manners sir, but in the rush to get out this mornin' I didn't even stop to ask your name?" asked Alice.

"They call me Ivory." he said.

"Ivory, what a strange name for a black man, how did you come about it?" inquired Alice.

"I suppose it's not so strange ma'am, folks call me Ivory, 'cause they say my teeth white as the keys on a piano. Yes, ma'am, Ivory Carl's my name," he replied flashing an extremely handsome and toothy grin that made both the ladies blush.

"Ivory Carl, hmmm I guess that's a fine name, for a fine driver," replied Alice.

"Um hmm, he's fine alright!" said SeRina under her breath laughing to herself as they stepped just out of earshot.

The ladies hugged and said their goodbyes. Ivory helped Alice into the big house with her package turning to see SeRina once more before he entered. SeRina had turned to get a quick glimpse of him once more and their eyes met again. Averting her eyes when they met, SeRina she rushed away down the pathway to the side of Aunt Tempie's house to open her gift. Alice had been very generous to put $50 in the satchel along with a note that read:

My Dearest SeRina,

I still cannot shake the thought of you being here treated as property as I go on day-by-day on this plantation. I wish I could free all of the slaves here, but I am only one woman of meager means. The slaves could free themselves if only they knew they were slaves. In many cases, they outnumber the masters by hundreds yet they remain docile and live the lives they were handed. I quietly muse and imagine that with ease they could band together and form a revolt and overtake their vicious owners.

In my heart, I know that such talk will get one killed, so I could never speak on this publicly. And as much as I long to free them all, I cannot help them. But God saw my thirst for change and gifted me you. I regret to inform you that by the time you read this letter, Morris and I will be heading back home. I could not find the words to tell you goodbye. So instead of goodbye, I leave you this gift of parting. I will give you the key to survival here in this ratchet land.

Avoid the sun. Allow your skin to pale. Learn the ways of a lady in this day and age, speak as they speak, walk as they walk, eat as they eat. Learn to think as they think. Avert your eyes for no Negro. Speak with confidence. Act as they act, even if only in pretense pretend you are better than your Negro brothers and sisters. at least in public. Demand the reverence of the Negro. Never under any circumstances reveal your truth to anyone. Hide it, and forget it forever.

I know $50 is only a start, but it is enough for you to make your way North and make a new life for yourself. You are a beautiful lady, which any man would be happy to have. Meet someone, court him and marry quickly to secure a happy life. In time, all will be well.

With Sisterly Love,

Alice

SeRina was so torn, she wanted to escape to a new reality, one where her skin didn't determine her fate, but she only wanted that future if Timothy was a part of it, especially if she were to be stuck in 1859. At least now she had a plan B in case she couldn't make it back to 2009. So she tucked the letter and money away in the satchel for safe keeping until one way or another, she was ready to make her next move.

CHAPTER TWENTY-SIX

The Barn

The evening was fast approaching, and Ivory had watered and returned the horses to the barn for the day. He was sweeping and tidying up the barn when he noticed the toe of a man's boot sticking out. He replaced the broom in hand with a pitchfork as a weapon and slowly approached the man hiding there.

"What you doing here?" he said as he turned the corner pitchfork in hand and pointed dead at the man hiding there. The black man was wearing a torn and bloody shirt and was obviously wounded.

"Help me, help me, sir, I don't mean no harm, I won't be no trouble, I just heard you could help me."

"Help you how?"

"I heard you can read and write sir, can you just help me and make me some traveling papers and get me some food and some water to dress this wound? If'n you can, I be leavin' straight away." The runaway slid back his shirt to reveal a gunshot wound to the shoulder.

"See I wasn't gonna run, honest to God, that is until they sold off my wife and my boy and now I just gots to run, I have to get them back sir. Help me please."

"Who told you to come here?"

"Pastor Edwards, sir..."

"He did, did he? Well, I got a thing or two to say to that damn Pastor when I see him next."

Just then Pastor Edwards entered the barn.

"Well, here I am Ivory, iffin you got something to say. But before you speak, remember the Lord sayeth in the book of Colossians, 'Now you must put aside all such things as these: anger, rage, malice, slander, and filthy language from your mouth.' "

"Well, since you can quote that bible so well Pastor, I suppose you can read it too which means you can write, which further means that you shouldn't have sent this nigga here! I got enough trouble trying to convince my own self to stay put!" Ivory replied.

"See that's where you wrong Ivory. The good Missus and Massa teach me the word, but I never did learns to read it for myself. Furthermore, son, this man ain't no nigger, this man is your brother in the eyes of the Lord. And he has suffered a great injustice losing his family to the hands of a vicious and greedy Massa who sold them just for profit. Now I thought that you, a man with enough freedom and access to the Massa's wagon could take me with this man over to the next town to the church for a special meeting. There is a Pastor there who knowed how to help him along the way to get his wife and son back and who can help them to follow the drinkin' gourd to freedom," said Pastor Edwards.

"Why would I do that and put my neck on the line?"

"You are a child of God are you not?"

"Yes, sir."

"God says to love thy neighbor as you love thyself. Does he not?"

"Yes sir, I s'pose you are right."

"Well, Ivory ..." said Pastor drawing closer to him in an attempt at being discreet, "who says it is just to be helping him?"

Ivory's face lit up, completing the thought Pastor Edwards was trying to convey.

"I see. So when is this so called meeting?" asked Ivory.

"Night after next..." said the Pastor. "It's a special evenin' service." He then walked over with the water and rags and started tending to the wounded runaway. Ivory removed the bullet fragments as and dressed his wound and the runaway winced from the pain. Soon after Lillybird appeared. She had been listening just outside the barn door and heard the whole plan. She was following Pastor Edwards' orders and was discretely delivering some food from the cookhouse for the wounded man.

"Good evenin' sir, hope I'm not disturbin' ya'll," said Lillybird.

"No, darling thank you Lillybird. Now before you go, you remember what I told you and keep this between us you hear?" said Pastor Edwards as he stooped eye level to make sure his message sunk in.

"Yes sir, I be quiet as a church mouse," said Lillybird, and she disappeared from the barn as fast as she had appeared.

CHAPTER TWENTY-SEVEN

Crossed Paths

SeRina was in a daze as usual standing walking down the dirt road back to Aunt Tempie's cookhouse when out of nowhere appeared LillyBird, Big Sam's not so little, little sister who invited herself on the walk.

"What's in that satchel?" asked Lillybird.

"None of your business!" replied SeRina

"I sawed you wit' a letter from Ms. Alice. Can you read?"

"Well, of course, I ..." SeRina caught herself mid-sentence and changed her can to can't. Everybody knew Lillybird was a blabbermouth and couldn't hold water...a secret to her was a good as printed in the local newspaper.

"I s'pose that's a silly question, folks know slaves can't read. Well, everybody says you been flittin' round with Massa Abbington son in love like you's white and courtin'," said Lillybird.

"Everybody needs to mind their own business!" said SeRina.

"Momma says you best be careful and that white mens mean you no good," said Lillybird.

"Your momma and everybody around here love talking about me huh?" asked SeRina.

"Yes indeed, you's the talk all around these parts," said Lillybird, proud to be relaying that tidbit of information.

"Look, Lillybird is it?" asked SeRina stopping briefly in the road and bending down to get a bit closer to the little girl.

"Yes ma'am, that my name," said Lillybird wide-eyed, wooly

headed, and grinning proudly.

"OK, Lillybird, I'm not interested in your little status reports about what everyone thinks they know about me. See I don't belong here, I don't know how the hell I got here and frankly I don't plan on staying very long."

"What? You gone run!" asked a shocked Lillybird.

SeRina hushed her loud mouth by putting her hand over it. Lillybird's eyes, big as saucers, peeked over her hand and looked back and forth like an owl-eyed cuckoo clock.

"Has anyone ever told you that you talk too much?" said SeRina with clenched teeth and a furrowed brow.

"Well, yes, momma told me that too..." replied Lillybird this time in a whisper. "It's just that I never knowed anybody who really tried to run. Massa Abbington treats us real kindly like round here so folks stay put most times. Folks 'fraid they gon' get caught by dem dogs and hangin' mens on patrol. But today, that handsome driver feller and Pastor Edwards was talkin' bout runnin' too, over on side of the barn. I just can't believe we gonna have ourselves a whole heap of folks runnin' all at once."

"Lillybird, have you told anybody else this?" asked SeRina.

"No ma'am, not a soul but you."

"Good, and you better not tell a soul. It could mean life or death for the ones running. Do you understand me?"

"Yes ma'am, I understand. I won't tell a soul, I be quiet as a church mouse, yes indeed I will!"

"Good, now GO HOME and keep your big mouth shut!"

"Yes ma'am, I be quiet as a church mouse," said Lillybird as she cautiously looked over her shoulder and made her way back to the cookhouse. SeRina turned down the path toward the barn. Her mind was racing with the possibilities, she needed to find Ivory and she needed to fast.

Just then, SeRina noticed Big Sam coming from the big house. She had been avoiding him since the day he saw her and Timothy together. She knew she had hurt his feelings and didn't have the words to say to him, none that she felt would get through anyhow.

"SeRina, SeRina, there you are my flower," said Big Sam now barreling toward her. SeRina forgot all about the trip to the barn and did an about face in order to avoid him.

"Wait for me pretty flower," said Big Sam, and she obliged him turning reluctantly to face him again.

"I been missin' you," said Big Sam.

"That's nice," said SeRina insincerely.

"Well, hows come we ain't friends no more." asked Big Sam with childlike hurt.

"I'm sorry Sam it's just complicated."

"What's complimated?" said Sam mispronouncing the word.

"Complicated, Complicated!" said SeRina impatiently. "Look, we *are* friends OK!?"

"Yes indeed, that make Big Sam awful happy."

"Good, I'm glad you are happy," said SeRina, just then Big Sam gave her a huge unexpected hug to which at first she resisted then she gave in. She hated to admit it, but it was nice to have her friend back.

"Momma makin' beans fo' supper," said, Big Sam.

"Beans... yum!" said SeRina sarcastically.

"You comin' to the cookhouse fo' supper?"

"Hadn't planned on it," said SeRina.

"Well, you better, 'cause momma say iffin you go in the Big House Millie gwine' to work you clean to death. Tomorrow is Ms. Eliza's birthday and she gots to make cakes and pies, and ham, and biscuits, and collards, and yams, and taters, and carrots, and snap peas and..."

"I get it, I get it!" said SeRina, interrupting the list. "Sure, I will come for dinner!"

"It will be like old times," said Big Sam.

"Just like old times," said SeRina. She smiled genuinely as they entered the cook house.

"Now, look-a-here at who Sam brought home," said Aunt Tempie wrapping SeRina in yet another unexpected embrace. SeRina was glad she had run into Big Sam and she was happy to see Aunt Tempie welcoming her with open arms. It was as close to home as she had felt since she arrived there. Together they sat, laughed and talked over the warmth of Aunt Tempie's beans.

CHAPTER TWENTY-EIGHT

It was a busy day in the big house, all hands on deck as they prepared for Eliza's 18th birthday celebration. Massa Abbington had spared no expense and had invited nearly everyone in town. Mrs. Abbington stood pacing back and forth in front of the picture window overlooking the garden commanding the slaves to and fro for this and that and fussing over every minute detail. Millie was almost back to her old self, barking out orders and SeRina mindlessly complied all the while her mind torn between waiting for her lover to make his move or escaping to live as a free white woman like Alice. She missed Alice tremendously and wondered how she was and if Morris was treating her any better.

The cakes were baked, the chicken was roasted, the beans were boiling, the best candles had been put out, and the lanterns refilled, bows adorned the staircase and the most musically inclined slaves were there tuning up their fiddles and the like. The house was alive with hustle and bustle as the guests were set to arrive soon. SeRina walked over to the window to set the last pie on the windowsill for cooling when she saw Timothy standing outside the window smiling and signaling her to come to him. Without a word, SeRina complied and slipped out of the back door.

"What are you thinking, you know Millie is going to have a fit!"

"I know, I just had to see you, it has been days. Here, keep my watch again and tonight meet me at 10:00 near the barn when the festivities are kicking up."

"Alright," said SeRina excited about the secret rendezvous. She thought Timothy had forgotten her, as their meetings had become few and far between. He had been so different since his family was home that she had found herself hoping for the best but preparing herself for the worst with regard to their relationship.

"Don't be late," he said, with a smile, and warm and inviting eyes. He kissed her hand which now held the watch and turned to walk away.

SeRina stood and watched until he rounded the pathway and returned to the big house, this time with a little fire lit under her. She smiled and daydreamed, sliced and peeled potatoes until her fingers were numb.

"SeRina, come here?" called Mrs. Abbington.

"Yes, ma'am," said SeRina.

"Eliza needs you to tend to her in her dressing parlor," ordered Mrs. Abbington.

"Yes, ma'am," said SeRina.

SeRina removed her apron while getting the side-eye from Millie for being able to escape potato peeling for more exciting ventures. She made her way up the big house stairs to the familiar room where Eliza was standing in her undergarments talking to her friend who was also getting dressed.

"Finally, there you are," said Eliza. "What is the point of having your own slave girl, when she is nowhere to be found?"

"Truly, I don't know what the point would be of that at all," said Eliza's friend laughing and turning to face SeRina.

SeRina about passed out when she saw her face. This was all becoming too much. This girl looked identical to her friend Michaela from 2009. She even had the same horrendous laugh. Was this a parallel universe or what? She thought in her mind, taking every precaution not to let on that she recognized the girl.

"Why Leslye, do you see what I mean, she stares at you as if she has seen a ghost!" said Eliza.

"Indeed she does," said Leslye. "What's the matter with you girl?"

"Nothing, nothing at all" said SeRina trying to pull it together.

"Come, help me then you impudent girl!" said Eliza, turning and putting her hands against the wall. SeRina pulled at the threads of her corset, wanting to pull them so tight that it choked the life out of her.

"Tighter!" said Eliza.

SeRina pulled.

"Tighter, Tighter, I say... I must have the smallest waist at my party."

"Then I *must* have your share of the birthday cake," said Leslye.

"No, you must not if you still have your heart set on my brother Timothy. I'm certain he won't want a fat pig for a bride."

SeRina froze and her heart dropped at hearing these words, but she dare not say a word.

"True, dear, well you know if our mother's had their way we'd be married already, cake or no cake," said Leslye.

"Pull you idiot," said Eliza to SeRina. She hadn't moved a muscle since she heard Timothy's name.

SeRina pulled this time with all her might, channeling every ounce of frustration and nearly cracking a rib.

"What on God's green Earth is the matter with you, are you trying to kill me?" said Eliza as she turned and slapped SeRina. Stunned by the sting of the slap and by natural reaction, SeRina wanted to knock this girl back into 2009, but she gathered her composure and finished tying the corset and then walked over to grab the dress to help Eliza put it on.

"The help these days, is absolutely worthless. I hope your father got her for a bargain," said Eliza.

SeRina assisted in silence as the girls chatted on and on about how incompetent the help seemed to be these days, the night's festivities and what they would wear to each-others make-believe weddings. SeRina felt so detached from reality and angry for believing Timothy would ever really want to be with her. She felt silly for getting her hopes up about meeting him later that night. She walked to the window and took out the watch opening it, winding it, and willing it to send her back home again. It didn't work. In fact, this time, absolutely nothing happened. Tears filled her eyes but she refused to let them fall.

"SeRina, SeRina, are you hard of hearing girl?" yelled Eliza. "Fetch me my earbobs and come help with my hair, now, you idiot!"

SeRina quickly tucked away from the watch in Timothy's handkerchief and returned to assist the ladies with preparing for the evening swallowing her pride and the choking feeling in her throat from suppressed tears.

Meanwhile, the guests were arriving and it was time for Eliza's grand entrance. A handsome boy from the neighboring plantation was her date for the evening and he waited at the bottom of the stairway for her next to her brother Timothy and her adoring parents. All of the visitors hushed and the slaves struck up the makeshift band as her entrance music. She was followed by Leslye and then by SeRina. Leslye had her eyes locked on Timothy the entire way down the stairs and at first thought, his adoring gaze was for her. Little did she know, it was for SeRina.

Timothy could sense something was the matter with SeRina as she looked at him and quickly looked away. He sensed a hurt in her and had no idea where it had originated. When Eliza reached the bottom of the stairs she was greeted with a kiss on the hand and locked arms with her escort. In similar fashion, when Leslye reached the bottom of the stairs, Mrs. Abbington nudged Timothy to follow suit and so he did, kissing Leslye's hand and taking her by the arm into the parlor. SeRina stood frozen on the stairs as she watched them walk away. Mrs. Abbington noticed him looking back at SeRina concerned over his shoulder and took note of the interchange.

The party was in full effect, and SeRina lost track of time as she served and refilled the glasses of the guests. She was so upset about Leslye and Eliza's conversation earlier, and the way Timothy was playing along with the charade, that she had lost herself in the work willing herself to forget all about it.

"SeRina, hurry and take the cake into the parlor, it's time," said Millie.

SeRina carefully picked up the beautiful cake and carried it from kitchen to parlor just as she had been asked. Upon entering, the guests all ooh'd, ahh'd and made a path for her to sit it upon the table for Eliza. Eliza's eyes lit up with excitement at the sight of it, the cake was simply beautiful.

"Thank you, dear," acknowledged Massa Abbington. "Tonight, we wish to celebrate the coming of age celebration of our beautiful and only daughter Ms. Eliza. May you have many more and continue to grow in grace and beauty!"

On cue, Eliza's beau came up and on bended knee said, "What better night to ask such an amazing beauty to make me the luckiest man alive and be my bride. Will you marry me?"

"Yes, Yes, Yes, Yes!" Exclaimed Eliza with increasing intensity, jumping up and down and hugging her Bo back to his feet. The room erupted in applause and well wishes, which were interrupted by a ping to a glass with a second announcement from Mr. Abbington.

"Ladies and gentlemen it is my pleasure to also announce that my son will be soon making a similar request to the lovely Leslye, merging our families and creating the largest Tobacco Empire in the South. Tonight is indeed a night to celebrate!"

Timothy nearly spat out his drink when hearing the news. He knew it was inevitable as all his life and that their families had planned on the two of them being married. However, he felt Leslye was a pretentious snob and he couldn't stand the thought of spending the rest of his life with her.

Upon hearing the news, SeRina tore through the kitchen and out the back door of the big house. She ran down the road as far and as fast as her legs could carry her, past the well, past the cookhouse and through Grandpa George's garden to the clearing tearing her dress along the way.

Timothy wanted so badly to run after her, but Leslye held on to his arm and insisted on a dance after the announcement. He obliged so as to not embarrass her, but the moment the song ended he ran after SeRina. He knew just where to find her, in their special place, the clearing beyond the garden. After running down the road in the darkness, he made his way to the clearing, and there she stood. She was so beautiful under the moonlight even with her face covered in tears. She felt him near her and felt a sense of temporary comfort at the thought that at least he came after her. He approached her from behind and wrapped his arms around her.

"I'm sorry, I wanted to tell you, but I didn't know how. She is not what I want, but it is out of my hands, our parents have been planning this for as long as I can remember."

"And when were you going to tell me?" said SeRina, breaking free from his embrace. "If your future isn't in your hands whose hands is it in? Your father? When are you going to stand on your own two feet and stop basking in his shadow? You know you don't love her. Follow your heart. Run away with me, we can start a new life somewhere. Somewhere far, far away from here."

"It's not that simple, darling, you know that. My family needs me here."

"What about what I need?"

"I know what you need." He said hushing her lips with a kiss so powerful she felt the Earth move beneath her feet. He pulled her into him and although her first instinct was to push him away, his urgency was so compelling that it took her breath away. She felt her heart's beat intensify as he lay her on the grass.

KABOOM... came a noise from the distance, startling them both. Then suddenly, the sky filled with the color spray of fireworks.

"It must be 10:00," said Timothy smiling as he looked upward.

SeRina, curious, took out his watch and opened the case. She strained to see the time under the moonlight and sure enough it was 10:00 p.m. on the nose.

"Father is always prompt. The fireworks are a special surprise for Eliza."

"Wow, aren't they beautiful?" said SeRina staring into the sky while laying on her back.

"Not as beautiful as you," said Timothy observing her and feeling some fireworks of his own. "And stop all that dreadful crying." he said taking out his handkerchief and handing it to her to wipe her eyes.

"Do you love me?" asked SeRina as she tucked the watch away again, in his monogramed handkerchief. She was still, and stood breathing shallowly, awaiting his reply.

"More than air," said Timothy without hesitation. "It may sound foolish but sometimes, I feel as if I will just stop breathing if you aren't near me."

"You're the only thing that feels real here, the only thing that makes me ever consider staying. But if I stay, I can't stay as a slave, we have to get away from here," replied SeRina.

"I don't know how, but I will make a way for us to be together. I love you with every ounce of my being," said Timothy gently turning her head toward his, and caressing away the tear gliding down her cheek. "I promise I will find a way, even if you run, I will follow you to the ends of the Earth." He lowered his lip to hers and kissed her with unbridled passion holding her in his arms as if his life depended on it. She lost herself in his kiss, took him in and breathed his air slow then fast until their heartbeats subsided and collided into the same rhythm. Afterwards, they lay looking at the stars as if they had never seen stars before. The sulfur had cleared from the fireworks and the stars were brilliant and stark against the black velvet sky.

"The stars, they make me feel like maybe I'm not so far from home after all. I remember my mom and dad used to take me outside and we would look up at the stars and try to name the constellations. I loved that," said SeRina.

"In time, we will have a home of our own and our own garden to lay in to worship the stars, we can count every single one together. Perhaps I will even name one after you my love. "

"That's the only way I will stay," said SeRina, turning to face him. "I will wait for you, if you promise me that."

"I promise you, you will be free, a slave to no man nor woman, and you will be mine. Forever."

She wanted with every ounce of her being to believe him, and she felt at home in his embrace. They lost track of time as they lay beneath the stars sharing stories of their past and fantasizing about their future together. Before long, the conversation dwindled, the sound replaced with the soft lull of crickets, and they fell fast asleep in each other's arms.

COCKLDOODLEDOO! Crowed the rooster from Grandpa George's cabin. Grandpa George came out in usual fashion to gather some wood for the day's work, and noticed some crushed vegetables from where SeRina had torn through the garden the night before. He followed the path to the clearing and found the lovers still lying there entangled in each other's arms.

"You best, be getting on home Master Timothy," said Grandpa George in a heavy and commanding voice which startled the lovers both awake. SeRina quickly covered herself and jumped to her feet. It was her only other time seeing Grandpa George since the day he stopped the overseer from having his way with her and this wasn't how she wanted him to see her at all. She wanted to ask him the secrets of the watch and tell him about where she was from, but all she could do is cover herself in an attempt to avoid his disapproving gaze.

Timothy also jumped to his feet and dismissed himself realizing the time. "I'm sorry, I must go. Goodbye my dear." he said in parting he grabbed her hand for a quick squeeze before tearing through the woods in record speed toward the big house.

"You know, I heard you looked like my Alice, but I had to see you up close to see for myself. I must admit, I thought perhaps the rumors to be untrue. When I saw you before I did not come close enough to truly see the resemblance."

"Yes sir, I hear that often, especially from Aunt Tempie, she mistook me for her for days when I first arrived here."

"The two of you look like you came from the same womb. Practically twins, well, I shall say, this is the most-uncanny thing I've ever seen," replied Grandpa George, his English accent still heavy after all the years gone by.

SeRina, embarrassed, readjusted her dress and straightened her hair.

"Don't worry now my dear, your secret is safe with me. But be careful, not everyone will be as understanding as I. Now you better be running along."

"Yes sir," said SeRina, humbled by his presence. She left the clearing and made her way back through the garden toward the road, they would just have to have that talk about the watch at another time.

Meanwhile, Timothy had made his way back to the big house. Little did he know his parents and Leslye were all up awaiting his return.

Leslye had alerted his parents the night before that Timothy had come up missing, and the news had not set with either of them very well, especially Mrs. Abbington.

"Do you have any idea the time, boy?" asked Mr. Abbington.

"No sir, I don't," said Timothy startled by his father. It was still early and his eyes had to readjust to the light as he entered the house. He was shocked to see his mother, father and Leslye all sitting there.

"Where is your watch? Perhaps you need a lesson in looking at it to tell the time!" said Mr. Abbington.

"It is lost, or perhaps someone stole it, I don't know I have looked all around for it, but to no avail," said Timothy lying, he had forgotten to get it from SeRina in the hurry to get back to the big house.

"Really, you don't know where it is?" said Albert entering the room. He had an inkling of who had it since he had been alerted by Misses Abbington earlier to keep an eye out for the two of them sneaking about.

"Find it!" said Mrs. Abbington to Albert and he left out with the task of finding it and a little something more in mind.

"He had better know where it is. I paid a fortune for the gold it took to make that watch and it took Grandpa George months to perfect it in time for your birthday."

"Really this is not about the watch at all!" said Mrs. Abbington.

"Everyone knows you've been running around with that slave girl and it stops today! You will not be an embarrassment to this family and to your fiancé!"

Leslye sat hurt and fuming in the parlor chair.

"My fiancé? Mother, I can't marry Leslye, I don't love her!"

"What do you know of love dear? Who do you love?" said Mrs. Abbington.

"He loves that nigger!" exclaimed Leslye.

"She's not a nigger!" said Timothy.

"How dare you disgrace this family by lying with that beast!" retorted Mrs. Abbington. Timothy was mortified by his mother's statement.

"Darling' can't you see the girl is upset, take her out. I will handle things," said Mr. Abbington. He stood his ground until his wife conceded.

"I simply cannot believe it. Why, the embarrassment of it all. Come along dear," said Mrs. Abbington as she comforted the now sobbing Leslye and took her upstairs.

Mr. Abbington exhaled relieved at his wife's departure. He turned to face his son and said, "Son, allow me to be frank. SeRina is a beautiful girl, she's a quadroon, and about the lightest nigger I've seen, but she's still a nigger. And not to say I haven't sowed a seed in a negra every now and again, but it was just to fulfill my urges and not my heart. Now you don't want to go and ruin the family name do you son?"

"No sir," said Timothy, sincerely seeking his father's approval.

"Then you know what to do. You need to make things right with Leslye, and if you decide to carry on with the negra behind closed doors, do it discreetly as I do to keep the Misses happy."

Just then, Millie entered the room with lowered eyes and a glass of brandy for Massa Abbington.

"A vision like no other." Mr. Abbington said, approaching her, caressing her face, and running his hands down her jawline past her neck and over her breasts in demonstrative fashion. A single tear descended from her ebony eyes and she closed them tightly to subdue the others to follow. Without a word, Massa Abbington then took her by the hand and she walked behind him into the spare bedroom.

"Yes sir," said Timothy stunned and seeing his father for the first time with unveiled eyes.

CHAPTER TWENTY-NINE

Red Handed

The sun had fully risen around the time Albert trudged down the road toward the slave shacks, stopping at every one on the hunt for SeRina, Timothy's watch, and a little something more if he could find it. On his quest, he stopped at the cookhouse hoping to spot her. Entering unannounced he said, "Tempie, have you seen SeRina?"

"No, sir, not since yesterday," said Tempie honestly.

"Lillybird? You see her?"

"No, sir," said Lillybird. "Not at all."

"Big Sam? How 'bout you?"

"No sir, I ain't seen my pretty lil' flower, but if you sees her tell her I been missing her a mighty heap," replied Big Sam.

"Hush boy, now that gal ain't thinkin' bout you I told you that before and you up and made a fool out yourself anyhow. I heard she been runnin' round with Massa Timothy. That gal ain't nothin' but trouble. Her skin is her curse make her forget her place round here!" interrupted a dark voice in the shadows, he emerged and Albert saw that it was Sam's father, Big Joe.

"I never thought I'd see the day that I agree with a nigger, but I do concur, she is trouble indeed!" replied Albert just before leaving. As soon as he stepped out of the cookhouse, he spotted SeRina walking toward him on the road. SeRina was smiling, twirling and laughing aloud with no regard to her surroundings. She had Timothy's watch in hand and was lost in reminiscent thought about the night before.

SeRina looked up and saw Albert, her smile instantly fading as she quickly put the watch in the crumpled handkerchief, stuffed it in her bosom, and made an about face and a beeline back toward Grandpa George's house.

"Not so fast there girl, what do you have there?" asked Albert.

"Nothing. I'm just going to see Old Man George," said SeRina.

"Not before you show me what you're hiding," said Albert walking toward her.

Instinctively, she turned to run but tripped and fell on the hem of her dress that was torn the night before when she ran through the garden.

"Give me that watch you little thief!" he said as he jumped on top of her and started tearing at her clothes to get to the watch.

"Aunt Tempie! Sam! Help!" yelled SeRina. Hearing her cry Big Sam barreled out of the cookhouse door just as Albert mounted SeRina. Overcome with rage, and remembering how Albert had hurt SeRina before, Big Sam mustered every ounce of strength and began beating Albert savagely in the middle of the road.

"You a bad, bad man, Mister Albert, you ain't gon' hurt my flower no mo'!" yelled Sam as he pounded Albert over and over with all his might.

Albert lost hold of SeRina in an attempt to protect himself from the savage beating, but not before the watch fell from her ripped dress and rolled out of the handkerchief.

"Stop Sam you're going to kill him!" yelled Aunt Tempie as she ran out of the cookhouse.

"Boy, turn him loose, what you trying to get strung up for hurtin' a white man?" yelled Big Jo, while running over to break up the fight.

"Turn him loose, turn him loose I say!" said Maurice, Albert's sidekick who had overheard the ruckus and come to his friends aid. He cocked his shotgun and fired a warning shot into the air, bringing both the brawlers to their feet, Albert much slower than

Sam. Albert brushed off his clothes tasting the blood from his now split lip and said, "This nigger attacked me, get 'em boys!"

Maurice and his accomplice grab Big Sam and subdue him. "That gal there, she's a thief, she had Massa Timothy's watch," said Albert.

"No, she was holdin' it for me, I tooks it, I tooks Massa Timothy watch," said Big Sam breathlessly in an effort to protect SeRina.

"No Big Sam, don't..." interjected SeRina.

"She ain't do it, honest I took Massa Timothy pretty watch, don't beat her, beats me! Beats me stead of my flower, don't you touch her no mo', no mo' sir no mo'!" said Big Sam.

"Shut your mouth fore you get yourself kilt Boy!" said Big Joe.

"Be quiet baby, shut yo' mouth and save yourself," pleaded Aunt Tempie, next turning to Albert. "Now Massa Albert, you know he ain't mean it, please let him be Massa Albert, you know my Sam ain't never hurt nobody, give him mercy, mercy I say," begged Aunt Tempie teary eyed. She grabbed hold to Albert in an attempt to pull him from her son, and he backslapped her down to the ground. Big Joe rushed to her side to help her back to her feet.

"Albert you's a rotten man, you don' slapped my momma and hurt my pretty flower. I's g'wine kill you dead iffin it's the last thing I do," said Big Sam.

"Is that right nigger, you done gone and done it now, you don't threaten no white man's life. You done clean lost your mind!" said Maurice hitting Big Sam in the back of the head with his gun, knocking him unconscious.

"Boys, take 'em in the cookhouse, I'm gonna teach him a lesson in submission," said Albert, wiping the blood from his mouth. Maurice and his accomplice did as they were told and despite the pleas of his parents, they took Big Sam inside the cookhouse tying him face down on the bed.

Albert remained outside for a time, tying SeRina hands together around the dinner bell post and giving her 10 lashes to the palm of her hands and forearms for taking part in the watch theft.   This punishment paled in comparison to what they did next to Big Sam.

Albert, walked into the cookhouse and dismissed the two men.

"I will take it from here," he said as he unfastened his belt and pants. The men nodded and left him there alone with Big Sam to do the unthinkable...again.

CHAPTER THIRTY

No Escape

Aunt Tempie, Lillybird, and Big Joe and several other slaves gathered and stood outside the cookhouse for what felt like an eternity afraid of what could be going on inside. After a time, Albert called the two men standing guard to the cookhouse to help carry Sam's still unconscious body out.

Albert untied SeRina's hands and next ordered the men to tie Big Sam face first to the dinner bell post where SeRina had been tied moments before.

"This is all your fault you little thief, so you get right there down on your knees and watch it and don't you dare look away!" said Albert to SeRina.

She did as she was told. She had seen but dismissed the beatings she saw in the movies with the rehearsed agony she almost found the scenes in the films a bit comical, and felt that surely they were exaggerated. But to be an arms-length away from the horror, the blood splashing upon her with every lash, to smell the fear and see the sweat dripping from Big Sam' brow, to watch his strong rigid body go limp from submission devastated her in ways that she could not explain. The lump she felt in her throat as the tears flooded her eyes was a combination of choking back pain and vomit. Albert joked and cackled as he twirled his whip cracking it once more across his back, saying over his shoulder to his side-kick Maurice, "Spose' I beat the piss out of him this time, that'll learn his black ass to steal from Mr. Abbington!"

SeRina watched in horror with the man holding her by the hair to keep her eyes focused on Sam with every lash. The final lash landed on his back sending another splash of blood across SeRina's face as a stream of urine trickled down his leg, his final release before he expired. *At least now he was free*, SeRina thought.

They all felt it. Aunt Tempie, Lillybird, Big Joe and the others gasped when the final lash took him. Tempie collapsed to her knees and her son/man Big Joe joined her on his knees holding her closely as she sobbed into his chest. Lillybird was speechless for the first time in her life, she stood frozen in disbelief as her brother was untied and fell lifelessly to the ground.

Although SeRina usually was an escapist, one able to easily

disappear into herself blocking all thoughts, all pain, all anger, she found herself unable to go into her usual trance. She could not shrug off the tragedy before her. She couldn't treat this untimely death as she did the death of her adoptive mother with cold shrill resistance. She couldn't dismiss it for hope of focusing her attentions elsewhere because there was no hope. Optimism was drained from her just as the blood drained from him onto the dirt pathway. Every single prospect of escape dwindled away and traded itself for fear and sheer pathetic hopelessness. She wondered where Timothy was and why he hadn't intervened.

She stared brutality in the face and subdued resistance just as the others had. She, the one who always said that she would never stand for such vile atrocities had not only witnessed it and done nothing, but it was all her fault. None of her knowledge of the future and how things would someday be could save her now, she felt as if there was no escape. No one questioned the conditions or the fact that they were owned, no one stood for him or rescued him from death. The bleakness of it all was as commonplace as the cotton in the fields to them. That is when she felt broken, that is the moment that the terror set in and the fear that she may never escape took over her very soul.

That night after the blood was washed from her face and ropes removed from her hands, she walked bemused back to the big house passing the dimly lit shanty cookhouse that Big Sam called home. Her thoughts consumed her on her journey as she found herself chained to an ancestral past that she never knew. She couldn't escape, she had no idea how she had gotten to this horrible place. She was trapped in every essence of the word, and there she shuffled forward unable to sob.

Her hopes of making a getaway now doomed to failure, she found herself floating adrift not only down the road but in a seemingly endless cycle of systematic oppression. This was her America, the one she loved and used to pledge her allegiance to every morning in her homeroom class. "Freedom," the once insignificant, simple and presupposed word now held a new value in her mind and she wondered if she would ever taste it again.

CHAPTER THIRTY–ONE

Follow the Drinking Gourd

A darkness settled over the Abbington Plantation the morning after Sam's passing. Aunt Tempie was devastated and for the first time in her adult life, she was confined to bed unable to work. She had always been able to engulf herself in the work needed in the kitchen and kept a cheery and hopeful disposition but for the first time in her life, she felt trapped. She *felt* like a slave. Aunt Tempie lost her joy, Lillybird her flit and even Big Sam's brother/father Big Joe was more sullen than usual.

That morning as Lillybird made her way to the field to take

water to the slaves as she always did, she noticed SeRina sitting on the side of the main road covered in dust, staring wildly off into oblivion with her back resting against a tree.

Lillybird couldn't bring herself to speak to SeRina because it was all her fault. Albert had even said so. Her brother had died for her stupid affair, and she resented her for it. And so she passed SeRina by without uttering a word. SeRina had hoped for a word from Lillybird, she wanted to scream I AM SO SORRY, but instead, she laid her head in her hands as they rested on her knees. Finally, she cried, she cried long and hard and until there were no tears left to fall and until her chest ached from heaving. She longed for Timothy to hold her, for her father to summon her back to 2009 and wake her from this nightmare. In the distance, she heard a familiar sound coming from the fields. A strong and low voice led the slaves in song...

Follow the drinking gourd,
Follow the drinking gourd,
For the old man is a-waiting for to carry you to freedom,
Follow the drinking gourd.

She raised her head her swollen eyes refocusing in the sun's light and the song continued ...

When the sun comes back and the first quail calls,
Follow the drinking gourd.
The old man is a-waiting for to carry you to freedom,
Follow the drinking gourd.

Now the river bank makes a mighty good road,
The dead trees will show you the way.
Left foot, peg foot, traveling on,

Follow the drinking gourd.

Finally, it hit her why this song was so familiar. Ms. Parker, her history teacher had played that song during history class and had told the students that this song was often sung by slaves as a signal to indicate they were going to run. The song held clues as to how to escape north to freedom. The song coerced her to her feet and all in an instant coursed through her veins igniting her adrenalin and revitalizing her strength. She took out running wildly down the dusty road her mind engulfed with thoughts of Big Sam, how he had loved and cared for her, how she had hurt him, how she avoided him, and how he was no longer there because of her. She thought of her mother and how if she had have just been there where she was supposed to be, that she would still be alive. It was all too much the thoughts surged through her mind like electricity fueling her pace to quicken. SeRina knew she had to escape, NOW, with or without Timothy. Fire and heat seethed through her body as she ran almost faster than her legs could carry her. She had to find Ivory before he left, he was her ticket to Freedom!

When she busted in the barn, she caught Ivory completely off guard.

"Take me with you!" she said without warning tears still streaming down her face.

She ran toward the horses and grabbed a saddle with her cut hands as if she were going to mount it right then and there and ride off.

Ivory looked her over, SeRina was not the polished, confident and flawless beauty he remembered from the carriage ride, instead he saw a lost, frightened and frenzied girl covered in dust and dried blood, her hands and forearms heavily ladened with cuts and welts that needed tending to. He had been away driving Massa Abbington overnight and hadn't heard the news about Big Sam, and further had no idea what happened to her or where any of this was coming from.

"Whoa there missy, slow down. What is going on? What have they done to you?" he rushed over to her taking her by the wrists and looking at her lacerated hands.

"He's gone, he's gone, and it's all my fault!" SeRina snatched away her hands and continued preparing the horses.

"Who's gone? Slow down!"

"Sam! They killed Big Sam!"

"What? Who would ever hurt Big Sam?"

"Albert! Look it doesn't matter, please just take me with you. I know you are running. It sounds like everyone may be running. I heard them singing *Follow the Drinking Gourd* in the field."

"Shhh!" said Ivory and he pulled her inside the stall and ran over to close the barn door.

"What you trying to get us all strung up? Here sit down," he said.

"Sit? No, uh, uh, I've got to get out of here!" said SeRina.

"SIT!" he said. And he gently pushed her down by her shoulders on a nearby stack of hay. SeRina was thoroughly annoyed.

He walked over and gathered the bowl and rag that Pastor Edwards had there earlier for the runaway. And emptied it.

"Hello ma'am," said the runaway slave who was still hiding there in the barn.

"What in the world, who is that?" asked SeRina, startled. She had assumed that she and Ivory had been alone. Her breath caught in her throat as she asked, she was still winded from her expeditious journey to the barn.

"He's harmless, said Ivory. Now you stay put, I will be right back!"

"My names Benjamin," said the runaway.

"SeRina..." she said nodding in his direction.

"Nice to meet you ma'am," said Benjamin, tipping an invisible hat.

"Look I'm not here to chit chat, I have to get out of here," replied SeRina impatiently.

"Runnin' could get you kilt. You gotta know when to run, how to run and you gots to know how to follow the stars or them woods and swamp will make your mind go to pieces and you's find yourself gettin' nowhere fast. But I s'pose gal like you could almost run in the light of day, cause you ain't no everyday nigger like me. You's whiter than some white folks I know," said Benjamin.

"That's what I keep hearing, but my whiteness hasn't kept me from suffering the same as you," replied SeRina showing Benjamin her lacerated hands and forearms. Just then, Ivory returned with some fresh water and rags and salve.

"Humpf, 'fore you even tell me who did this to you, I bet I can guess. Weren't nobody but that damned Albert," said Ivory incensed.

"You guessed it." confirmed SeRina.

"He gone get what's comin' to him in this life or the next!" said Ivory.

"God ought to strike down folks like him dead in their tracks 'fore they can hurt another soul," said Benjamin.

"He ought to, but God obviously doesn't care about anybody around here... Big Sam had the biggest heart in the world and God just let him die!" said SeRina. She had started to wonder if God was even real after seeing how he let people suffer in this day and age. If he cared, why did God take 246 years to end slavery? How many people have to suffer and die before he decides to do something?"

"You got it all wrong little missy. See, God doesn't cause the suffering, he just lets things take their course and well the devil' he's the one you should be cross with. He aims to kill, steal and destroy and is the father of the lie, besides, how do you know when God's gonna end slavery?" said Benjamin.

"You wouldn't believe it if I told you," said SeRina.

"What, you can tell the future?" asked Benjamin wide-eyed.

"Sort of... said SeRina... Actually, I'm *from* the future. What the heck, nobody believes me so I might as well tell you. Slavery will end in 1865, so if we hang in here for a few more years none of this will even matter. And not that you will believe me, but in my day and time it is argued often if slavery actually started in 1492 or if it started in 1619 so if it wasn't 246 years, it was 400 years which from my limited understanding goes along with Gen 15:13 in the Bible you people love so much, so it's almost like God planned all this to happen!" SeRina exploded, she was so fed up with the barbarism and blind optimism all the slaves had, she was sick of being stuck there, she didn't care who thought she was crazy she was determined to speak her mind!

"Gen 15:13, Know for certain that your offspring will be sojourners in a land that is not theirs and will be servants there, and they will be afflicted for four hundred years," said Pastor Edwards entering the barn unexpectedly. "It does seem to some as if the good Lord had it all in his plan."

He always seems to come in at the most inopportune times, thought Ivory to himself as he entered the barn halfway through Pastor's commentary.

"Yes, I know that passage well," said Pastor Edwards smiling genuinely at all three of them.

"Just the person I'd like to ask what's burning on my heart... If your God is almighty and powerful why did he let Sam Die? Why did he let them do this to me?" asked SeRina as tears filled her eyes again as she displayed her wounded hands and forearms.

"My dear, SeRina is it?" asked the Pastor.

"Yes."

"Rumor has it that you are a time traveler of sorts, is that true?" said the Pastor.

SeRina was baffled as to how he knew that, but he had overheard her speaking with the runaway just moments before.

"Well, yes, sort of although I have no idea how I ended up here. Do you believe me?" asked SeRina, now calmed by Pastor Edward's calm demeanor and commanding presence. It was a bit surprising however to her that he knew about her past.

"With God, all things are possible. And well, if it is true my child, you better than any of us should know that in the stream of time and with the scope of eternity, suffering in this life is for only a moment for joy cometh in the morning!"

SeRina found herself speechless as she had a moment of epiphany. Suddenly, all her feelings of anger toward God and doubting his love and his existence felt moot. If Pastor Edwards were right, then maybe God let people suffer to make them closer to him... after all when bad things happen, the first thing people say is "Oh, my God!" It didn't make sense to her, but she thought to herself, *who am I to question God?*

The men had continued speaking to one another about the

plans later that evening for a secret meeting of sorts and SeRina refocused her attention mid-conversation.

"Now, Ivory, remember be there tonight in the clearing at sundown," said Pastor Edwards.

"We will be there," said Ivory, his eyes shifting from Benjamin to SeRina in confirmation.

Pastor Edwards tipped his hat to both gentlemen and to SeRina and exited the barn door just as quietly as he had entered.

"Now, you should know better than to doubt the existence of the Lord, who else can you credit for making a creature as wondrous as you?" said Ivory jokingly to SeRina flashing a flawless grin. She felt uneasy about the compliment. She found Ivory incredibly attractive and had never been quite so close to him. His breath touched her brow gently as he spoke, the nearness of him involuntarily spine-tingling.

He slowly and ever-so-cautiously washed and bandaged her hands and forearms applying the salve. She winced from pain but her comfort grew from his tenderness. "OUCH," she said as he wrapped the rags tightly creating a makeshift bandage.

"There, there, now it's not as bad as all that. You should've seen Ol' Benjamin when we found him. I almost run him through with that there pitchfork not knowing he already had near bout bled to death from a bullet. He was hiding over in that corner only problem was he forgot to hide away them big ol' feet's of his!"

Both the men laughed. SeRina didn't think any of it was funny.

"You know what this was a bad idea!" she said as she got up to go, but tripped instead. Ivory caught her by her waist, reflexes, and chivalry in full effect.

"Whoa, there, now don't be like that little missy. Let me help you," he spun her effortlessly by her waist back to face him holding her at the small of her back close to him holding her close and looking deep into her eyes. He took her breath away. Time stood still as she prepared herself for a kiss that never came. He knew what he was doing to her, but also knew they had an onlooker, and that the time wasn't quite right, so slowly he released his hold on the small of her back and she stepped away to regain her composure.

"We both know, you could use some nursing on these hands and arms, stop being so prideful and let me finish fixing you up," he said in a commanding whisper that trailed off into that perfect smile of his.

"Now come on over here and have a seat, that's the least you could do after all the trouble I went through to get that fresh water, salve and rags to get you all fixed up," said Ivory.

"Thank you for being so kind," said SeRina

"It's the least I can do. You gone be the ticket to my freedom," said Ivory applying the last of the bandages.

"Me?" said SeRina. "I was thinking that *you* would be the ticket to MY freedom."

"How's that?" asked Ivory.

"Well, seeing as though when we met you were just about free, I figured you knew your way around, weren't afraid to try again and that together maybe we could make a go of it," said SeRina smiling.

"Well, I figured that with you looking white and all we could write us up some papers as if you are transporting me somewhere or you could say I's your personal slave or something and that together maybe we could make a go of it," said Ivory mimicking SeRina and smiling all the while.

"Interesting," said SeRina almost flirting.

"Interesting indeed. Way I see it, one way or another we gon' be the ticket to each other's freedom. Just make sure you are in that clearing tonight at sundown."

"I'll be there, matter of fact, do you mind if I go with you?" asked SeRina.

"I'd be mighty obliged, I thought you'd never ask."

CHAPTER THIRTY-TWO

The Secret Sermon

The night was especially quiet and clear, the crickets not up to their usual noise-making, it was as if even they had a secret meeting to attend. SeRina had spent the evening with Ivory in the barn even dining there and avoided the big house and the cook house for fear of running into Lillybird again. She didn't even want to imagine what Big Joe may have to say to her, he swore from the moment he lay eyes on her that she would be nothing but trouble and she had proved him right, so she stayed clear of them all.

She and Ivory waited until just after sundown and he led her down the road, past the shanties, through Grandpa George's back garden to the hush harbor for the secret meeting. On the way, SeRina second guessed herself and wanted to stop and say some parting words to Aunt Tempie and to grab the dress and the package that Alice had given her, but she dare not face Aunt Tempie after the loss of Big Sam. She had written a short note to Tim during one of her daydreaming sessions about time and thought it ironic that she was stuck there and that his name included so many letters from the word TIME. She hadn't seen him in days and didn't want a run-in with Millie who she knew would immediately put her to work, so never had the chance to give it to him. The note read,

> T-I-M, no E can change the way I feel
>
> can't be erased by T-I-M-e ...

SeRina approached the hush harbor noticing something different in the open circle of the clearing she knew so well. There were stakes in the ground with string which had wet rags and quilts strewn about it to quiet the voices hidden within. A warm glow from the lit lantern illuminated the quilts like a firefly and created a safe and quiet haven for the forbidden meeting. Inside the circle, there were 3 black men 3 black women and 2 black children who looked unfamiliar to SeRina. All were huddled on their knees surrounding Pastor Edwards and an unidentified white man. None uttered a sound other than the Pastor who addressed the covert congregation.

"For I know thine are weary of the message found in Ephesians 6:5: 'Slaves, be obedient to your human masters with fear and trembling, in sincerity of heart, as to Christ.' So tonight as my heart compels me I bring to you a new message that our earthly masters forbid me to preach, a message of freedom and a message for our masters in this life, for if you look a bit further down in scripture you will see that Ephesians 6:9 states 'Masters, act in the same way toward them, and stop bullying, knowing that both they and you have a Master in heaven and that with him there is no partiality.' We have seen a great injustice with our poor Sam on this plantation, and with Benjamin who has come from the plantation with the others of you who are overseen by a horrid master. We have a plan that my good man and Christian Brother Mr. Owens, an abolitionist from the Methodist church up further North, will help us to execute. May the Lord bless and speed you all straight to the north by way of the drinking gourd." As if on cue, all the slaves looked to the sky at the big dipper as if it was speaking its own language and was beckoning them all to freedom.

SeRina noticed an uneasiness amongst the others as the abolitionist began to speak of the plan and as she made her sight plain to all around her. The slaves from the other plantation nearly gasped at her sight thinking they had been found out by a white woman nosing about in the hush harbor. Pastor Edwards eased their fears by interrupting his accomplice and stating, "Rest assured, the girl before you is evidence of the atrocities of slavery, as she looks as close to them to be one of their own, yet she still bears their scars and wounds upon her. Come and sit my child. My brother, you have two more to add to your manifest, the girl, and Ivory here." The Methodist nodded in approval.

SeRina sat, uncomfortable and self-conscious and looked around at all of the runaways. She examined the faces and found herself actually caring about each of their stories and what landed them there in the hush harbor on the cusp of running away. Benjamin, the runaway from the barn who had arrived with SeRina and Ivory, sat near the slaves from his home plantation and tipped his hat in humble acknowledgment of his brethren.

A stiff breeze meandered through the hush harbor sending a chill over SeRina, the hairs on her arms stood on end and Ivory sensed her discomfort. He removed his overcoat and wrapped it around her shoulders, and seated himself next to her. She looked up into his eyes and saw a tenderness there that wasn't there before, and for the first time, she exhaled, finding comfort in the nearness of him and in simply being "one of them."

CHAPTER THIRTY-THREE

The Methodist

Once the instructions were given, Pastor Edwards and the Methodist bid farewell, exchanging a brotherly hug and kind words.

"God speed you all to freedom," said Pastor Edwards as he disappeared back into the woods back toward the plantation.

"It is time, come, my brothers and sisters," said the Methodist motioning everyone to quietly make their way through the woods.

This time they took a hidden pathway SeRina hadn't noticed during her other trips there before. The pathway was hidden by the thickness of the trees but was well worn once you passed the threshold of brush. Benjamin held back the branches letting the children and women and other men to pass before following suit. After walking in total silence with shallow breaths and tapered steps, they arrived at a wagon drawn by 2 sturdy horses tied to a nearby tree.

"Careful now, children first, then women, then men into the wagon. Mothers keep your young'uns close and quiet like. I need to chain you all for the pretense that I'm returning each of you to your masters, so once you are seated, please put the chains on nice and loose so you all's still comfortable," said the Methodist. His name was Reverend Michael Kenneth and he was a Godsend for the runaways, a white man who was willing to risk his very own life for their freedom. He and Pastor Edwards had mapped the plan out to get all of the runaways to safety for the night and then up to the North by way of the Underground Railroad.

"Now some of you all will be strong enough to make it the furthest north out of the states and up to Montreal, Canada, some of you others with little ones or who don't wish to travel as far, may be split off and go your way North up to Buffalo, NY. No matter your path, I promise each of you to give my all to see you to safety. May the good Lord bless and keep us on our journey," said the Methodist.

The slaves did as they were told and quietly boarded the not so well-appointed wagon and shackled themselves one to another. SeRina hadn't worn chains since the day they found her on the road, so the gravity and inhumanity of the situation weighed on her more than the iron.

She cried silently and involuntarily, her eyes meeting Ivory's for a brief yet intense moment. The tenderness remained there in his eyes and beckoned her to rest her head on his sturdy shoulder. She obliged. The wagon slowly ascended the hilly terrain into the night carrying all eleven souls off into the darkness.

Meanwhile, at the plantation, Mrs. Abbington had just called for SeRina and discovered by way of Lillybird that she and Ivory were nowhere to be found and had somehow disappeared, together. Mrs. Abbington, then, of course, reported the news to her husband, who reported the news to his son Timothy and to Albert. So there they stood, two unlikely allies Timothy and Albert before Massa Abbington.

"Now Albert, you went without consequence for killing one of my hardest workers Big Sam, I won't stand by and see that happen again. So mark my words, I want them found, I want them found quickly, and I want them brought back to me UNDAMAGED! Get the horses, and get going without delay!" ordered Massa Abbington, speaking to his son and to Albert as if this time they were the slaves who had to adhere to his every command.

The news hit Timothy that SeRina had run away with Ivory and he felt enraged and betrayed. *Why would she chose him over me*? he wondered. Then he remembered how he made her a promise and then treated her as if she didn't exist in an effort to please his mother and pretend to court his now fiancé' Leslye. Although his feelings for here will still as strong as ever, he had avoided her following his father's advice. It hit him that he wasn't there for SeRina when Big Sam was murdered by Albert's hands and that perhaps she took his silence as concurrence on Sam's murder. He resolved to return her, quickly and undamaged just as his father requested. Part of him wanted to take out his rage on Ivory who had tried to steal off into the night with his precious SeRina and the other part of him wanted to rip Albert apart for damaging her and murdering Sam. But there he stood, caught between the choice of blatant disobedience and disappointment or coming out the hero, and he chose the latter despite the consequences.

CHAPTER THIRTY-FOUR

The Real Dish

Upon sunrise, the big house was alive and tensions were high the grandfather clock struck 6 a.m. in the parlor and it might as well have been noon with all the hubbub and people running here and there. Poor Henry was doing all the things that Ivory would ordinarily do, and Millie found herself overwhelmed without SeRina's help with all of the requests of the Misses. Mrs. Abbington seemed to be ordering her around like she had something to prove this morning.

"Millie, really what is the matter with you this morning? I asked for eggs, tea and toast an hour ago and still, I sit hungry. How difficult could it possibly be to prepare a breakfast so simple?" asked Mrs. Abbington.

"Yes ma'am but remember you asked me to fetch new linens for the guest room, dust the parlor, sweep the porch, and do the washin' and I am a hand short this mornin', ma'am."

"Are you sassin' me gal?" asked Mrs. Abbington.

"No ma'am."

"Really, the help lately has been in complete disorder," replied Mrs. Abbington, speaking now to her daughter Eliza and husband who had just joined her at the dining table.

"Well, perhaps we will get breakfast before our lunch is to be served mother," said Eliza with a snide scowl on her face.

"Perhaps," replied Mrs. Abbington, almost mimicking Eliza's facial disapproval.

"Run along Millie," said Massa Abbington looking over his spectacles and puffing on his pipe. He was looking over some documents and not paying much attention to the goings-on in the room.

"Really, must you smoke that at the table?" asked Mrs. Abbington thoroughly annoyed by the fuming tobacco.

"Yes, I must, especially when there is no breakfast and 2 missing slaves. Really it does soothe the senses," replied Massa Abbington.

Millie exited the dining area returning to the kitchen to plate the breakfast for the Abbington's. She felt a slight dizziness wash over her, but shook it off and headed towards the dining room tray in hand. She placed her back against the kitchen door to open it as she had a thousand times before, but this time when she did, the dizzy spell hit again and she fell clean through dropping all of the food on the floor.

"Honestly, Millie. I've never seen you so. Lillybird come, help Millie clean this mess and make a new breakfast," requested Mrs. Abbington clearly frustrated with her incompetence.

"I'm so sorry Misses, I'm just not feeling well. I can make a new breakfast tray ma'am," replied Millie re-standing and brushing off her apron her hand resting on her stomach.

"Why Millie, you are with child!" exclaimed the Misses jumping to her feet her eyes affixed on Millie's mid-section.

"Yes ma'am, I am," replied Millie sheepishly.

"Well, why didn't you say so? When we get SeRina back, we can have her take more of your duties. William, did you hear that? Millie is with child."

"Yes, dear," replied Massa Abbington mindlessly disengaged from topic of conversation.

"Why didn't you tell us, we could have a wonderful broom jumping ceremony for you, so you can at least be right in God's eyes? Pray tell us, who is the lucky young man? Thomas? Or maybe it's that handsome Ivory. My, my, he would be an excellent catch for you indeed," said Mrs. Abbington exuberantly.

"No ma'am."

"Well, who is it then?" asked Mrs. Abbington.

"I'd rather not say ma'am," replied Millie.

"Come on, don't be silly. Just tell us, you know how mother loves fussing over these things. Moreover, it would be amazing preparation for my wedding for her to arrange a broom jumping ceremony for you. So who is it?" asked Eliza.

"It's... it's..." stuttered Millie.

"My child spit it out for Christ's sake!" said Massa Abbington not even certain of what the fuss was all about, all he knew is that he was beyond annoyed with the racket interrupting his reading time. He put down his pipe and paper and focused in on Millie looking over his spectacles.

"Well, since you all insist. The child ... the child is yours," said Millie looking Massa Abbington square in the eye. The room stood so still you could hear a rat piss on cotton. The awkward silence was immediately interrupted by a knock on the door.

Old Henry came in the room hurriedly.

"Massa, you gots a telegram here from Mr. Morris and Ms. Alice."

"Pardon me, for a moment," said Massa Abbington to his wife, daughter, and mistress who all stood awaiting his response to the news. Millie, shocked at her own revelation, used this as her moment to escape back to the kitchen to gather herself. The Misses and Eliza sat in total deafening silence as he stepped away to read the telegram.

Massa Abbington walked over toward the parlor window to read it in the light, it said,

> Dear Mr. Abbington,
>
> We apologize for the lack of notice, however, are in route to you for a visit and wish to be retrieved from the station on Tuesday evening. We thank you for your understanding and hospitality in advance and hope this telegram finds you well.
>
> Cousin Morris

Massa Abbington could feel the eyes of his wife boring into the back of his head as he had his back to her to read the telegram. He simply could not deal with this news from Millie or his wife's reaction, so he couldn't be happier to have received a telegram in his life. To avoid confrontation, he decided to leave a day early to make his way a few towns over to the station to escort Morris and Alice back to the plantation. Little did he know, that they would arrive with some news of their very own.

"I beg your pardon ladies, I must be going. It seems we are to have visitors." And just like that, he walked out of the front door leaving his wife staring, mouth gaping and blood boiling.

CHAPTER THIRTY-FIVE

Discovery

By mid-day, the Methodist and his caravan of runaways had stopped to rest at a church and had just gotten back on the road in the light of day. Passersby never looked twice at them making down the road. Why would they, after all, things appeared natural. A white man with a wagon full of chained and shackled property being taken to a plantation in the grimy southern heat. The slaves were antsy with anticipation of reaching their destination. The children growing cranky in the afternoon sun under the weight of the chains. Approaching them on horseback were two patrolmen in search of several runaways.

"Where you headed there sir?" asked the first patrolman.

"Delivering these slaves from market to their new plantation home sir," replied the Methodist.

"Is that right, where are the papers?" asked the second patrolman.

"Just a moment sir," replied the Methodist. He knew he only had papers for the original group that was to attend and was 2 people shy on his manifest with the last minute addition of SeRina and Ivory, so fumbled around a little longer than normal looking for the "papers." He produced what he had, and the patrolman said after half a glance, "Looks alright to me, good day to you sir," allowing them to continue down the road.

The slaves and the Methodist said silent prayers of thanks and exhaled in relief. Several of them had tried this perilous journey and had been captured and this was literally their last time giving escaping north a shot. SeRina even found herself praying, her adrenaline in full effect when the slave catchers approached. Ivory held her hand which was chained to his to calm her until they had passed. He was nervous too, but never let on.

"So what keeps you running?" SeRina asked Ivory breaking the silence. As afraid as she was, she was so grateful to have him by her side on the perilous journey. He quietly felt the same, finding comfort that she was by his side no matter the outcome.

"I wonder that oftentimes myself. My father was strong minded, and sharp, he always told me that they can shackle my body but not my mind, and certainly not my soul. When we was just little ones, my father and mother gathered us up in the night and stole off in the night heading north. Trouble was, we didn't make it. Then Massa was so vexed that he sold off my daddy to one plantation and my momma to another and just left us behind. So I used to run just in hopes of seeing my folks again. Well, I done gave up on that dream, but, now I just want freedom for myself because I promised myself a long time ago that no child of mine would ever be born a slave."

The wagon forged ahead on the bumpy road, heads nodded in sleep and children giggled, others were awake and smiling and talking. SeRina was joyless in her shackles, her fair skin bruising from their weight.

"I understand, I wouldn't want children in this world either," SeRina replied with a half-smile. "So what do you want to do when we get north?"

"Well, folks say I can makes a decent wage coal minin' in West Virginia. So that's where I'm a headin'. Folks say a strong able-bodied man like me can make almost $200 a year. They hire women-folk too, iffin you want to join me," he said flashing that impeccable grin, again.

"That's not really what I had in mind," said SeRina with pouty lips.

"So what did you have in mind?" he asked.

"I'm not sure as far as work, but I do know I'm not slaving away in anybody's coal mine. I am going to earn enough money to buy myself some decent clothes and start a new life as a ..."

"What, a white woman?" interrupted Ivory, sarcastically laughing out loud.

"Well, honestly, yes. When I settle in I am going to send for Timothy and we can get married and just start a new life, since it seems I'm stuck here, I may as well make the best of it."

Ivory felt insulted. He felt they had a connection and she might as well have spat in his face when she said those words. Incensed, he replied, "Gal you don't get it do you?"

"Get what?"

"Timothy done moved on, he ain't bout to disappoint the almighty Massa Abbington and run off with a gal like you. He's fixin' to marry that Leslye gal from the other plantation. Folks say dat's been the plan since he came from the womb," said Ivory.

"He wouldn't do that. He promised," replied SeRina sincerely remembering the promise Timothy had made in the hush harbor.

"A white man's promises. Humpf, dat's what got all of us in this situation in the first place. How many of us been promised we can work our way to freedom? That man ain't got an ounce of integrity in his bones. He ain't never gon' choose you, that would be like choosin' courage over comfort, and that ain't in him," said Ivory.

"You can't lump every white person in together not all white people are the same. Look at this white man risking his life for all of our freedom," said SeRina looking toward the Methodist who was driving the wagon. The sound of the wheels and the horses' hooves against the road drowned out their conversation so the Methodist was oblivious to being the topic of discussion.

"You right, they not all the same, but most of 'em would rather see you hang than to see you happy. This dream life you done concocted in yo' pretty little head is just that a dream, and if you ain't careful it's gon' become a nightmare!" replied Ivory, he wished they weren't chained together so he could move as far away from her as possible in the cramped wagon.

"You don't know him like I do. He wouldn't break his promise to me," said SeRina not fully believing her own words.

"Suit yourself gal, you gon' see one way or another that to him you's just another nigga just like the rest of us."

Meanwhile, back on the Abbington Plantation, the shock of Millie's news had landed on the Misses. Millie had gone on about her daily chores and had no regrets about delivering the news. She had felt dirty and broken since the first day Mr. Abbington had his way with her and she wanted the Misses to know the filthy pig that he was. Millie had made her mind up to keep her secret, but when they all pressured her to tell who the father was, she felt maybe it was God's way of revealing the truth. When she uttered the words it was if a tremendous weight had been lifted from her spirit. What she didn't know, however, is that the news had triggered an ominous darkness in Mrs. Abbington that would soon be unleashed.

Timothy and Albert were well on their way on the dirt road north and were gaining on the Methodist Reverend and his caravan of runaways. There was obvious tension between the two men, so few words were spoken. Timothy was lost in thought about SeRina running away with Ivory. The feeling of betrayal was suffocating and although he loved her, he found himself wanting to punish her for breaking his heart.

Just then on the road, they encountered the patrolman who had not so long ago stopped the Methodist to check for the legitimacy of his cargo.

"Good day sir," said Timothy.

"Good day," replied the patrolman.

"Have you by chance seen a couple runaways on the road, a mulatto girl extremely fair and beautiful and a negro man tall, ebony, and especially strapping?"

"Well, as a matter of fact, there was a white man with a cargo of such down the road yonder, he had about 9 or 10 slaves on his wagon, all he claimed were runaways being returned to their owners. I checked his manifest and it seemed a couple slaves shy, but I thought nothing' of it. If you hurry you might just catch him just about 3 miles north of here."

"Thank you, you just made this search a whole heap easier," replied Albert.

"Indeed, thank you kindly," replied Timothy.

"Just doing my duty sirs. Best of luck to you both," said the patrolman.

"Yah!" shouted Albert with a slap to his horse to take off down the road, Timothy followed suit galloping full speed north.

The adrenalin charged through Timothy's veins transforming his love and passion for SeRina into loathing and disdain. He was furious with himself for allowing her into his head and heart and he would make her suffer for leaving him.

"There, over yonder!" yelled Albert, he spotted the Methodist and his wagon on the dirt road a half a mile or so in the distance.

"Yah, yah!" hollered Timothy pushing his horse to sprint at a feverish pace.

The wind tousled Timothy's hair, his clothes twining to and fro as they galloped faster and faster, hooves pounding on the dirt path and leaving behind a cloud of powdery dust. They were gaining way, the Methodist heard the hooves approaching behind him and slowed the wagon pulling it aside hoping and praying the ensuing parties were to race past him but he wouldn't be so lucky.

"Whoa, Whoa..." said Albert easing his horses pace as they neared the pulled over wagon. Timothy slowed his mare as well and both riders and horses took a moment to gather themselves and catch their breath as they approached the wagon. SeRina had fallen asleep as had Ivory in the back of the wagon, the other slaves that were awake, grew nervous as they heard the hooves approaching.

"You there, what is your business with these slaves?" asked Albert. Timothy, was silent as he circled the wagon with his horse. He spotted SeRina sleeping peacefully on Ivory's shoulder and his rage heightened.

"Here they are!" shouted Timothy startling both Ivory and SeRina awake. Ivory on guard tried to jump to his feet but had forgotten the shackles held him in place.

"Again I say, what business have you with these slaves?" said Albert.

"I discovered these runaways along the road and were returning them to their rightful owner Sir," said the Methodist.

"Ah, well let us make things a little speedier for you, these two belong to me and my father the Abbington's from the Abbington Plantation 12 miles south of here," said Timothy. Seeing him in this light sent a shudder of devastation through SeRina. Her plans of sending for him and living a life together felt displaced and foolish, Ivory was right, she was just another nigger to him *and* his family, property, and nothing more.

"Well, certainly, if you must, you may take the two, but the two only. The others are on my manifest," said the Methodist. He was trying to hold it together and really didn't want to lose any of his precious cargo but rationalized it better to lose 2 than to lose all so cooperated out of obligation to the others. He produced his manifest and Albert and Timothy took turns looking it over. They handed it back to him.

"Fine then, just give us the two, and we'll be on our way," said Albert.

"Yes sir," said the Methodist and he disembarked the wagon walking to the rear of it with keys to the shackles. Ironically he unshackled them and then returned them to enslavement with their master and overseer.

"Good day," said Timothy to the Methodist. The Methodist tipped his hat, returned to his wagon and continued on his way down the dirt road. Ivory and SeRina watched for a while, seeing their freedom disappear just as the wagon had down the road.

"I told you I'd follow you to the ends of the earth and this is how you treat me? Unbelievable," said Timothy to SeRina. "I thought...you know, damn what I thought, come along." He remounted his horse and motioned and reached down for SeRina to mount the back of the horse with him.

"I don't want to be near you. I will walk," said SeRina disgusted at the way he was treating her, she felt a sickness come over her at the thought of being treated as his property.

"Fine, suit yourself. You and your nigger lover can both walk," said Timothy.

"Lover? He isn't my ..." disputed SeRina.

"Shut your filthy mouth," interrupted Timothy. She had been soiled to him by this black man and he wanted nothing further to do with her. Seeing her sleeping on Ivory's shoulder had stepped his resentment up a notch and he wanted her to suffer and experience the agony he was feeling. Little did he know, she was feeling it, to the core of her soul, he had just broken her heart in two.

Albert tied SeRina's hands together and handed the rope to Timothy to pull her behind his horse. He tied Ivory's hands and held his rope as he mounted his horse. SeRina's heart dropped, the rope weighing on her more than any shackle as it was held by the man she had given everything to, her heart, her purity, her sanity, her hope. Timothy was everything she thought she ever wanted, now with no Sam, and no Alice, he was the only glimmer of solace she had found in this place so far away from home. She wished for her father's arms, her mother's encouraging words, the laughter of her friends, the comfort of her home in 2009.

She felt immeasurable sadness settle upon her and tears flowed silently and steadily washing away any hope she had amassed and trading itself for fruitless despair.

Ivory looked at her, his heart breaking for her. Instead of 'told you so's' he wished he could hold her and take away her pain, he hated that she had placed so much stock in Timothy and wished she would see that before her eyes was a man open, willing and able to love her and give pure unbridled devotion, a man who would be proud to call her his very own. Timothy never deserved her, he was a coward, unwilling to abandon his father's expectations to stand on his own two feet and give SeRina the unabashed love she deserved. Ivory wanted to cut the ropes from her hands and hold her. She needed to be held, to be kissed, to be loved, to be protected and he vowed within that he would be the one to do that for her.

Interrupting the heavy silence, Ivory said to SeRina in an undertone as they were pulled behind the horses side-by-side, "I'm sorry for my cruel words earlier today. I wish I could take them back. I pray my simple words ease your broken spirit. In time, God reveals all that is true all that is a sham. In time God will reveal genuine love and heal your heart. You are a strong, beautiful and resilient woman, in time you will accept yourself and embrace the woman he created you to be. Stand firm, dry your tears, walk strong and proud."

Without words, SeRina's eyes gratefully accepted the kind words given to her by Ivory. She lost herself in thought and walked behind the horse the 12 miles back to the plantation. Her legs numb, feet blistered, mouth dry, arms sore, wrists singed from the rubbing of the ropes. She couldn't believe her precious Timothy had treated her this way, but it no longer mattered, she would find a way to escape and this time for good.

CHAPTER THIRTY-SIX

The Tree

Eyes strained from the setting sun's light, SeRina became aware of her whereabouts when she spotted the tree. The massive tree she woke up under when she first arrived to this place and time. It was just as beautiful as she remembered, its leaves now sporting autumn's colors. It was just moments thereafter that they all arrived back to the Abbington Plantation. As they made their way up the familiar road, SeRina looked over at the fields and noticed the harvesting was done, the slaves had plucked every leaf from the now golden fields and now were grading and bundling the leaves in preparation for the tobacco barning process.

Months had passed since she arrived, and she couldn't believe that she was still there. As they approached the big house, Mrs. Abbington was sitting on the porch with Eliza reading a book and looked up for a moment spotting them coming. Lillybird was standing there fanning her Old Henry was serving the ladies a cool glass of lemonade. Mrs. Abbington had an unfamiliar and ireful look on her face, her eyes locked with SeRina's and peered through to her core. Mrs. Abbington sat her book down on the table nearby and slowly stood with her hands folded neatly in front of her.

"Alas my dear, you have arrived. My, they look awful, did you have them walk a long ways?" said Mrs. Abbington to Timothy.

"Yes mother, we found them about 12 miles or so north of here with the old Methodist Reverend from Sharontown. He claimed to be returning them to their rightful owner, but was not at all headed in the right direction," said Timothy sarcastically.

"My, my. Well, it is good that your father set you out after them before they made it too far north. Henry, do take them to get them some water before they pass out from exhaustion," ordered Mrs. Abbington.

"Yes ma'am," replied Henry.

Timothy untied SeRina's hands freeing her to go into the big house. She never looked him in the face and the closeness of him turned her stomach. Albert loosed Ivory's hands as well, and Ivory rubbed his sore wrists then helped SeRina up the stairs to the big house. When he reached the top of the stairs Ivory turned and looked wrathfully at both Albert and Ivory.

"Watch that reckless eyballin' nigger," said Albert. "We don't want another Sam situation."

Ivory broke his stare and walked inside the Big House. He knew if given the chance he would wring both Albert and Timothy's necks for treating SeRina so poorly.

"Eliza, do find something to do with yourself child, I need a word with your brother and Albert.

"But of course mother," said Eliza before going into the house.

"So, it appears we have a little situation. One that requires management before it get's too far out of hand. Apparently, our niggers have all lost their minds, and well, I frankly have grown tired of it. Your father is away doing heaven knows what, so I have decided to take matters into my own hands. It is time to set an example for the others so they understand that we have been a loving and fair Master and Mistress but that our fairness and kindness cannot be mistaken for weakness. Albert, gather all the slaves about, the tree there. Man, woman, and child, every hand, every cook, every mammy, old, young and indifferent. Timothy, go to the barn and fetch the whip, and rope. Make haste, before nightfall. As God is my witness, there will be a lesson learned by these niggers today!"

Meanwhile, Mr. Abbington had arrived at the busy train station to pick up Morris and his bride. The train pulled into the station puffing and screeching to a halt. The passengers disembarked one by one and Mr. Abbington paced in anticipation of his guests.

Milie's announcement was still fresh in his mind, and he was overcome with emotion. What was initially just desire needing to be quenched had turned into unexpected feelings for Millie. He had fallen for her wit, her beauty and had lost desire for his wife. It had been months since he and Mrs. Abbington were intimate. His desires lay elsewhere and Mrs. Abbington had noticed but hadn't complained. Now that the cat was out of the bag, Massa Abbington dreaded facing the Misses upon his return. He nervously paced, his mind playing through one scenario after another on how he would handle things upon his return.

"Mr. Abbington, Mr. Abbington, oh there you are," said Alice approaching with a smile.

"Why hello there, aren't you as beautiful as ever, replied Mr. Abbington, kissing her hand.

"Vincent, how are you sir?" asked Morris.

"Fine, fine indeed. And what's this I see? It appears there is a bit more to you this time than the last," said Mr. Abbington looking at Alice's pregnant belly. She looked to be very far along.

"Why yes, indeed, we are so excited to be expecting. I'm hoping for a boy," said Morris.

"And, well, I'm just hoping for a healthy little one be it boy or girl. Indeed a healthy child, bright and clever, just like his father," said Alice beaming.

"We were hoping that we could stay here until our child is born. We will then be looking to purchase some land nearby and start our family here," said Morris.

"But of course my boy, you are always welcome. If my inklings suit me right, I predict it's a boy. The Misses will be delighted to know you all are coming and that we will soon have a little lad running about," said Mr. Abbington smiling earnestly and thinking to himself there would soon be TWO little ones running about the big house. "Come along now, let's make haste, it looks as if it may rain."

They made their way to the horse drawn carriage and mounted making their way back to the plantation in high-style with warmhearted conversation.

She was unraveling... Mrs. Abbington had clearly lost her marbles. After having Albert gather all the slaves around the big tree, she had all the house slaves come out to watch as she ordered Timothy to beat Ivory 20 lashes for running away and 5 for the reckless eyeballing incident. Timothy did as he was asked without hesitation unleashing all his anger and heartbreak with every lash. Ivory stood tall firm and rigid tied to the tree never a whimper, only a wince. He took his 25 lashes was untied and with weak legs was ordered to remain standing to watch the barbarism continue. It was SeRina's turn.

"Do it quickly without hesitation!" ordered Mrs. Abbington to Timothy.

"Mother, must I. Please can Albert do it?"

"You know full well why *you* must do it. So carry on, and do it with haste!" ordered Mrs. Abbington.

Timothy did as he was told, at first half-heartedly then as the tears flowed he increased the intensity of his lashes. Ivory looked at him with a menacing gaze that let him know that should he ever get the opportunity to return the favor, that he would without hesitation. At the 15th lash, Timothy became overcome with tears and dropped the whip.

"Mother, I can't, I just can't."

"You can, and you will. She is an animal, a filthy animal, you lay with her demeaning yourself and humiliating our family, you will beat her and beat her well. Do it! Do it now!" screamed Mrs. Abbington.

Timothy refused and fell to his knees sobbing.

"Finish it Albert!" ordered Mrs. Abbington. "I've never been more disappointed in you Timothy than I am right now!"

Albert obliged with lashes 16, 17, 18, 19, and 20 and added a couple more just because. SeRina had long passed out from the pain and was tied lifeless to the tree. Timothy went to her and untied her and she fell in his arms the warmth of her blood running through his fingers. He pulled her close and cried silently into her neck.

"Take her to the barn with the rest of the animals," said Mrs. Abbington.

Timothy obliged, and took her in his arms to the barn. His heart was heavy with guilt. He didn't want to feel anything anymore but had nothing to numb his emotions so he let the tears flow. He had destroyed the one woman he loved, he was ashamed and felt like a corrupt, heartless failure and a coward. Aunt Tempie had been watching along with all the others and unbeknownst to him had followed him back to the barn. Without warning, she put her hand on his shoulder as he lay SeRina on a bed of hay.

"I takes care of her now Massa Timothy," said Aunt Tempie. She hadn't talked to SeRina since the loss of her beloved Sam, and although she had some resentment toward SeRina for causing his death, she couldn't help but feel sorry for her as she lay there lifeless and bloodied.

Timothy kissed SeRina on the forehead, stood and walked over to the barn door looking out, and then turned back to Aunt Tempie.

"Take care of her. Tell her I'm sorry, I'm so sorry about all of it."

"She knows Massa Timothy, she knowed you love her, this just ain't the time for ya'lls kind of lovin' but maybe someday," said Aunt Tempie.

"Perhaps ..." he replied.

Just then Ivory walked into the barn and stared Timothy down. No words needed to be said, Timothy knew he had lost her forever.

"You don' did enough damage, get on out of here, I see to it she taken care of." Ivory had no regard to Timothy's power. In that moment, they weren't slave and master, they were simply two men, standing in love with the same woman.

Timothy couldn't move. His heavy heart and the burden of guilt weighed down upon his feet making them feel anchored to the floor. Ivory turned from Timothy and rushed to SeRina's side. He scooped her up and cradled her in his arms kissing her and saying a silent prayer. Tears welled in his eyes, from both his pain and the pain inflicted upon her. Aunt Tempie left to fetch the salve and some rags to clean SeRina and Ivory's wounds and passed Timothy with lowered eyes.

Timothy stood and watched Ivory hold the woman he loved and turned and walked out of the barn, defeated, heartbroken and guilt-ridden. Once he closed the door behind him, he turned to make his way toward the big house. What Timothy saw in the tree obliterated every ounce of normalcy of the brutality surrounding him, and took the breath clean from his lungs. His knees gave way, and he dropped to them right there in the middle of the road, mouth gaping, tears flowing, heartbroken and in complete and utter disbelief.

"The ride was quite pleasant. Thank you again for your hospitality Mr. Abbington," said Alice politely as they pulled up to the Big House.

"Don't mention it," said Mr. Abbington with a nervous smile, tension mounting in anticipation of facing Mrs. Abbington after Millie's announcement.

"That was indeed a mighty kind gesture sir, we are most thankful," said Morris to Mr. Abbington. Remember your manners and the things I told you," said Morris to Alice with a freezing glance. He would not be embarrassed by her acting like 'one of them' again.

"What is that there?" asked Alice.

"Perhaps Millie decided to be creative with hanging out the laundry this time," joked Massa Abbington. He was anxious to get Millie alone and have a talk with her about her announcement with the Misses amongst other things. "Let us get a closer look." After rounding the wagon, his smile quickly faded into disbelief. Thunder rolled, and rain began to fall. Through the falling rain, here in the tree wearing a beautiful gown which flowed with the breeze of the storm, was his beautiful Millie; suspended and swinging in the wind from the boughs of the tree like a pendulum.

CHAPTER THIRTY-SEVEN

The Arrival

Weeks had passed since the untimely arrival of Morris and Alice to the Abbington plantation. Lillybird and SeRina were both now in the big house acting in place of Millie. SeRina had healed on the outside but was still broken from the prior weeks' events. She missed Millie and Sam tremendously and wished for the life of her there was something she could do to bring them both back. She even wondered if somehow the watch could turn back the hands of time just enough to undo their deaths but hadn't seen the watch since Albert nabbed it the day he killed Big Sam.

Timothy had tried time and time again to apologize to her but to no avail. The damage was done. It was over.

She found solace in her occasional meetings and conversations with Alice which had become fewer and fewer as Alice had neared her due date. Alice had changed and it became increasingly difficult to get a word in with her, she was so caught up in the pretense of being the perfectly convincing white lady that SeRina's plight had eluded her thoughts.

That particular day was just as the others had been. SeRina had awoke to the sound of the rooster crowing at the crack of dawn, she had dreadfully made her way from her bed in the attic to the lantern, and continued her way outdoors to the privy hole and done her business while holding her breath to avoid the stench. When SeRina returned to the big house, Alice, Eliza, Leslye and Mrs. Abbington were all sitting in the parlor having a chat.

"SeRina, dear, please fetch us all some tea and cakes," asked Mrs. Abbington.

"Oh, yes tea sounds marvelous." co-signed Alice. Now, being ordered around by Mrs. Abbington was one thing, but having Alice chime in, got under SeRina's skin for obvious reasons.

"Sure, no problem," said SeRina sarcastically.

"I think she be forgettin' she ain't even white," said Lillybird, as SeRina rounded the corner to the kitchen.

"Hmm, somebody ought to remind her and knock her down a peg or two!" replied SeRina. She and Lillybird laughed. It was nice working with Lillybird. Yes, it was awkward at first because of Big Sam's death, but as time progressed they had grown fond of one another. It was a bit warm in the kitchen from all the baking that had gone on so SeRina opened the window to let in some fresh air. A couple of houseflies used the open window as their opportunity to come in and have a taste of the cakes cooling and Lillybird popped them dead with a rag.

After steeping the tea SeRina poured into the decorative kettle and trayed the saucers and teacups.

"Hold on now, I think you forgot the special ingredient," said LillyBird and she squished the two flies and added them into the tea kettle.

"Oh my God, I can't believe you just did that!" said SeRina.

"You best believe it," said Lillybird and the two girls cracked up laughing.

"OK, pull it together, shh, we don't want them to suspect anything."

"Yes ma'am, I be quiet as a church mouse," said Lillybird still giggling. The girls took a moment to gather themselves. SeRina led with the tea kettle and trayed saucers and Lillybird followed behind her with the assortment of pastries.

"Rumor has it that there is a black woman who married a white man and who has been parading around passing for white over in Sharontown. Seems everyone ought to be able to tell, how on God's green earth could someone get away with such a thing?" said Mrs. Abbington.

"Not quite sure how one could manage," replied Alice.

SeRina placed a saucer and teacup and poured a cup for Alice with a steely-eyed glance that screamed 'YEA RIGHT!'

"Your tea ladies..." said SeRina as she served each lady a cup of tea. SeRina and Lillybird could barely contain their giggles as they exchanged mischievous glances as the ladies all drank their tea. SeRina sat the tray down on the table in case anyone wanted refills.

The ladies made small talk about the state of politics, then started the usual fussing over Alice and the baby to be.

"Your little one will be here any day now. I bet you can barely contain your excitement," said Eliza tea in hand.

"Indeed, Morris and I have been quite beside ourselves of late," said Alice sipping her tea and making eyes back at SeRina. SeRina and Lillybird about lost it when Alice and Eliza both drank a sip at once.

"I can only imagine. I can't wait for Timothy and me to be married so we may start a family of our own," said Leslye, intentionally timing her statement with SeRina's arrival. SeRina hoped she would choke on her tea.

"A double wedding, wouldn't that be divine," said Eliza exuberantly.

"Absolutely splendid idea!" exclaimed Mrs. Abbington.

SeRina and Lillybird left the parlor returning to the kitchen.

"She just tryin' to get under your skin, Timothy still love you not her," said Lillybird.

"Doesn't matter, I gave up on him a long time ago," said SeRina.

"Well, a lil' birdy told me that you may have your sights set on

another fella anyhow. One a might darker than Timothy."
"Well, that lil' birdy might be right," said SeRina. She had grown quite fond of Ivory since they were recaptured.

"Ahhhhhh, there's a fly in my tea!" shrieked Alice jumping to her feet much too quickly to be 9-months pregnant.

CRASH! Just then, a loud crashing noise came from the room which sent SeRina and Lillybird running back into the parlor. When they entered, Alice was on the floor with a pool of amniotic fluid beneath her.

"Quick, Lillybird, have Timothy fetch the Doctor, Alice's water has let down!" said Mrs. Abbington.

"Yes ma'am," said Lillybird. She quickly ran out of the front door down the dirt road to find Timothy as she was told.

"SeRina, help Alice up to bed," ordered Mrs. Abbington.

"Yes ma'am," said SeRina. She helped Alice to her feet and their eyes met, this time with softer glances. For the first time, Mrs. Abbington looked at the two of them noticing the uncanny resemblance and the fact that Alice's skin was only a shade or two lighter from SeRina's. It didn't set well with her at all. She followed the two up the stairs to the guest room and sat inside in anticipation of the Doctor's arrival.

SeRina and Alice chatted familiarly, SeRina saying kind and encouraging words to ease Alice through the pains of labor.

"My father back home is a doctor. The way he coaches women through childbirth is by having them to breathe slow and steady like this..." SeRina demonstrated breathing and Alice mimicked her desperate for any help she could get to take the discomfort away as her labor pains had grown more and more intense.

Mrs. Abbington sat in a chair in the corner of the room, never taking her eyes off of the two of them and her suspicions started to grow into wild imaginative assumptions as she closely observed the all too familiar ladies who looked nearly identical.

The Doctor arrived within the hour and rushed to Alice's bedside. She was in active labor and the baby was well on the way.

"Hello, SeRina. Good to see you faring so well," said the Doctor to Mrs. Abbington's surprise. She wondered how the doctor knew SeRina.

SeRina excused herself upon his arrival stepping into the hallway and encountered Morris pacing nervously just outside the doorway.

"How is she?" asked Morris.

"She will be fine, the doctor is helping her now. You will be a father before you know it!" said SeRina.

"I know, that's what I'm afraid of," said Morris.

"I'm sure she will be fine, just pray," said SeRina. She shocked herself with this statement. Before she became lodged in this day and time, she rarely if ever prayed or even thought of God for that matter. But now, more and more, prayer had become part of her daily routine and coping mechanism. She felt inspired by both Ivory and Pastor Edward's words and had to her own surprise, taken them to heart.

She and Ivory had seen each other only on occasion since the day they were recaptured. He had taken care of her alongside Aunt Tempie caring for her day and night until she was well again despite his own injuries. Whenever their paths crossed, he was always kind and genuine. Although it was obvious he was interested in her based upon the words he said to her when they were recaptured, he was patiently waiting on her to see that the love she sought was right before her, so kept his distance.

More and more lately her conscious screamed for her to stop avoiding him and instead to find him and tell him she had been foolish for ignoring him. She wanted to tell someone the news of Alice's baby, so used that as an excuse to make her way out to the fields to catch a glimpse of him preparing the seedbeds for the coming crop and perhaps tell him how she was feeling.

No time like the present... she said to herself and decided to go see Ivory while the household was all up in arms and busy with the birth of Alice's baby.

SeRina rounded the back of the big house and took out running, making her way to the dirt path that led to the fields where she knew she would find Ivory.

"Hey there, SeRina. What's the hurry? Where you off to?" said a familiar voice from behind her. She turned to see Timothy standing there and found herself speechless.

"You look so beautiful today," said Timothy.

He took a few more steps near her and she froze not knowing if she should run to or from him. She didn't know who he was anymore since he had beaten her and treated her so savagely. Part of her still loved him and always would, but the other part of her was finally reconciling who she was and trying to own that.

"Thank you," she said and turned to walk away carefully and slowly, not knowing what he was capable of. He caught her by her arm and spun her back around to face him pulling her close to him with a firm grip.

"SeRina, please, darling, I'm so sorry, I love you."

She pushed away," Timothy, please let me go! You are hurting me. Don't you get it? You can't undo the things that you did to me. You broke me, you took everything from me... everything I thought I ever wanted, but that's not who I am anymore. So let me go!" she said as she broke free from his grasp.

"SeRina please, let me explain, he said pulling her to him again.

"Don't touch me ever again!" she said firmly standing her ground. When he reached for her again, she slapped him with all her strength and ran as fast as her legs would carry her towards the fields. Tears flowed uncontrollably the wind blowing her curls in her face, her heart racing as her feet pounded leaving a cloud of dust behind her. Timothy stood there broken as his love ran from him into the distance.

Ivory was out in the field breaking the soil with a heavy hand plow preparing it for seeding when he looked up and saw her. She was even more beautiful than he remembered. She stopped as their eyes met panting for breath. Tears still flowed but she smiled through them as she finally was right where she belonged. The sun seemed to radiate from her, her smile beaming and resplendent in its light. She simply took his breath away. He put down the plow and walked toward her slow at first, pace building to match the pace of his heart. SeRina thought he had never looked more amazing. This strapping and powerful man had said the most graceful and delicate words to her that willed her to get through her heartbreak. His words echoed in her mind and warmed her heart...

In time God will reveal genuine love and heal your heart. You are a strong, beautiful and resilient woman, in time you will accept yourself and embrace the woman he created you to be. Stand firm, dry your tears, walk strong and proud ...

And so she did, she walked toward him stronger than before, resolved to find the love that God had in store for her in the most unlikely of places. When at last they met at the edge of the field a gust of wind inched her even closer to him, their eyes and hearts meeting in a moment of all-encompassing understanding and harmony. He lowered his lips to hers and kissed her as if he had waited his entire life to do just that. She gave into its fervor forgetting place and time and losing herself in the safety of his arms.

CHAPTER THIRTY-EIGHT

Bait

The cord was severed on the infant as was the connection between Alice, Morris and Mrs. Abbington. The baby boy was beautiful no doubt with a head full of ebony curls, but his hue was caramel and golden serving as evidence of Alice's unspoken truth about her heritage. The doctor washed and blanketed the baby and handed the infant to his mother. Upon exiting he grimaced knowing that there were some heavy conversations to be had in his absence.

"I knew it!" exclaimed Mrs. Abbington.

"You knew?" asked Morris.

"Yes, she looks identical to SeRina, then it occurred to me that she knows everyone a bit too well for my taste, so I snooped around and I noticed her talking to old Aunt Tempie as if she were family. Turns out she is related to the nigger," said Mrs. Abbington. "Turns out your wife has been all the talk. She's the Sharontown negra that's been runnin' round passing for white!"

"I'm sorry, I loved her before I knew," said Morris tearfully disappointed. The secret was out and there would be no more pretenses.

"It's fine. Your secret is safe with me, now what are we to do with the blasted animal."

"My son?" asked Morris.

"He's not your son, he is an animal! She is a nigger! Haven't you noticed how much she looks like SeRina? They are practically identical. It took me seeing them side by side to really notice. Something is definitely not adding up. Let me get this through to you. You listen and you listen well, you absolutely will not disgrace our family with such a scandal. Now if we get rid of the baby you can carry on with your marriage and just be certain that you do not have any other children. Having a nigger in our family is shameful and I simply will not allow it. Do you want to keep your dirty little secret or don't you?" demanded Mrs. Abbington

"I do," replied Morris shamefully looking over at his unsuspecting wife. She had fallen asleep with the baby in her arms.

"Good. That's my boy, now, go get Albert, tell him your plight and I'm certain he will know what to do with the dreadful thing."

"Indeed," said Morris, head hung low he left the room stopping momentarily to look over at Alice sleeping peacefully holding his son.

After his departure, Mrs. Abbington paced back and forth in the room playing out scenarios of how to dispose of the infant. She had heard rumors from a relative in Florida that they would throw unwanted black babies to the swamps tied by ropes to bait alligators which they captured for the making of purses, shoes and the like and so she decided to throw the piccaninny to the 'gators in the Great Dismal Swamp. They could have a funeral for the baby with an empty casket saying it had died at birth and none would be the wiser.

By the time Albert had returned, the plan was solid, and he was told to execute it. Just as he was taking the baby from Alice's arms she awoke. Her husband Morris stood sniffling and cowering in the corner of the room without uttering a word.

"What, wait, Albert, what are you doing with my baby?" said Alice. She looked at her son for the first time seeing his complexion and gasped in disbelief. He was the most beautiful infant she had ever seen his curls framing his face, his cheeks a golden rose hue. She held him so tight that he awoke and started to cry as Albert snatched him from her arms.

"This here baby bout to be alligator bait. If'n I was them I'd throw you to the gators too for lyin' bout being a nigger!" said Albert as he exited the door carrying off the baby boy.

"Now, there, there child, it was either the baby or you," said Mrs. Abbington. "You will not disgrace this family, so this is what's best, I'm sure you understand," said Mrs. Abbington as she too exited the room. Morris had no words, so left behind Mrs. Abbington not making eye contact with Alice.

"No, not my baby, Morris, please, he's your son! Please, please, don't do this!" she screamed to no avail as the door closed. She was too weak to run after them, she was too broken to continue screaming. They had ripped her child from her arms without a second thought just for the color of his skin and she could do nothing about it. She glanced over at the nightstand and saw the knife the doctor used to sever the umbilical cord and she reached for it.

"God forgive me..." she said before slicing the soft flesh of her wrists. The blood rushed from her wrists staining the white quilt, she watched it and felt her body go from warm to cold and death quieted her sobs into a dark silence.

"Just the person I've been lookin' for," said Albert to Ivory as he approached him holding the baby. Ivory was standing near the edge of the field with SeRina's hand in his.

SeRina looked over to see Albert holding Alice's baby and wondered what he was doing with him. She knew he had to be up to no good.

"The Missus has a job for you Ivory," said Albert.

"What job?"

"Well, seems as though dem gators down in the swamp need a feeding," said Albert.

"What? What are you talking about?"

"Rumor has it them gators love them some pickaninny meat," said Albert laughing maniacally. "Dem gators gonna snatch this lil' nigger right on up and you going to be the one to feed him to 'em!"

"I will do no such thing, you tell the Misses I ain't no baby killer. No sir, I can't kill no baby," said Ivory.

"I've got my share of repenting to do to the Lord, but killing babies, now that's where even I draw the line."

"I can't do it I say!" said Ivory.

"You can and you will," said Albert shifting the baby one side and pulling his pistol and pointing it at Ivory.

"Don't shoot! I'll do it, I'll do it, said SeRina to Albert's surprise.

"You will, will you. Boy, what kind of hex you don' put on dis gal, got her ready to kill a baby to save her man!" said Albert laughing.

"We will both go!" said Ivory not wanting Albert to have a moment alone with SeRina.

"Suit yourself," said Albert handing SeRina the baby and poking the gun in Ivory's back. "Now I've got myself a lil' insurance."

"Go on down to the swamp you know how to get there," said Albert. As they turned from the field and made their way down the dirt road, the other slaves stood reactionless and watched them pass by. They made their way to the garden behind Grandpa George's house and the baby began to fuss from hunger.

"Shut that thing up!" said Albert. The baby continued to cry, missing the warmth of his mother and in hunger as he hadn't yet had a chance to nurse.

"Shh, it's okay," said SeRina to soothe the baby. She was rocking him on her shoulder, holding him close. She was praying that Ivory would come up with a way for them to save the baby. She was grateful that he was with her as they entered the woods behind Grandpa George's house and walked through the all too familiar clearing down the hidden path to the swamp.

"Don't you go gettin' no ideas in that pretty little head of yours!" said Albert as SeRina's pace quickened in front of him. "I got this pistol in your man's back and I ain't 'afraid to pull the trigger if you get to runnin' with that there baby."

SeRina crunched through the dried leaves down to the banks of the swamp. It was a little cooler than usual which she hoped would keep the alligators at bay. The water near the banks of the swamp wasn't very deep so she was thinking if they dropped the baby in the shallow part of the water that at least he would be easy to rescue.

"Give Ivory the baby," said Albert.

SeRina obliged. Albert was facing SeRina and Ivory, gun drawn, locked, loaded and ready to fire if they made any fast moves.

"Ivory, go on and throw the baby in," said Albert.

"I told you I ain't no baby killer, you wants this baby to drown you gwine' do it yourself," replied Ivory.

"Is that right, see I'm bout sick of you niggers thinkin' you have a say in the matter. I tell you what," he said, "it's obvious you don't realize I have the upper hand in this situation." He dug in his pocket pulling out Timothy's watch and popping the face open with his thumb. "Way I see it you have ten seconds to do what I said or SeRina's gonna catch one of these bullets and go for a lil' swim in this here swamp with the baby. Ten, nine, eight ..." he started counting down, SeRina looked at Ivory and looked at her lost and not knowing what to do, not wanting Albert to harm the baby but not wanting her to be harmed either. One! The gun fired just as a sharp blow hit Albert over the head. It was Grandpa George. The bullet grazed SeRina in the shoulder and she and the baby both fell into the swamp, the water taking them both away with the current. SeRina gasped for air and tried to stay afloat holding on to the baby.

"Help, help!" yelled SeRina.

Ivory dived in to her rescue and caught up with her and the baby. The water rushed over them both and they were both mortified to come face to face with a huge gator swimming in their direction.

"Quick, you and the baby head for the shore," said Ivory.

"No, I won't leave you," said SeRina.

"Go on now, the gator will come after me, and I can handle him better than you holdin' a baby, so go!"

SeRina swam with the infant as fast as she could with one arm toward the shore. The gator was just feet from Ivory and Ivory found himself struggling to stay afloat his clothes and boots weighing him down. He looked back and forth, searching the water for something he could use as a weapon or barrier between him and the gator. The gator was now just inches away and opened his mighty jaws to tear into Ivory when out of nowhere three shots were fired.

POW, POW, POW.

Just then, SeRina and the baby made it to the shore where Grandpa George stood holding Albert's gun. He wasn't sure if he had hit the gator or Ivory as they both had disappeared beneath the surface.

"Oh, no, Ivory! Ivory!" screamed SeRina fearing the worst.

"Don't fret, he's a strong man, that alligator has a fight on his hands." Reassured Grandpa George surveying the water gun in hand to see if another shot was needed.

"SeRina, SeRina, yelled Ivory. He had resurfaced and was swimming toward the shore against the current.

"Ivory, over here!" yelled SeRina, hoping he would swim in their direction.

"Hurry SeRina, put the baby down for a moment and help me with Albert," said Grandpa George.

SeRina sat the baby down in his blanket on a soft patch of grass and grabbed hold of Albert's feet. He was out cold, if not dead, and was bleeding profusely from the skull where Grandpa George had struck him. They together grabbed him, one by the feet the other by the arms and threw him into the swamp. His body made a big splash distracting the alligator from Ivory long enough for him to make it to shore. Moments later, the gator pulled Albert's body underwater and both disappeared from site.

Ivory climbed up the rocks to shore and SeRina and Grandpa George helped him up. When he made it to his feet, Grandpa George hugged them both with all the might of his 75-year old body.

The three of them walked over to the patch of grass where the baby was laying and next to the child was the pool of blood where Albert was laying and the watch which he had dropped when he was struck by Grandpa George.

Grandpa George picked up the watch, tucked it away in his pocket and said, "Go, go now quietly to the cookhouse and wait for me there."

And so Ivory scooped up the infant and they ran as fast as they could back up the bank to the dirt path, through the clearing and the garden back down the dirt road to the cookhouse. There they knocked and waited patiently for Aunt Tempie to open the door. When she saw SeRina bloodied at the shoulder and Ivory carrying the baby, she hurried them in quietly closing the door behind them. They played back the events to her word for word.

Just then Lillybird arrived from the big house. She was rattled, screaming, crying and banging on the door. Aunt Tempie swung the door open.

"Lillybird, what's the matter child?" said Aunt Tempie.

"Momma, Momma!" she said as she burst through the front door wrapping her arms around Tempie.

"What is it child?" asked Aunt Tempie.

"It's Alice, she dead!" said Lillybird.

"Oh, heavens no," said Aunt Tempie collapsing into her rocking chair. "What is goin' on around here, nothing but death and misery all around? Not my sweet Alice Faith, God, not my Alice too," said

Aunt Tempie.

Oh my God, poor Alice, thought SeRina, she wished she had stayed behind to be by her side once she had the baby instead of leaving but then again if she hadn't the baby might not be alive.

Ivory rubbed his temples and then let his hand glide over his face to his chin where it rested, he then shook his head, walked over to the window and looked out, then turned back to the women.

"Look if we run and take the baby with us, no one will hurt the baby. Besides I can't stay here, when they find Albert dead, they won't suspect Grandpa George, they will suspect me. I will take the baby and go."

"Take me with you," said SeRina.

"It's too dangerous, and you're hurt."

"I can help care for the baby," SeRina pleaded, walking over to him and putting her hand on his shoulder. "Let me go with you please, Ivory."

"You know what that means," said Ivory. "No more plans of passin' for white. Are you sure that's what you want?"

"Yes," Said SeRina.

Alright," said Ivory, conceding and a bit relieved that she wanted to join him.

There was a knock at the door. SeRina went to the corner of the cookhouse behind Aunt Tempie's chair holding the baby close to her and Aunt Tempie got up from her chair motioning Ivory to go with them into the corner. They were all afraid of who it may be.

"Who's there?" asked Aunt Tempie.

"George and Pastor Edwards," answered the voice.

She opened the door and Grandpa George entered holding some rolled up papers. Pastor Edwards entered behind him, removing his hat out of respect for the ladies present.

"I knew someday these would come in handy again," said Grandpa George as he walked over to the dining table and sat down opening the scrolled papers and revealing that they were maps of the roads of all the major cities of the South. He had kept the maps from his days as a traveling English salesman, selling his watches and carvings across the country before he was captured and sold into slavery.

"SeRina, Ivory, come here," he said. "These maps will lead you to your freedom. Guard them with your lives. There are maps here of every city I traveled to during my time on the road as a salesman. They are many years old but should guide you to the North once you make it past the state line. For tonight, Pastor Edwards will escort you to the Methodist Reverend Michael Kenneth's home where you may stay until morning. Thereafter, he will escort you as far as he can and provide you with wagon and horses and supplies for you and the baby for you to make it north."

"Before I go, I want you to have this SeRina," he said, placing the watch in her hands. "This watch was created out of love and I give it to you in love, I leave you with this reminder that time is precious and not to be taken for granted and the poignant but simplistic words of William Shakespeare 'Time is very slow for those who wait. Very fast for those who are scared, very long for those who lament.

Very short for those who celebrate. But for those who love, time is eternal.' May God be with you and may you find your way home in time."

SeRina wondered how he knew she was lost in time. But it didn't matter. She felt so connected to this man she knew she was his blood she could feel it in her very soul. She hugged him tightly, tears welling in her eyes feeling finally connected to the family she had always hoped to know.

Grandpa George shook Ivory's hand, gave Lillybird a squeeze, and kissed Aunt Tempie on both cheeks as Englishmen do.

"Farewell on your journey," said Grandpa George before leaving the cookhouse.

"What is the baby's name?" asked Lillybird.

"Well, Lillybird, I think we should call him Little Sam," said SeRina with tears in her eyes as she walked over to Ivory and looked down at the beautiful baby boy in his arms.

"I think that's a fine name," said Aunt Tempie and she walked over taking Lillybird by the hand over to SeRina and Ivory for a group hug.

"Ouch," said SeRina, her shoulder tender from the bullet graze.

"Now, let's see bout dat shoulder," said Aunt Tempie. She was such a nurturer, always bringing the life back into everyone around her. And so she patched SeRina up to get her ready for the perilous journey ahead.

Once SeRina was patched up she walked over to Lillybird who was sulking in the corner.

"Lillybird, I think I'm going to miss you most of all," said SeRina. "You are like the little sister I always wished for."

"Really, dat's the nicest thing anybody ever said to me," said Lillybird and she threw her arms around SeRina, forgetting about her shoulder.

"OUCH!"

"Sorry," said Lillybird.

"That's OK. I love you anyway. Big mouth and all. Oh, I have something for you. Look under... Big Sam's bed over there." It was still hard for SeRina to say his name.

Lillybird got up and walked over bending down to pull out the package from under her brother's bed. It was the dress and the note and $50 that Alice had left for SeRina.

"You keep it. I won't be needing it where I'm going," said SeRina.

Lillybird's eyes grew big as saucers as they tended to do when she felt excited.

"Thank you so much! It's the most beautiful dress I ever seen!" Lillybird caught herself just before hugging SeRina and gave her a kiss on the cheek instead.

"Now, you keep quiet about that money, put it away, you will need it someday," said SeRina.

"Quiet as a church mouse," said Lillybird, tears flowing down her shiny brown cheeks.

Aunt Tempie was so happy to see SeRina letting go of the idea of passing and not just embracing who she really was that she felt tears of joy warm her cheeks. "I'm gon' miss you SeRina. You will always have a special place here in my heart no matter where you go. Now, ya'll be safe, and here's some vittles for the road. Now these here, these called hushpuppies. If'n they set the dogs after you, throw 'em way out yonder in the field to get them off your scent and hush dem puppies!" She laughed as she wrapped the last of the hushpuppies and placed them in a carrying basket and bid SeRina, Ivory, Pastor Edwards and precious Little Sam farewell.

CHAPTER THIRTY-NINE

New Beginnings

The sun had set, and the evening was crisp and cooler than usual. After an hour walk, mostly through woods off the beaten path led by Pastor Edwards, they finally arrived to the Methodist's home. It was a lovely two story on a lot of sprawling beautiful rolling hills. The house sat perfectly and neatly on a small hill with a cobblestone walkway and exuded a golden light that spoke of warmth and comfort to SeRina and Ivory. After a special knock, the Methodist appeared with a smiling and adoring wife at the door and invited in SeRina and Ivory and Little Sam, who bid farewell to Pastor Edwards.

"Hello and welcome, you must be exhausted," said the Methodist's wife. Oh and what a precious little one, you look so young, is he yours?"

"Yes," Ivory and SeRina said in accidental union.

"He is ours now..." answered SeRina, "His mother didn't make it."

"Oh, I'm so sorry to hear that," said the Methodist's wife.

"Do you have milk for him and a bottle? He hasn't eaten," said SeRina.

"I have just the thing," said the Methodist's wife and she took SeRina and the baby to the kitchen to make him a bottle of milk.

"I didn't fancy I'd see the two of you again," said the Methodist.

"Life has a funny way of comin' back around, just in time," said Ivory.

"Just in time..." echoed the Methodist. "Well, it isn't much but we have a room in back with a fireplace where you all can sleep for the night, it will be warm and comfortable until we get on the road tomorrow morn'," said the Methodist.

"Please, won't you join us for dinner?" asked the Methodist's wife inviting them to all take their seat at the table. It was the first time Ivory had ever sat at a table with white people and ate a meal and he was obviously uncomfortable.

"It's alright, here we are all brothers and sisters," said the Methodist placing his hand on Ivory's shoulder and pulling out a chair for him to sit. Ivory obliged and sat uncomfortably at first but his discomfort dwindled into warmhearted and genuine conversation and fear and apprehension waned and morphed into a fullness of mind, heart, spirit, and belly.

The Methodist's were the most genuine white people SeRina had encountered in this day and time and she felt at home, happy and worry free in their home. She found herself laughing and enjoying their company and Ivory's company and lost complete track of time.

When the meal was over she stood and mechanically began to clean up after everyone and the Misses, stopped her. "My dear, you don't have to do that here, you are *my* guest, go, take the baby and rest, I can take care of the cleaning."

SeRina's eyes filled with tears and she hugged the woman and held on longer than she ordinarily would. She scooped up baby Sam and took him into the back room that they had prepared for her and Ivory.

"I could get used to this," said Ivory. "This is livin'."

"Funny, when I lived this way every day, I took it for granted, not appreciating simple freedoms, not appreciating family, warmth, love, and peace of mind, now it's all I can think about. Everything else that I thought mattered doesn't, if I don't have those simple things," said SeRina. She was holding Little Sam and feeding him, he was so handsome and had drifted off to sleep in her arms.

"Can I hold him?" asked Ivory, reaching his arms out to hold baby Sam.

"Sure," said SeRina handing him the infant.

"He is a handsome lil' Devil. Funny, he looks somewhat like you," said Ivory smiling that gorgeous smile. SeRina loved the way little Sam looked in his giant arms. She felt herself getting used to the idea of them being a family.

Ivory sat down on the makeshift bed and rocked and hummed an unfamiliar lullaby to the baby. SeRina walked over and sat next to him laying her head back on his chest and resting her arm across him and the infant. And there she lay, holding the golden timepiece in her hands and watching the minutes tick away. The ticking lulled Ivory to sleep with both she and baby Sam in his arms.

Laying there, SeRina realized that in this moment she was happiest she had been since she arrived to this day and time and that everything she thought mattered, never did. Her life had somehow unexpectedly become interwoven with this baby and this man and she was finally alright with abandoning the idea of running and pretending to be a white woman just to get by. Suddenly, the idea of being with Ivory and baby Sam felt warm, inviting and embraceable. At that moment, the thought of being in her skin as a black woman didn't feel so foreign and intolerable.

The soreness of her feet and legs was relieved by the makeshift bed and before she knew it, she had slipped off into slumber lulled asleep by the ticking of the timepiece.

CHAPTER FORTY

In an Instant

The warmth of the sun warmed SeRina's cheeks as she slept and lured her into a dream so real she could reach out and touch it. She was in a beautiful meadow at a house of their own, out back hanging a basket of laundry. Little Sammy was about 3 years old in her dream, and she was expecting another child of her own. He peek-a-booed and giggled, darting in and out of the sheets she was hanging which blew in the breeze. Ivory sat on the porch steps nodded off with his hat over his eyes and she looked over at him with a loving glance. Suddenly, a pair of men's boots appeared beneath the last sheet she hung and she dropped the clothes pins and gasped. Little

Sammy ran to wake his father and there before SeRina's eyes stood Timothy, whip in hand. She turned to run and he chased her wildly through the wildflowers. Ivory awoke from his nap hearing her screams and ran into the pathway calling for SeRina to stop running, and Timothy shot him straight through the heart.

Not him too? In an instant, he was gone, the man she had finally grown to love, who had been true to her and who had her back from the very first encounter when she arrived in this time and place. The ponderings of "how" no longer mattered. Despite how she tried to rationalize her presence in 1859, the method of which she got there eluded her. She suddenly felt a sharp pain in her wrist, then in her neck, then in her back, then there was a blinding white light that flooded in. A light much too bright to be the dawning sun.

"No, Ivory, I'm sorry, I love you, I want to be here with you, I accept who I am, I don't want to pass, I want us, I want our life together!" she screamed. "Please, no, don't leave me here, please." She agonized over the thought of his demise, her breath quickened her heart raced and then she was snatched back into reality when in the distance she heard the baby crying. It was baby Sam. After a sharp pain to the chest she fully awoke, breathless, tears still in her eyes.

Ivory was still laying there, the baby was awake fussing and squirming, and she was still holding the watch. The tear that had wedged itself in the corner of her eye escaped falling on the face of the watch which she must have left open as she slept.

DRIP.

THUD.

She fell to the ground, or at least she thought. She felt herself twirl uncontrollably and then reopened her eyes.

The incredible DIZZYNESS sent everything around her twirling uncontrollably.

Had she lost her mind? She was there in a room surrounded by the voices of ones she loved... she swore she had just been inside the home of the Methodist family, how was she here in this place. What was this place? Had she died? Was this heaven? Was this all a bad dream? The light blurred the faces and there were the voices again... those familiar but haunting voices. It was her mother, Darrene, she heard her clear as day, why was she crying? How was she even here? She wanted to reach for her to hold her but couldn't see her. SeRina felt as if she were nailed to the ground. Then there was another voice, familiar but unrecognizable, it was a voice from the past, or was it the present? She was lost in confusion, her eyes felt glued shut, her tongue frozen, cold dry and speechless.

Light, Darkness, Light... blue light, flashes of memories flooded her mind, she recalled it all, the party, the storm, losing her mother, her not being there for her father. She revisited the funeral recalling the sun's light reflecting from the silver casket, the scent of the countless flowers, her inability to mourn. It was as if she were at the funeral again, she felt the pollen of the flowers tickling her nostrils and smelled their sweet perfume. The few whispering voices echoed and became many angry voices. Her back was cold her hands felt tied. Suddenly, the darkness swallowed the light and enveloped her into silence.

She awoke, sore and stiff, this time the sun not so bright. The field was greener now, the flowers in full bloom, the field hands working diligently as the overseer watched. How did she get back to the plantation? She was back here again, not certain of how she arrived or if she had ever left. Her body ached from head to toe, she couldn't understand why. She tried to rationalize what just happened but came up blank. She lifted herself up and looked around surveying the land, the field, the big house, the row of shanty's, the privy, the children playing. Where was Ivory? She was just there moments before. She looked down and had the watch in her hand, its hands were spinning uncontrollably and she felt herself plummeting into light and darkness, a soothing whooshing sound filled her ears, then the a hum, then deafening silence interrupted by a beeping noise and voices. She opened her eyes slowly and faces started to come into focus.

"Oh my God, Dr. Kwaisi, she is awake!"

"It's a miracle!" said Dr. Kwaisi hugging Mr. Salvatore.

"Oh, SeRina my darling. I'm so happy you are awake!" said Mr. Salvatore with tears in his eyes. "We didn't think you were going to make it. I just called the family in, we were to make the decision to remove you from life support today."

"Huh?" mumbled SeRina still confused. She couldn't speak, something was in her way, it was the tubes.

"Sweetheart, there was an accident. A terrible accident," said her father. "You are lucky to be alive. I'm sorry to have to tell you this but, Christophe... he didn't make it."

"What?" said SeRina, this was all too much, she looked around the room, seeing it for the first time in the months she had lay there. The heart monitor was beeping and the whoosh of the respirator was filling the air. The tubes in her throat made it nearly impossible for her to speak, so all she could do was cry.

"It's going to be alright darling, said her Father. Dr. Kwaisi will get the tubes out and get you all cleaned up. I will be back in a moment love I need to make a few phone calls. I'm so happy to have you back. Thank God you are going to be OK!" He kissed her on the forehead and stepped out of the hospital room consulting with Dr. Kwaisi in the hallway.

"I never thought I would say these words to you due to her condition." Dr. Salvatore paused, tears of joy welling in his eyes. "Please remove her from the ventilator, start the CPAP trial and extubation. And thank you, thank you from the bottom of my heart my friend, I don't know how I could've gotten through this tough time without you," said Dr. Salvatore.

"You don't know, don't you mean WE don't know how we would have made it without you," said Darrene catching the doctors by surprise. "I'm praying there is some good news here... since we seem to be celebrating."

"Yes, well, as you know the lady is always right, you know what they say, happy wife happy life! Darrene, yes, darling, I have some tremendous news, she is awake honey! SeRina is awake and responsive and well we have some tests to run but I anticipate she will make a full recovery!"

"What, oh my God, that is incredible news! After all these months, she is awake, wow, it's practically unbelievable! Can I see her?" asked Darrene.

"Yes, of course you can, she can't talk yet, but go on in," said Dr. Kwaisi. "I'm sure she will be happy to see you."

Darrene entered the room locking eyes with her daughter and rushed to her bedside bursting into tears.

"My baby, I'm so happy to see you awake, I never thought I'd see those beautiful eyes looking at me again," said Darrene. SeRina began crying hysterically, little did Darrene know that SeRina's tears were for a totally different reason. In her coma, her dreams of her adoptive mother's death were so real to her that she couldn't believe she was right there before her very eyes. She finally would have another chance at showing her how much she loved her. She couldn't speak so squeezed Darrene's hand as tight as she could in response.

"Your teacher Mrs. Parker and some of your friends from school were here the other day. They all decorated your room with pictures and memories of you. We all thought we were going to lose you so we told them all to come back today to say goodbye. Imagine their surprise when they walk in and see you alive and well. Thank heaven for miracles!" said Darrene still flooding with happy tears. Although SeRina's tongue was frozen from speech due to the respirator tubes, she cried the same happy tears as she gazed around the room and saw images of her and her friends from school, along with countless cards, balloons and drawings. Her eyes landed on a photo of Christophe with R.I.P. written on it in sharpie. Strange thing is she had already mourned him in her comatose state and didn't even know why. In reality he was really gone and it cut her heart to know it.

"Sweetheart, I hope you aren't upset, but since we thought we were going to lose you, we reached out to your biological family so they could come and say their goodbyes. But it looks like instead of goodbyes, they will get to say a few hellos. Now if it is too soon, you let me know and I can call and tell them not to come."

"Uh, uh!" SeRina managed to utter from her swollen throat. She did indeed want to meet the family she had always longed for and wondered about.

Moments later, there was a knock at the door, it was Ms. Parker, SeRina's Social Studies teacher along with a few of SeRina's friends from school, Miki, Bri, Wes, Alex, and Tamika from school. SeRina tried to smile around the tube in her throat but was unsuccessful. Everyone understood she couldn't smile or speak, but rejoiced at her awakening nonetheless. Darrene stood to hug and welcome each one of them and make room for them to get nearer to SeRina's bed.

"Honey it is so amazing to see you awake again. I was beginning to wonder what on Earth I would do in class without your smart mouth?" said Ms. Anderson squeezing SeRina's hand and smiling ear to ear. SeRina, squeezed her hand back in reply and smiled with her eyes.

"Look, I am going to go grab a cup of coffee and I will be back in just a second, I will let your friends have some time with you but will be back before you know it OK?" said Ms. Parker.

"I could use some coffee too," said Darrene, "Mind if I join you?"

"Of course not."

"Be right back Pumpkin," Darrene kissed SeRina on the forehead and joined Ms. Parker, leaving the girls behind.

SeRina felt so loved by the presence of her friends and family, but was still overwhelmed with her dream that had felt so real. She wondered how long she had been out of commission.

It was uncanny to her that her two best friends Briana and Michaela were oblivious to the fact that in her dream they were two snotty Southern Belles who couldn't stand her, and if she didn't have the tube down her throat she may have the mind to tell them about themselves. But instead, she listened and smiled inside as they told her the tales of her coma and caught her up on the goings on at school. Although she missed them, she was achy and tired so was glad when they left leaving her for a moment in the silent room.

Dr. Kwaisi and his attending nurses Valerie and Sandra entered the room, drew the privacy curtain, and removed the tube from SeRina's throat. When they were done they wheeled her away for some other testing. After having some blood drawn and an EKG, SeRina was given some fluids by mouth and was wheeled back into her room to rest.

"Now take it slow, you've been out for a while. Oh and looks like you have someone here to see you again," said Nurse Valerie before she left SeRina with her guest. There in front of the window with her back to SeRina, stood a black woman, short, old, frail, and gray headed.

"Well, it's about time," said the woman before turning around.

"Grandma Hattie?" said SeRina, her voice still weak, low and raspy from the tube.

"Why yes indeed. There you are. God, is good and he is always right on time. Now look at you layin' there finally awake, and much prettier that way if I may add," said Grandma Hattie.

SeRina wanted to spring from the bed and wrap her arms around her but was too weak so lay there and waited for her to come closer.

"I've been here with you now for months telling you all the stories 'bout your past and now, well you get to look part of your past square in the eye," said Grandma Hattie as she walked over and sat on the edge of SeRina's Bed. She laughed to herself again. She had in her hands a hand carved wooden box.

"Now they say when a person is in a coma, that they hear everything around them, know who is there, know what is being said. Well, if that be true, then you ought to know an awful lot about me and your history child," said Grandma Hattie.

"Yes ma'am, I do," said SeRina still softly. She was completely and utterly astonished.

"Good. When they told me today to come and say my goodbyes, I knew this would be the day. I knew it was time for you to open your eyes and call me Grandma. I started my evening in prayer, and I prayed from the time the sun set last night 'til it came up again this morning, and I know my heavenly father heard my prayers! So I bought you a mighty special gift for when you woke up, so you'd know that no matter where you are or the time of day that it is, that you my child are loved." And she handed her the hand carved wooden box with something special inside it.

Just as SeRina was opening the box, Darrene and Ms. Parker arrived back to the room, on their 2nd cup of coffee. As they walked in, Ms. Parker froze staring at Grandma Hattie as if she had spotted a ghost.

Grandma Hattie turned and saw Ms. Parker, and sprung up from the bed and ran over and wrapped her arms around her. "Diana, my baby, you came, I don't know how Jehovah worked this out, but you are here, my father in heaven is always RIGHT ON TIME!"

It hit SeRina what this meant. Her mothers knew too. Both of them. Ms. Diana Parker, her Social Studies teacher was SeRina's biological mother. How incredibly unbelievable. All this time, her mother was right there before her and neither of them had any idea.

They all exploded with tears and laughter celebrating the realization of it all.

Just then, SeRina's father walked in and saw Diana Parker standing there. Time stood still for a moment as they replayed their college years together and their love. He had broken her heart abandoning her for the sake of his family. He never even knew she was expecting a child, but seeing her there rejoicing in realization of finding the daughter she gave up for adoption hit him hard. It sunk in to his core, that the very daughter he adopted at 4 years old was the very daughter that he had abandoned unknowingly for lack of willingness to displease his family and marry a black woman. Things had truly come full circle. He hadn't accepted who he was and owned up to loving Diana and had punished himself through the years for what he felt was abandonment of her. All of this, while not knowing he was raising his very own daughter. It was all so surreal to him, to SeRina, to Darrene, to Ms. Parker. He had adopted his very own child.

A few days passed, and SeRina was discharged from the hospital. Her condition had improved and she was told she would make a full and total recovery. She had spent every waking moment with her parents and her newfound mother and grandmother and was absolutely looking forward to their bright and promising future together.

In preparation for checkout, Darrene gathered SeRina's belongings and Dr. Salvatore helped his daughter into the wheelchair to take her home. Hattie and Diana had come also to be a part of the festivities. It was a grand celebration, seeing as though days before they thought they would be bidding SeRina farewell.

This beautiful family, Black, Italian, White and in-between all walked the hallways of the hospital together, laughing, and joking and full of life as they bid the hospital staff farewell. As they exited the hospital, a young man ran behind them trying to catch them before they got into the vehicle waiting out front.

"Ma'am, ma'am, you forgot something," said the gentleman as he finally caught up to them.

"Ma'am, whew you were a tough one to catch. Looks like I caught you just in time. Look, you forgot this, and well, it looks pretty important, so I thought you should have it," he said catching his breath and reaching into his pocket.

SeRina, recognizing the voice, turned her wheelchair around to face him. She couldn't believe it, standing there in a pair of pale blue scrubs wearing a Medical Student badge was a very handsome tall black man with a familiar ebony eyes that spoke to her soul.

"Do you know who I am?" she asked, her eyes searching for the answer.

He pulled out the hand carved wooden box with the watch inside, and gently placed it in her hands. "It doesn't matter if I know who you, are as long as you do. By the way, they call me Ivory," replied the man, flashing one of the most beautiful smiles she had seen for a time.

About the Author

Joyce Licorish is the youngest of 7 daughters and mother of 2 beautiful daughters and 1 rambunctious son. She recently married film actor Jerome Davis. She was born and raised in the inner-city of Indianapolis, where she was bussed to a primarily white school and saw early on the effects of discrimination and racism.

Joyce, singer, actress, plus model and playwright, takes a turn toward another creative vein as the author of THE FORGOTTEN TIMEPIECE. Best known for her direction/production of Oprah Winfrey's Color Purple the Musical Tour, her powerhouse vocal abilities and stage acting, she takes a step away from the microphone and stage towards the pen to create her debut novel. Inspired by a dream about a watch left to her by her now deceased grandmother Hattie, Joyce is excited to have penned her debut novel and hopes that you have enjoyed reading it as much as she enjoyed writing it.

Your feedback about her debut novel is welcome via social media:
www.Facebook.com/JoyceLicorish
www.Twitter.com/JoyceLicorish
www.ForgottenTimepiece.com

Acknowledgments

First and foremost, thank you to my creator Jehovah, God, without you, there would be no me. Thank you to both of my late grandmothers Tempie and Hattie, with a special thanks to my grandmother Hattie B. Rouse for leaving me the watch that inspired this book. I thank my husband Jerome for being open and willing to share me with the world and endure my late night writing and reading sessions. Thank you to NY Times Best-selling author J.L. King for the encouraging words and for reading past page 65 to see the potential in this book (smiles.) Thanks to my two daughters for reading aloud with me on our road trips and helping mommy get the book just right! Thanks to Jayden my 5 year old who gives me so much inspiration!

I thank my best friend in the world Tina for staying up with me until the wee hours in the morning editing, being a shoulder to lean on and a voice of reason. Thank you Christa, for seeing the vision even before you had the opportunity to get to know me. Thank you Leith for inviting me to open my heart and my eyes to creating the possibility of actually seeing this project to completion. Thank you to my parents for instilling the love of reading in my heart, and especially to my father for blessing me with his genes of creativity. To my sisters, thanks to each of you for believing in me. To my readers, friends, family and supporters, without you, there would be no need for these acknowledgements, you are so loved and so appreciated!

Last but definitely not least, a special heartfelt thanks to you all for reading! Please add a short review on Amazon and on my website and let me know what you think of the book!

CPSIA information can be obtained
at www.ICGtesting.com
Printed in the USA
LVHW032322140720
660731LV00001B/138

9 781387 055982